Sara's Swamp Blues

For Kyra, Kevin and Daniel.

Many thanks to Gloria Ogo, my editor and motivator.

Cover design by RebecaCovers of Fiverr.com
Back cover photo by Don Shepard.
Thank you to the Stephen Center and Charles Washington Library in Omaha, Nebraska.

"Miriam Landry was the best damn musician I ever seen or heard, and I was raised in a juke joint masquerading as a whorehouse"
Sara Barnum 1963

Part 1

Chapter 1

1945, Caddo Parish Louisiana.

Miriam stared at me with big brown eyes that reminded me of the deer often seen prancing around the bayou. I needed to say no, but the look made it impossible. I understood why my father gave in to her charms after Mami disappeared. Them Creole lips protruded more than normal, and the girl begged so good; she always got her way.

"Miri baby, I don't want to, but I need to go. I ain't going to become a lawyer if I hang out in this old whorehouse we call home. Stop hugging me."

Her arms tightened around my shoulders. She hung onto me as if she climbed across a train trestle.

"I'm going to miss you too Miri."

"Ms. Sara, I want you to reach your dreams, but I don't want you to forget me."

I smiled and wet my lips with my tongue. "Baby, after the last few weeks, I'll never forget you. I don't think you were teaching me stuff. I think you were having some fun with me."

She smacked me on the shoulders. I love the way your boobs feel when they squish up against mine."

I kissed her on the cheek. Tears dropped from my eyes by the time she eventually let me go. I turned and walked away, headed for Baton Rouge.

I enrolled in Louisiana State University in the fall of 1945. The Nazis and the fascists already humbled in Europe, and the Japanese suffered from cancer caused by the nuclear destruction of the island chain. Not many women enrolled in the prelaw at LSU, and none were as mixed blood as me. My Papi, a Creole, gave me Caucasian, native and Haitian blood, while Mami's family came from Mexico.

Becoming a civil rights attorney was my destiny. My Papi fought for the rights of the minority. He died too early. This battle was for him, so the laws could change to give voices to the voiceless. I owned dreams and ambitions and most women attending LSU desired a Mrs. Degree. Most of these hincty dames believed in the wrong side of the civil rights fights. However, in 1945 Louisiana they voted on the winning side.

I pictured my dream at only nine years old and both parents are to blame. My father Bo Barnum fought the injustices of the world by speaking his mind and singing folk songs with his banjo and guitar. He sang for the people from Louisiana, Mississippi, Arkansas, and Mexico. He ain't never sang nothing from Texas.

Mami, born to revolutionaries of the Mexican War. She fought battles with my father, but the woman was on the run all her life. Exhausted, she craved peace in her life, and found it in prison, where she sang with the infamous Goree Girls string band based out of the Huntsville, Texas state prison. I thought she became incarcerated. Perceptions of family history are often wrong.

Daddy, born to a moonshiner in Texarkana, Arkansas, and thought my grandpa hated all but in fact that crusty old whiskey maker loved more love people, in addition he raised my little brother, Tomas, me and took in Miriam, after daddy's premature death and Mami's disappearance.

At LSU, my roommate was also in the pre-law program, as well as the pre-Mrs. program. Priscilla was your run of the mill sharecropper, and I don't mean no red dirt farmer, who worked on her daddy's mega plantation. Pricilla was to me the perfect college roommate, since I never saw her. She returned to the room around six in the morning, brushed her teeth, forgot her class books, and ventured out again. I spent my days at class, the library or back in the dorm, reading and writing. I budgeted no time to mess with these petty active duty drugstore cowboys who hung around Indian Mounds with their cigarettes dangling from their mouth, taped to their lower lip, and wearing an oversized fedora and non-matching argyle sweaters. They got their highs giving us freshman coeds catcalls, and unwelcome hollers. I ain't ever give them the time of day. The sharecroppers stayed and chatted and left with different boys.

Me and LSU did not get along. I attended for an education, and worried that I couldn't pass as a white woman. In addition, I failed to make friends. My dorm mates were southern belles, the gals with fanciest clothes, swankiest hats, and up-curled red lips. I heard the whispers as I wore my overalls, and straw hat, and walked right past them, with my head high. These stuck up bitches meant nothing to me, since laws would soon change. While the world evolved, Sara Barnum stood right dab in the middle of the movement. Getting an education and changing the world remained my focus. So, I attended school for the degree, instead of looking for Southern white men seeking a lucrative profession. I didn't make any friends down there with these society girls, since these princesas would have taken me to Indian Mounds, and rape me with their unused golf clubs, tennis racquets, or whatever tools they located. Once finished I'd be lynched for rush week.

My social life was me taking my guitar, harmonica, and my singing voice out to the mounds, where I played some of Daddy's tunes, or some of my own. My blackness emerged as I played the swamp blues, and the white folks didn't listen to it. They had their Cajun music, and country, but some gal wailed the blues. I failed the one drop rule. I lasted one semester.

My favorite song I wrote called Cornbread, Crawfish and Me.

Springtime in Louisiana
A Lot better than Alabama
At least that's what I've seen

Cornbread is Sweeter
Crawfish are boiling
And this lady is waiting on the banks of the Sabine

Oh Yankee Man keep rolling
Oh Cowboy keep on a strolling
Let me grab that Creole man,
with the banjo in his hand
and two step the night away.

Cornbread, Crawfish or Me
Cornbread, Crawfish or Me

You don't have to choose,
You can have all three,
Cornbread, Crawfish and Me.

The accordion is a rocking,
The guitar is chopping,
and the ladies are prettier than me.

The music much sweeter,
The night getting hotter,
Come love on me down on the banks of the Sabine

Oh Yankee Man keep rolling
Oh Cowboy keep on a strolling
Let me grab that Creole man,
with the banjo in his hand
and two step the night away.

Cornbread, Crawfish or Me
Cornbread, Crawfish or Me
You don't have to choose,
You can have all three,
Cornbread, Crawfish and Me

Well, someone researched on my family and discovered slave ancestry in my blood. The one drop rule applied to me, so I evolved into a full-blooded Negress and all public institutions in Louisiana or anywhere else in the south disallowed my attendance. Louisiana became my home five years earlier, and my heart belonged to the state. In addition, Grandpa Cecil's declining health made me choose a college closer to him, so I enrolled at Grambling College, an all-Negro college 90 miles from Grandpa Cecil's place. The short distance made taking care and visiting the geezer easier.

I finished my studies at Grambling in three years. My little brother Tomas also attended the Northern Louisiana College and played linebacker for their famed football team. He didn't play football after he graduated. Instead he pursued a degree in criminal justice, and later went on to work for the FBI.

I took a year off from college and went to Chicago to meet my old friend and tutor, Miriam Landry. Miriam, also Daddy's old lover taught the family nuances of the Zydeco music. She and I played music together, on the docks, in the boat or in the house. I missed the music, but I'll never forget her magical touch, her genuine smile, but most of all I'll never forget our friendship. In fact, I always thought there wasn't a better musician than Miriam, and I grew up in a whorehouse masquerading as a juke joint.

The Greyhound bus waited for me as I punched my ticket on the northbound headed to Chicago. For the second time in her life, Miriam Landry ran off with a pig of a blues man. This time she decided to move out of the South, and this man became a key figure in jump-starting the Chicago Blues scene.

I didn't like that Chicago crap. I preferred a juke joint player, or even some dude playing a Stella on his front porch with his neighbor harmonizing with a rusty old harmonica while they spit out snuff but he spit blood, from the untreated gum cancer. I loved the Blues, I knew what my Papi played, and what I learned how to play.

I sat in the rear of the bus by choice. Showing my respect for the Southern Negroes I strutted past the Caucasians with my head held high, in torn overalls, and daddy's favorite straw hat, carrying both guitars and a small suitcase, with my other pair of overalls and a change of undergarments.

"Damn agitating Negro," one white woman said as I bonked her head with my guitar. I scrunched my face, stuck out my lip, wagged my tongue at her, and continued gallivanting down the aisle.

I found a seat next to no one, I preferred to sit alone so my long legs and stinky feet stretched out. I tuned Stella up, aware that Miriam soon would shred the steel strings with it. Sliding my switchblade knife across the steel, I carried her home to the swamplands of Louisiana.

I started the blues shuffle, the shuffle I played before I walked. Papi taught me that, while I sucked milk out of Mami's boobs it. I set the Stella down, grabbed my bag, broke out my harmonica holder, and put the Marine Band in it. I put the holder over my neck, the harp next to my waiting lips and recreated the train whistle. Papi taught me the whistle at age four when we hopped freights together. Soon, Stella cradled in my arms as I played the shuffle and blew the harp.

Hoots and hollers rained from the teethed and toothless men migrating from segregation. I invented lyrics and toe tapped as the bus headed away from Shreveport towards Texarkana. The Negro ladies clapped in rhythm, waiting for a chorus from the men, who joined in like a gospel choir. I felt fantastic.

The screech of bus brakes drowned out my musicianship. Soon a stale stench filled the air, as a fat white man in his early 40's made his way to the back of the bus. He smelled like cheap whiskey, bad cologne, and cigarettes and the aisle reeked and creaked with each step he took. My hat covered my eyes, so he couldn't tell I noticed him, but I knew he paced our way. I kept an eye on him as he waddled past the white folks.

"Ma'am. Get off the bus now. You're an agitator and no agitators ride on my bus."

"I ain't agitating; I'm entertaining these peeps back here. It's a long way to Chicago and we need some music."

Next thing I knew I stared down the barrel of a Colt 45 pistol. My switchblade wasn't the most reassuring thing in my pocket. After all, slicing things is only a second purpose. I protected myself with the guitar. The fat driver glowered, ready to toss me off after we crossed the state line. I saved him the trouble and jumped off rolling into the Welcome to Arkansas sign, as the bus bounced towards Papi's birthplace in Texarkana.

Papi had hopped a freight to get to Omaha, so I ventured through the cotton fields, and the bayou carrying Stella and my Regal. I ditched my suitcase, and threw my clothes in a guitar case, continuing my hike across plantations. After a two-mile walk, I emerged at the steel rails. I set my tired self-down and waited, all the while calling the train home on the harp. I kissed the harmonica, my mouth all the first three holes, inhaled and exhaled, and repeated thrice. Finally, I breathe on the fourth and fifth holes, holding my breath if possible. I shook my hand over the harp and sent the sound waves back to Louisiana. I repeated until the southern sky turned a dark gray, as if a springtime thunderstorm approached. I gathered my belongings and hid behind some foliage. When the engine passed, I ran with my gear, threw the guitars on first and with all my mighty strength, I heaved 120 pounds into the box car.

Hobos galore rode the train. Most of them Negroes, eager to make the great migration I wasn't too worried, since my slide rested in my overalls. After all it served another purpose. Those Negroes all eyed me, I guess they wondered why a lonesome dame rode a freight all alone. A few preying eyes enveloped my body, but words weren't exchanged. I got Stella out of the case and opened my slide.

Snap came the blade, and I played the blues the way I knew how. Sad, mean, full of dirt, grit, and swamp. I knew that in order to save my life I needed to entertain these folks from Texarkana to Chicago.

Half-way up Arkansas, sanity took over, and I jumped off, tumbling into the forest. No one followed me. Thank God! I jumped off the freight short of Little Rock and hitched into town and bought a ticket to Chicago. I figured it will be nice to become a good girl for a change.

I napped through most of the ride, and I arrived in Chicago early the next afternoon. I ain't seen anything like this, not even in Narleans as people scrambled everywhere, moving every which way but loose. I noticed a lot of Negroes in Louisiana, but they never seemed free. They seemed happy up here. These folks roamed the streets, going to and from work, dashing to the market and department stores, cutting in and cutting out. They wandered like they owned the place, and on the street corners, guitarists cut heads. My fingers itched to teach these fools a couple of tricks.

The music, passionate, energetic, soulful, electrified and loud. Folks shook their bottoms so hard I thought their butts would fall off. Negroes danced, drank, sang, swayed and smiled. This weren't back home, but to this Louisiana girl, the city life lacked something. Absent sat the lone singer, with his cigar box guitar, playing on his front porch, spitting out his tobacco into an empty can of Sanka. He played with a buddy who wailed harp, and better yet, a blind washboard player, and a hip cat playing an accordion. In Chicago for only a half hour, I already craved the Swamp Blues. Miriam needed them too.

I wandered through the projects of the south side in search of her home. The buildings all huge, all connected, as folks hung outside playing on the stoops. Kids played stickball in the streets, handball games against the front stoops became cut-throat, and folks seemed jovial in the ghetto. A sharp-dressed-man showed me where to go, and I rushed to her unit. I found a three-story building where laundry and dishes hung and stacked on the back porch, and a young skinny woman bent over washing both piles by hand. The girl was a petite thing, and I recognized her right away.

"Miriam Landry, get your scrawny butt down here."

"Sara Barnum? Get your mixed ass up here."

I returned her smile. "You get down here, I've been hauling this stuff since Shreveport, Let's hit the bus station. We're going back home."

"You come up here. My man playing a show tonight. I want to walk in on him while he's trying to give it to those other women."

"Leave his cheating ass. We gonna play some shows down home. I need to make some money for law school."

She looked at the pile of clothes that the dirty blues man left for her to wash, while he drank on a street corner and hit up some underage girl who he'd knock up and leave fatherless. She looked behind at the dungy apartment they shared, before her eyes fell at her finger which still missed a ring. When she peered down at me from the second story, there was a new set to her chin that was never there. Then her face broke into a smile as she leaped over the broken railing, and landed on a rat-torn abandoned mattress, took a tumble and sprinted out of the complex. She grabbed me into a hug. She smelled like a combination of a beautiful woman living in a ghetto, sleeping on rotten, torn and tattered mattress.

"We need to get you out of the ghetto. This place ain't fit for rats to live."

"You should see the inside."

"I ain't going inside."

"Good it's dirtier. I need some new clothes and a shower. I ain't putting no clean clothes on this dirty body. My man doesn't like me smelling to pretty, unless we go out. Thinks some bourgeois suitor will steal me away from him."

"Bourgeois?"

"Yeah an old uppity Negro, not some strange and made up Barnum conspiracy."

"I say let's get on the bus and steal a shower somewhere before we get to the South. I'll get you some clothes. You're going to spend the summer with me."

We showered at the bus station, and I bought her a few pair of overalls, and a new grungy looking hat, and boarded the Southbound. We went straight to the back, because once we got out of Illinois, we knew that's where we'd sit.

We looked at each other

"Sara, I miss you." Her lower lip protruded. I miss my lala and my Bobo. I really loved your daddy. He was a good man, even though he died trying to save your mama."

I smiled back at her. "C'mon Miri, you'd run off with another dirty gunslinger."

"I feel real guilty, Sara. If I wouldn't run off with that dirty man, Willie, Bobo might still be alive." A small tear dripped from her eye. I snapped it away like a bug.

"Lots of folks wanted Daddy dead. It probably wasn't even those two Mami ratted on."

"Sara, I blame myself. If I wouldn't have been with him, I wouldn't have gone to jail and met your mama. You guys would have thought she be dead, and Bobo would get over her. He needed more time." She looked deep into my eyes, hoping she figured correct.

"Don't blame yourself. Papi didn't need to run after her." I paused for a few minutes trying to recollect everything and putting my own spin on the situation. I peered deep into those brown eyes. "He needed closure. I know you're right, if he had more time, he'd love you deeper. Papi fought for you and chase that dirty man's caddy down." I stopped, took a deep breath, and stared back at those eyes. "Part of this is my fault. I knew Mami was alive."

"Your Daddy didn't love me?"

"I don't know. Like I said if he needed closure from Mami, he'd die fighting for you. He would have chased that dirty man in the caddy and roped him down like a cowboy. That was Papi."

Miriam bowed her head for a second or two, and her pretty face turned and smiled at me. "Bobo couldn't rope and ride."

"He'd chase you down, if you're willing to come back."

"I'm not sure if I be willing."

"We all fucked up. Did I ever tell you I tried to get with your baby brother? You know your man-child little bro. Whatever happened to him?"

"Well Bobo and me heard you sneaking up. I didn't know you tried to get with him, and I remember you sneaking off with him down in Morgan City. Sara, the last I heard he's drinking and drugging it up and making babies and playing all over South Louisiana."

"You know he's the only boy I kissed. I didn't mess with no one at Grambling. I didn't have any time, so I'm taking a year off from school. We're gonna have some fun." I saw my smile reflect in my friend's eyes.

"I'm ready for some fun too Ms. Sara. That dirty singer done worn me out, with his drinking and slapping me around. I'm ready to chase some boys and play some music." She stretched her legs out across mine. First Sara I need to rest my mind and body."

"Me too." I stretched my legs across hers, and we both napped until the bus halted in St. Louis.

We hopped on another bus that took us to Memphis, where we caught one to Texarkana and into Shreveport. We got in my car which I left parked on the bustling Fannin Street.

"I ain't never told you this Sara, but I use to work on Fannin back in the days. That's where that other dirty old fat man found me. The one I ran away from, when Bobo picked me up. Your Papi was a good man."

"So, you whored yourself, when that raper got to ya?"

"I'd rather whore myself and making money, than pretend to be a maid, and some fat slob's mistress. Bobo saved my life. Now, Sara Barnum you're doing the same."

"Miri, you're my best friend. Ain't no dirty drunk blues singer going to put you down, and you only going to sell yourself to a dirty fat pig over my dead body. I'll make sure you do not whore out to some stinky fat guy ever again. I flipped around and laid my head in her lap."

"Ms. Sara," she interrupted. "If it's to save our lives, I'll to do it."

"I'm protecting us, Miri. Ain't nothing going to happen to us. We're going to play some gigs across the south, and maybe meet some smart, clean, skinny pigs to have fun together. I'm starting to listen to protest songs, you know Woody and Pete, there are plenty of others out there. We can put our own style to it."

"I'm up for that Ms. Sara. Let's get to the bayou."

Chapter 2

The cypress trees stood tall as if they anticipated her return. With the wind blowing through the bayou that evening, it seemed as if my girl received a standing ovation for her arrival. Miriam had spent seven years of her life in or around Shreveport. She worked the streets in St. Paul Bottoms on Fannin Street whoring herself out until the fat judge, Paul Mitchell rescued the girl but used her as his personal slave. Papi took her down to Zwolle and made her our maid, and at age eighteen, they became lovers down on the Sabine. After Papi's passing she moved up with the family to Pawpaw's place on the Black Bayou. She stayed there until she ran off with her second Blues singer. This man became a legend, the first guy never got a chance. He received a premature death; attempted rape of a tough, spunky young woman can do that.

I tried to avoid the bull snake stretching across the road that leads into Grandpa Cecil's place. I almost missed him but didn't quite, and that didn't sit right with me. I didn't like killing nothing. I'm the type of girl who thinks that once you killed a creature, his friends and family will come back for you, and haunt you until you're dead. You have no idea when they will attack. I did not like snakes, so I knew my old friend and I needed an early start, so the bull snakes or water moccasins won't try sneaking through my window that overlooks the bayou. I'm not sure about other snakes, but I knew critters chased me. Sometimes snakes do not always form the shape of those scaly creatures that slither along the ground, but they also take the form of younger siblings.

"This place hasn't changed a bit." Miriam craned her neck to see more of nature as we zoomed past. "I liked Bobo's better, but I called this place home too. I loved sitting out on the dock watching all the critters float by while singing with you Ms. Sara."

I smiled and observed the vegetation, trying to see it through her eyes. "That's always the best. Let us see if Angeline got some grub on for us. I'm hungry."

Her smile lit up the interior of my sedan. I hopped up and down the driveway, as the car bounced like a rubber ball as we approached the entrance of pawpaw's place. Gator III, my coon dog, came out to greet us, with a wide grin, tongue hanging out and tail wagging and dashed straight to Miriam once he saw her. After slurping her up and all, I received my puppy kisses.

Cecil, still spry as he aged, as he hobbled on his cane, but his toothless grin said it all. Pawpaw seemed elated at Miri's homecoming, and ecstatic that I made it back in one piece. We trooped inside, and Miriam and I inhaled the aroma of homemade Mexican food. The chilies and pork called us to the other room down the long hallway.

"Sara, Miri, I made tamales." The voice from the kitchen hollered, welcoming us back to Louisiana, and Miriam back to segregation. Miriam raced into the kitchen and yanked Pawpaw's girlfriend into a big hug. The two of them, always kindred, because they shared a past profession. Time was generous to pawpaw's lady who at about fifty, still remained beautiful, with her dark skin and long straight hair.

After dinner, we retired to my room.

"I need me a bath Sara." Miriam yanked off her overalls and tossed the dirty outfit on my bed. She paced in her lower undergarments, encouraging me to look at her body. I couldn't help but notice the little bruises on her chest, legs, and arms. She walked by me again and turned around, while pretending to search for a towel, showing me her bottom. She slipped out of the remaining garments and sprinted into the bathroom naked. I debated taking one with her, but wondered if such experiment before college was practice or real couple sex. I waited for her to finish her bath and retired to take mine. That bus made us stink.

After my bath, all nice and fresh, we played music and talked. In the morning the road called.

Miriam and I planned on hitching our way to Virginia, but something sinister changed our mind. Cutting through the bayou, and looking up at the cypress trees, we noticed two young women dangle from the tall trees, ropes around their neck, and they swung in the Louisiana breeze.

I clutched Miriam's hand, "Miri, that could be us hanging from that tree."

"Hell yeah, Miss Sara. Let's catch the bus to Clarksdale." She shuddered and turned away from the ghastly sight.

A desolate road isn't the best place for partial and full blooded young pretty Negro girls to stand around. We crossed Louisiana, headed for Clarksdale, and then our destination, Richmond, Virginia. The Blues waited for us in Mississippi. The city appeared nearly vacant; I guess the Great Migration happened. We found a street corner where some ol geezer set up. He downed a bottle of coke and smashed the bottle on the ground. "Damn, I forgot my slide," he screamed. He grabbed the end of the bottle and played the stuff I remembered.

"Sara you're right. Much better than the amplified stuff back north."

"Darn tooting Miri, let's go find us a place to play."

We found what looked like an abandoned gas station that doubled as a juke joint after hours.

"Let's sit our asses down and play some stuff."

Miriam dropped a dime in the machine. She pulled out a coke bottle and took a few big swallows. She took another drink and spit it out all over the curb.

"Do you want to finish it Sara?"

I grabbed the bottle and chugged the rest down and gave it back to her.

She grabbed the bottle and whipped it down; looking like she wanted to smash a dirty ol blues singer's head with it. The bottle shattered, as the ol blues man's bottle up the street did. Miriam placed the busted bottle on her left ring finger, as if she married my Stella guitar. Stella already tuned down in open G tuning, Miri slid the bottleneck across the strings, looked at me and smiled. I played the shuffle, while Miri sang about a light skinned woman and a brown skinned woman, on the road for adventure, and not meeting any men along the way.

We made up songs, be-bop standards, and music we heard some old Negro codgers and their partners crank out on their back porch. We took turns and played about six songs in all. Then we switched back on the slide and shuffling. No one stopped by at first, except this one hip white cat, who happened to stare and smile right at me.

"You ladies sure are purdy; you're a couple of pretty things. I hope you don't have some big old redneck boyfriends or some jealous, pistol toting husbands waiting, because you my lovely dark haired, and dark-skinned women are having dinner on me." He tipped his hat to me and only me, however Miriam disagreed. "My name's Robert Greene. There's an extra e on the end and that E is for elated to meet you. I go by Cisco, like the Cisco Kid."

I smiled up at him. "I'm Sara, and this girl's name is Miriam. She's living with a Blues singer up Chicago way."

He stood there. The man I searched for. Cisco wore wire rimmed glasses, a goatee, and long dark, thick curly hair, which he stuffed up into his fedora. Blue jeans torn and tattered, which I liked. He wore an old work shirt with a non-matching vest. He looked like no man I ever met, but that ain't saying much. I never met any man for dating anyway. He played guitar and wrote folk songs about unions. He didn't possess the best singing voice, but I guess a guy's voice don't need to sound pretty. He sang with passion and got his message across. He also wrote poetry, but not in the boring, pretentious way. In no time, he broke out in poem.

"Sara, oh pretty Sara
Carry me to Ol Virginia.
We got these guitars,
And we'll play to the stars,
Way on down to Richmond town."

I smiled as he made up more five-line stanzas. My index finger twirled my long dark hair, and unknowing I kept tracing my tongue around my lips.

"I made that up" he confessed at the end, his smile, somewhat awkward, but seemed sincere, as he continued. "Say pretty Latina girl and her dark-skinned friend, with that long dark hair, and those big brown eyes. I'm playing a show down in Jackson, at the college, and hoped it speaks to some of the Negroes about freeing their mind about integration. I've another show fixed in Oxford the next night. I'd love it so, so much, if you girls turned up. I like what you play, and you can do a few numbers with me."

"We'd love…"

I interrupted Miriam. I cut her off like there sat a switchblade in my overall pocket, resting comfortable next to my harmonica. "Of course, we do. You can teach us the songs on the way down."

We threw our belongings in the trunk of his Desoto and rode the legendary highways of Central Mississippi. A white man, a black woman and a fine blend. Cars followed us and looked our way, but Cisco didn't pay no mind to them, or who rode in his vehicle. He turned up the radio and we sang along to Hank Williams about jambalaya and crawfish pie, which made Miriam and me think about Daddy. Crawfish pie, his favorite meal, and my traveling companion cooked it better than anyone.

We entered Jackson around ten o'clock. We found a black motel for Miriam. I planned on sleeping in her room, but the folks prohibited me. "You ain't colored." They told me.

"Yes, ma'am, I'm colored."

"Well you don't look colored."

"This here's my stepmom, and sister. We're traveling together."

"You need to go to a white motel." She closed the door on me as Miriam departed to her room.

Cisco sat in the car smiling as I headed back to his vehicle. "They wouldn't let you stay?"

I shook my head, "I don't think they got rooms for my blood. It's so mixed up."

He gave me a pitying look. "You can stay with me and sneak around in back."

My heart beat faster, steadying myself on legs that shook, and other things happened to my virgin body. Just like when I was sixteen, and a younger but more experienced man child of a Zydeco musician showed this girl a premature lesson in love. In Morgan City, as a schoolgirl, I felt petrified, but still eager. Tonight, I wasn't scared, but my legs wavered like a pecan tree in a hurricane. A lot happened to me in those five years, losing Papi, graduating from a black college, and not allowed to stay in a black hotel, in the mix of it all, I anticipated a love life.

Cisco came out from the lobby with the key, and he drove to our room at the little roadside inn.

"It's got two beds, cause I'm a gentleman." He opened the door for me, as I tossed my bag on one of the beds. He dropped his stuff next to mine and sat beside me. "Do you want dinner? I can get us some grub, pretty lady."

"I'm craving so much. You can get me a big slab of crawfish pie, some fries and a coke."

"I'll get us a bottle of wine."

"Cisco, you don't know me that well." I walked up to him. "I don't drink. I've seen booze ruin a lot of people. Plus, I need to stay in control." I kissed his lips, wrapped my arms around his neck and played with his wavy hair. "See I'm in control, so get us some grub."

"Sassy Sara, I'm hungry for some pie, but I also crave something else." He put his left arm around my waist, and his right hand caressed my shoulder.

I closed my eyes and he dipped me down like we did a waltz, or some other fancy dance, leaned down and kissed me long on the lips. "Sexy Sara, I best be getting some grub. Looks like we're going to need some energy."

He left me alone in the room for what seemed like an eternity. I wasn't sure if I wanted him tonight or not, but these feelings nagged like that stupid little devil and angel that jumps on one's shoulder. I'm not a virtuous girl by any means, but I'm no whore. I've never been laid by any guy, but that's because I didn't have time. Coupling for the sake of it wasn't going to happen with me. Cisco needed to warm me up, until I couldn't say no.

He arrived back with dinner at the time I was ready to eat an entire horse. We sat on his bed while we ate. His fork slashed into the pie, and dangled on the utensil, as he raised it towards his open mouth.

"Oh, sorry sexy, sassy Sara. I'm a gentleman. Ladies first." He moved the fork towards my waiting mouth so I could take a bite of the crawfish pie. My lips grabbed the tip of his finger and gave it a quick lick. He fed me dinner, and I continued my seduction of this man, as I sucked on his finger. The pie soon got tossed across the motel room. It splashed across the bad painting that hung up on the wall. I wanted to tantalize him, and feed him dinner, but I fed him other ways.

After we finished the steamy entanglement, Cisco laid there snoring beside my naked body, while I wondered if I gave up my virginity to the right man. He didn't give me total pleasure. It felt good, but I heard it felt like a California earthquake on the Fourth of July. I expected the ground to move and shake and fireworks and such. None of it happened. Maybe he needed another chance or two.

Things got better the next few weeks. The ground did shake, not like a California quake, but maybe like a rare Oklahoma quake. The fireworks resembled a backyard display, not one a city puts on overlooking the city park.

When Miriam and I got a moment to ourselves, which didn't happen often, she asked, "So how was he?"

"Not bad." I tried to look her in the eye, like I attempted telling her the truth. She knew I told her fibs.

"Oh Sara, my best friend, sister and daughter. Does he..." she stuttered for the words. "Does he make you quake inside? I mean does he get you off?"

"He did." Again, my eyes focused on the mountains in Eastern Tennessee. My lips curled up as I made a face, and I heard laughter."

"You don't know if you got off, do you? Sara, do we need to go back so I can re teach you stuff?"

"Miri, you don't need to teach me nothing."

"No Sara. You must relax and enjoy. Girl, you want him to get it over with. You know Bobo's the only one that made me shake and quake. Those dirty blues singers I ran off with, don't do it for me either. They just bigger." She smiled when she said it. "So is Cisco pretty big, or little?"

I glared at Miriam, resisting the smile that tugged the corners of my mouth. "I ain't got nothing to compare him. He ain't a bad lover, does some things good. I enjoy his kisses and touch. He ain't no passionate lover. I mean, the guy's all about passion for his songs and poems. But he needs to give me the passion. Dat man just goes through the motions."

Miri smiled. "How do you know?"

"I don't. I guess I still want to feel the way I did when your brother kissed me, and when..." I stopped. I did not want her to know I still loved her.

Miriam's lips twisted. "Sara I've fucked bunches of guys, and every guy's different. For me nothing compared to your daddy. I felt he's the only one who ever loved me. Give him more time and relax."

Cisco returned to visit us in the Tennessee Mountains with the chicken we requested. I grabbed the greasy drumstick, and scarfed it down, while enjoying the mashed taters and gravy.

Cisco started talking. "I grew up in these hills with my Mama cause Papa roamed the country since he's the best fiddle player in the world. Mama played in an all-girl string band but stuck around Johnson City. She didn't like Pa always running around. I went out on the road to find him and lost his trail down in Louisiana a few years back. I wanted him to play some fiddle on some folk tunes I wrote."

Miriam and I looked at each other, her reaction the same as mine. At least I hoped she grasped the idea that this young, clumsy but dashing poet and folk singer evolved from the sperm of the man who killed her lover and my father, and my grandparents I never met.

"We share everything here, wealth, property and each other." He tried to sound like a wannabe hipster.

"Sweet sexy Sara, we're about sharing here. Sharing Sara, Sara sharing sex. Baby, oh baby. My whole band sharing Sara. I even wrote me a song. Sharin, Sara. My band gonna love ya Sharing Sara. Got your dark- skinned lady friend, can play along. Can't wait til Mama meets you both." Cisco snorted forgetting he possessed a cool nickname he made up himself.

He removed the spectacles, winked at me, and put them ugly glasses back on. He raised Miriam's legs over his scrawny shoulders and stared at her hoochie.

My friend smiled at him and parted her lips. She turned at looked at me as if we're going to get busy again. Her smile vanished, as mine did.

"This girl ain't no swinger, and I don't do orgies. I'm not into commies, and I don't do commie orgies." I pushed the weakling over on his back, stepped on his chest, forgetting about the non-violence I studied. I crept away from him, waiting for Miri to follow me, and she soon came running.

Huffing and puffing she tackled me laughing. "Sara, I stomped on his head. He said, 'What da fuck happened? I thought she sweet on me, and you gals' game.' "I told him I thought we were too. I hoped so anyway. He moved in to give me a kiss and felt up my leg while at it. But I grabs my guitar and told him I wanted to play him a song first. He's like okay my dark-skinned lady friend. Play me something. I whipped out the slide and pointed it in his face. Don't ever do my friend and sis like that, he said. Watched him run to his car crying. Guess we need to hop the freight to Richmond. We got a gig in two days."

Chapter 3

"Miriam, I say fuck the commies, and the American commie folk music scene. We gonna play what we know, and that's good down-home Zydeco."

"That's the best music. We're gonna show them hillbillies out here something."

We did stop in Johnson City, Cisco the Commie's hometown, to listen to him play, but we weren't going to meet his Mama, Daisy. I remember Papi mention that she came to my third birthday party, and they came to town a few times when I was a baby back in Nebraska, but I don't remember who the hell she was.

We watched a lot of the music in Johnson City, and I thought I'd enjoy this lifestyle. I liked the music and the way the community gathered up to do some square dancing and clogging, people twisted like a cyclone, and kicked their legs up. Miriam giggled and her eyes sparkled as she joined the action.

The guy with the banjo played like no one I heard before. He wasn't cranking his hand like he attempted opening a jar of Mami's pinto beans, or Papi's blackberries, but instead his right hand sat still, and he only moved his thumb, index and middle finger. Daddy never played like that. That man played as fast as lightning, while the rest of the band consisted of a mandolin player, stand-up bass player, a guitarist and the fiddler kept up the pace.

Miri shook her goodies until I grabbed her. "Over there." I pointed to the railroad tracks to the North. "All them ugly white guys. They're all dressed in white, with capes and masks. It's the damn Klan. We need to make a run for it."

Miriam turned and smiled.

"I got a better idea. You got your slide?"

I snapped the blade open. "I don't go nowhere without it." Her smile widened.

She popped hers open too. "The train tracks are that way. Sara, the only way us folks can't fear those chicken shit bullies, is to go after them. We're armed. Let's head for the tracks."

I nodded, knowing Klan members had something to do with Papi's death, at least killed him like cancer. I shut the blade, and a grin as wide as the Tennessee valley appeared on my face. I put my hand on my chin, inhaled, snapped the blade open again, and watched it rise in the Tennessee air. I repeated the act. "Let's go sis."

We set of toward them on what would either a death sentence, or a groundbreaking moment. I heard that Bessie ran the Klan off at one of her shows. The cold eyes of Miriam, my big sis, former sex tutor, and step ma, made me think of someone who does not care if they lived or died. There were at least six of them guarding the track. Our guitars strapped on our backs, and our small bags with our clothes all tied up tighter than a flea's ass over a rain barrel. The guitars slowed us down quite a bit, with Miriam leading the way. She darted through the thick trees and I followed until we came to a clearing, and soon we were exposed. Miriam focused on her prey, like a hawk, waiting to scoop down and carry one of those rodents away. The woman tasted blood as she shot one of those dirty old blues men.

"I'm leading the way, Sara. Is your slide ready?" Snap went the blades. Stares and smiles exchanged. We went off like rebels in the war between the states, did the classic rebel yell, ran as fast as we could with them guitars bouncing on our backs. I figured we both resembled painted turtles and I hoped we weren't moving like them. The fat, ugly, caped and masked white men seen no fear in Miriam's eyes. She didn't care if she got killed; the girl, bound to take at least one out. These masked apes were nothing but cowards and retreated deep into the forest.

I learned something that day. Bullies are cowards, who you need to stand up to, even if you're little like Miriam. Life's lessons are learned anytime and anywhere. You'd never think two women standing up to these pigs disguised as terrorists, in the mountains of their home territory would be one of these lessons. Before the Klansman regrouped, an eastbound freight chugged past, and we hopped it. In that moment, I earned my first victory against the Klan and it wouldn't be my last. I knew that Richmond sat on the other side of Virginia, so we'd remain on this train for a while. It stopped in Bristol and resumed its venture towards the coast. The squeal of train brakes woke us, and we tumbled in the boxcar, while somersaulting our way towards the front. After we gathered our senses and balance, we took off towards the night, not knowing what direction we headed. We heard from the outside. "There were two of them. They gotta be lynched."

Not sure where we were, or which way we were going, one thing we knew was we were being hunted like game, and tomorrow may never come for either one of us. The best we could do was hide in the railyard, and keep our big yappers shut. Flashlights beamed, and we heard voices.

A guy not 5 ft from me said, "Dem niggers ain't getting out of Abingdon. We got a special place for niggers like them."

I wanted to exhale, but he stood too close, emitting an odor that choked me. He hadn't showered, plus he'd hear the air releasing from my lungs.

We hid pretty good and when we awoke, the sun was up and there wasn't anyone around. I craned my neck to see where we hid. A house, whose back yard sat adjacent to the train tracks. I couldn't live there since I'd hop freights take it to wherever I wanted to go. We hid underneath the back step that meets the back door. No trains sat in the yard, So Miriam and I walked down the street, taking in the sights of downtown Abingdon.

"I could live in a little mountain town like this Sara."

"Not me I need a swamp. Ain't no gators around."

"We could get a hound and call him gat …"

A shiny Desoto stopped. A dorky commie orgy-wanter, tipped his Fedora to us. "Sexy, sassy Sara, and her equally sexy and sassy dark-skinned friend, I come to your rescue. The Klan's got you surrounded, but I grew up here so I can get you out of town. I got friends who played a civil rights rally last night; the same as we'll play tomorrow night. So, your sassiness's, do you want to run across Virginia, or do you want a ride in the big old bus that's parked at mama's house? Sexy sassy Sara and Sara's equally sexy and sassy dark-skinned friend. What's it going to be? You can even sit in front. That big old machine is leaving soon."

The wimp smiled at me, and through his spectacles I saw him stare and eye what he used to have. He wasn't a threat, since we both carried our slides.

"Let's go Miri."

We crawled into the back of his Desoto. Cisco tossed blankets over us and we sped up into the mountains and bounced like we hopped a freight. He hollered at us to take the blanket off, and we swerved up the old mountain road.

"My mama lives up here. Her name is Daisy. My Pa might be home, since he comes and goes. You might meet him sometime." He barked the kind of laughter that I only heard in scary movies. It reminded me of a raccoon stuck in a trap. Miri tensed up, and I thought about jumping from the car. We swerved a dusty lane that led up to their house, and I noticed a big bus parked there, with a bunch of musicians standing outside waiting.

I heard the banjo player yell. "You're the two girls who took on the Klan? Thank you. They popped in to bust up the anti-Klan rally we played. For our appreciation, we will give you a lift to Richmond. The bus leaves in an hour, so you're welcome to get yourselves cleaned up and grab a bite to eat. That's from Ms. Daisy Greene."

We were both reluctant, but the reek from our bodies and with our stomachs sounding like a black bear that hangs out in the mountains, we went inside.

The owner a busty redhead, wore short shorts and talked with a sweet little accent. She smiled at me. "Sara Barnum. I haven't seen you since you were knee high and chewing grass. Whatever happened to your Ma and Pa?"

"Ma'am? How do you know my name?"

"I know a lot about your family Sara."

"Then where's Early?"

"He drops by for a few weeks. Say, Robert when was the last time your pa visited?"

"It's been a couple of weeks mother. I think he's playing the show in Richmond. Did you know Sara and Miriam here play real good? I hope Daddy makes it back. He'd love to play a show with these gals."

The kitchen door creaked open. My eyes followed the creaking sound, and a tall man emerged from the shadows. He adorned a straw hat just like what Papi used to wear and a slashed scar across his cheek. He carried a fiddle in his left hand and his bow in his right. I looked at Miriam and she took a step backwards.

The voice came from the shadows. "Sara Barnum, I was present the day you were born."

Chapter 4

"How do you know my name?" I asked Mr. Greene.

"I know a lot about you. Like I said, I was there when you were born, and you spit up on me. I don't forget faces, and I don't forget people vomiting all over me. I don't care if you were a day old." He cranked the fiddle up and rosined up his bow, while playing *Zydeco Sont Pas Sale.* "C'mon Girls let's play along. You know them beans ain't salted."

I sweated like a whore in church, as was Miriam, while we remained motionless. I knew Early Greene killed Papi by slashing his throat, and I wanted to ask, but that damn cat kept biting my tongue. Miriam crept backwards attempting to hide in the shadows. Her face had gone ashen and I could tell that man made her feel ill. The fiddler continued to play, finished his first number, and started on *Jambalaya.* I couldn't stop myself from strumming along. Miriam on cue, burst out singing. We played three more songs together.

"Damn you girls can play. Your daddy taught you well. God Bless Bo."

The cat relinquished my tongue, and I blurted. "What do you know about my daddy's death? I know you know something." *I stressed on the know.*

"Come here." He pointed to their parlor room, and Miriam and I followed the suspected killer. I always doubted that he killed Papi, but I didn't think Mami could lie to me. "Sara, you can't tell anyone, not even your brother." He pointed to Miriam. "You need to leave the room."

"You can tell her, we're sisters," I snapped, not about to be left alone with my father's murderer.

"No. I will only tell you. Besides, you must promise never to tell anyone."

In silence Miriam retreated from the parlor room which stored record albums, and on the wall set mounted deer antlers. The parlor looked like a hunting lodge, and a music studio combined. Early walked across the floor, went over to the door that Miriam left open.

"This is confidential, Ms. Landry," he said unapologetically and slammed the door in her face. He turned to face me. "take a seat on the green davenport, under the large antler rack."

I looked straight into his eyes, "So what do you have to tell me?"

"I know you think I killed your dad. It wasn't me or your uncle, and I know the people involved. Let me give you a little background on who I am." He stared at me, chin resting in his hand. "I worked for the government and was hired by a former president to kill the Fuentes family, which included your mother. I made a mistake when hiring my accomplice. I picked the wrong Barnum brother since Zeke possessed Klan affiliations, making it a Klan killing. I took a liking to your Dad. He's a great guy, and we made some amazing music together. Then, I saw him with your mother, and admired the way he loved her. They evolved into the perfect couple and I couldn't have her killed."

I sighed. "So, if you didn't do it. Who did?"

"Bourgeois. Maybe the deputy, or the old man in Huntsville. Your Mami never got kidnapped. She left on her own free will. It's a conspiracy."

I lowered my tone to a whisper. "Mami knew about it? She wanted Daddy dead. Why?"

"Your mother wanted her freedom, and craved stardom, and being a Fuentes married to a Barnum, she'd never receive fame."

"My brother Tomas and I'll never get that will we?"

"I can't answer that, but I want to play some music with you at the folk festival in Richmond tomorrow. I've listened to you play. I loved your pa's playing, but you got more talent in your little finger than he had in his right and left hand. He carried no rhythm." The man laughed for the first time. "Your dad made up for his lack of timing with passion. You got them both young lady. A total cross between your ma and pa."

"Thanks, I know I'm blessed that they're my parents, but I need to know how to lead my life. Are folks after me and my little brother? Hell, I don't even know where he is at the moment. I suppose you know what he's up to."

"Sara," he sighed and said in a passionless voice. "I can't answer anything about that. Live the life you want. That's all I can tell you. Let's rehearse some songs."

My squinted and curled my lip, a perplexed swamp girl out of place in Virginia at the home of the man who I always thought killed Papi. I just found out he might not have killed my father, and folks wondered why I carried a befuddled look on my face all the time. I followed him out of the room and grabbed my guitar and Miriam, and an accordion player joined us, and soon we jammed on swamp songs in the Virginia Mountains.

Our song ended, and there to greet us stood Cisco's mother and the commie, orgy-wanter lifesaver himself.

"Miss Barnum." The aging Southern lady stared at me, like a school marm.

"Yeah, what?" I wasn't trying to disrespect her, but since the age of twelve I grew up in the bayou. Papi didn't teach me no manners.

"That's yes ma'am," she spoke in a thick Tennessee accent but attempted to act all proper. "Why did you dump poor Robert back in Tennessee? He says you pushed him over and walked across his face. Remember this, young lady, this boy's a talented young man. He has a bright future ahead of him in politics, or anything he wants to do. Anything Robert wants, Robert gets. So little Sara Barnum, whatever you do, don't cross him." She folded her arms below her chest, lips protruded while she scowled at me.

I wanted to laugh. I turned to Miriam and she held her hands over her mouth. She opened her hands, and I witnessed her smirks

. I turned my head, wiped my grin off, and in my best Southern belle voice said. "Yes'm," Miriam and I turned around laughing and bolted from the parlor.

We rode with the Greene's on their bus which turned out quite an adventure. Miri and I went to the back, as we'd been taught and conditioned to throughout the years of Jim Crow. We sat next to each other, and that damn fool Robert, aka Cisco tried to squeeze his scrawny butt in between. He ended up on our laps, with his arms around us.

He whispered to me. "Mama wants to see us get along. Give me a quick kiss my sweet, sassy, sexy Sara."

I wriggled my butt, and his arm tightened on my shoulder. "Don't move sassy Sara. I know all about your father. You don't want to see him yet. We need to let my ma and pa know that we're back together."

He sang a little folk song,

"Together again, it's been so long since I've seen your face, it's been so long since I felt your embrace. It's been so long since I held you tight. We will be together again, tonight."

Somewhere near Roanoke, the bus pulled over. Fuel, food, and peeing required by all. Miri and I hopped off last. Our eyes met in a "Let's run for it." Rucksacks and guitars nabbed, we sprinted from the bus, retreating the short distance to the railroad tracks. We ducked behind some dogwood trees until the sky turned gray. Steam filled the air, and the lone sound we heard became the lonesome whistle of a passenger train. We jumped on without a ticket and got booted off at Christiansburg. We strolled down the tracks towards the southeast and waited for a freight train. The moon stood high while the night took over, and animals howled in the mountains. There weren't no gators here, and I trusted the reptiles, but had no clue about bears or wolves. We sat in the dark, and I called the train on my harmonica. It soon called back, and we hopped it. The box we climbed into carried no hobos, so we caught a break, and the freight rolled all night and didn't stop until morning.

We stopped in Knoxville, Tennessee and there we washed dishes for food, and played on a street corner to earn some money for a bus trip to Shreveport, where we hitched home. We arrived at Grandpa's after a wild adventure of having ran into Early Greene, chased the Klan, played some music, and I lost my virginity to a commie, and the son of Early Greene. I was pretty sure I'd run into Cisco and his family again.

Despite my coaxing against it, Miriam boarded the bus out of Shreveport returning to Chicago. I would be alone and missed my little brother Tomas. Tommy grew into a man from what Grandpa told me. A young man who played football at Grambling, even though he grew into the lightest complected Barnum in the family and passed for a white man. He should have played at LSU, but got rejected, because his sister was a nigger.

Part II

Chapter 5

Baton Rouge, Louisiana 1954

Even though I owned a car, and was able to drive to work at the East Baton Rouge Parish court system as a public defender, I rode the city bus. Two women worked there, while I was the lone minority in the office, and I had my work cut out for me. The public defenders attempted to defend the guilty, but this was the South, and I got to defend many innocent Negro clients.

My most famous case was a rape trial which received national attention. I defended Isaac Begnaud, a twenty- year-old student at Southern, accused of raping a white LSU coed, a nineteen- year-old Jayne Delaroche. Ms. Delaroche happened to be the youngest daughter of Miles Delaroche, the owner of a small grocery store chain in the city known as the Red Stick. Mr. Delaroche was a known Klansman as were his two sons, one who worked in law enforcement in the capital city, and the other managed the small local grocery store chain.

Mr. Delaroche and his wife also had three daughters, the two eldest, were graduates of LSU, and married prominent businessmen in the capital city. Jacquie Delaroche married Michael Timmons, an executive of Mobil Oil, and Jeanette Delaroche married a young banking executive.

Jayne, the youngest Delaroche and rowdiest. She reminded me of myself, back when I was a young freshman at LSU for that one semester.

The girl never acted polished and sophisticated, always in torn clothes that were either a little big, or too small. I thought she was pretty, while her sisters whom I met at the trial, seemed way too snobby. Most people thought the opposite, since Jayne's style wasn't appropriate for a Southern Lady. That's what Miles Delaroche said anyway about his youngest daughter.

Isaac Begnaud came to Baton Rouge from the peninsula. A young musician, who hailed hailing from the same town as Miriam and studied music at Southern. The young man wanted to be more than an accordion, and washboard player, and went on to study jazz trumpet at the Negro College. Isaac never knew his father, they said he played guitar, and dropped in and out of the area.

Isaac's mother, a schoolteacher down in Morgan City. She taught history in the black school, and had two other children, not yet in college. She told me that all three kids were born to different fathers. I wasn't sure if that had anything to do with the case or not. Having gone through the case, I felt Isaac didn't rape young Ms. Delaroche. My gut feeling hinged on her and Isaac became lovers, and the Klan family felt ashamed. After speaking with Isaac for five minutes, I knew I stood correct.

My job became an easy one of trying to convince the jury that what the defendant and victim had was consensual, and not rape. I wouldn't blame Jayne Delaroche. She wasn't asking for it, hanging out at jazz clubs and rubbing up on young jazz musicians. That would be victim blaming, the coward's way out, and disrespectful to the grocery store heiress.

Isaac told me the whole story, "My band played a lot in Old South Baton Rouge. We hadn't quite made it to the Lincoln yet, but we were working on it. I hoped we'd open for Pops or Ella someday. The combo gathered a good following, not exclusive to Negroes from the area, but these white girls kept showing up. One gal was Miss Delaroche. She showed up every Friday night with her two girlfriends, I think one's name was Clara, while the other gal went by the name Eve.

"Anyway, Jayne always stared at me. At first, I wasn't sure if it was because I played the leads, or because she liked me, but as time wore on, I knew she liked me. The way her eyes lit up when I blew my horn, and when I stared back at her. I mean we built a connection. I took her back to my pad, where we smoked up some reefer and messed around. I really loved the girl and wanted more to our relationship. I wanted to take her to the Chicken Shack for dinner and spend all my free time with her. Damn, Ms. Barnum." He placed his head in his hand and looked down as though he preached to the dirt floor inside his jail cell. "I got ready to take her down to Morgan City to meet my mama. Mama can witness this because I called her up saying; I got me a white girlfriend." He looked up at me. "Her name's Jayne. Mama told me to be careful, and don't trust no white woman from a good family. They are using you."

Isaac stared at the other end of the jail cell as he continued, "Anyways, me and Jayne finished up our lovemaking, and I told her I loved her and wanted to take her home with me one weekend. She looks at me, and says I don't want to meet your mother, and I don't love you. I go, why are we doing this? She laughed weird not like she thinks I'm a funny boy, but she laughed at me, and not with me. Guess she thought me a little naïve. I tried to tell her I loved her, even hugged her, but and she looked up at me, and said don't touch me ever again. Stupid me reaches out to hug her one last time, and she slapped me like a drummer beats his skins. I looked at this thing, walk away in her ripped short dress. Next thing I knew the cops came and arrested me."

"Well, let's say we're lucky this is going to trial. I've heard horror stories, as I'm sure you have about black men engaging in sexual activities with white women. Isaac, I know you're innocent. I grew up with music, and your stuff grooves. I go down to Old South on Fridays, mainly to see some Zydeco, but I came in and seen you play, and I'm impressed. I came in a few more times, and I've seen Ms. Delaroche there, and there was one night I wanted to talk to you, cause I play guitar, but I see her come up and kiss you as you left arm in arm. Also, Isaac, I can round up several witnesses who saw you leave together. This should be an open and shut case. Of course, we live in the South, and they've hung folks down here for less. You, Isaac Begnaud, will become a free man once this trial concludes."

"I sure hope so, Ms. Barnum." He doesn't sound hopeful.

"Isaac, this is why I became a lawyer. My daddy's family fought this for generations. I'm the first who's trying to do it legally."

"Ma'am, I'm glad they appointed you."

"Call me Ms. Barnum, and I wish I didn't have to. Innocent men shouldn't be on trial, but I tell you what Isaac, it's going to be an honor defending you."

The young Southern student and Jazz musician smiled at me, and I got some of the same feelings I felt years ago, when I was fifteen, and some young guitarist gave me my first kiss, and even stronger than Cisco Greene. I couldn't react on it since there's a code of ethics. And that young boy who kissed me, and whose room I snuck up to, only to be humiliated by him, may be kin to this young man. I smiled back at him and patted him on his shoulder."

I asked for a fast trial, which I did not receive. I argued that the boy, a student at Southern, and a prominent musician in town, would miss way too much school, and too many gigs. The trial was scheduled two months from the time I appointed as his attorney.

I spent a lot of time in Old South Baton Rouge, which was normal for me anyway. The best music and food were down there, and I lived right across the tracks. I found several witnesses, who saw Ms. Delaroche leave with Isaac, and interviewed neighbors who watched the grocery store heiress head out for class the next morning, hand in hand with my client. I talked to the young heartthrob's neighbor who claimed the squeaking, pounding, and moaning kept him up all night. The old black man was in his 70's, and when he told me the story of their lovemaking, he smiled at winked at me. I wasn't sure if he hit on me, but I thought it was cute.

Finally, the day of the trial arrived. The Delaroche family hired the best attorney in town to prosecute Isaac. The man, Klan all the way, was noted for getting the maximum sentence against the blacks in town, regardless of the crime. I know, because I went up against him on a couple of occasions. Once when I tried to defend a sixteen-year-old boy for shoplifting a bag of beans and a bag of rice, to prevent his large family from starvation. I lost the case, and the boy got five years in jail.

My plan appeared simple. It wasn't to disgrace Ms. Delaroche, but to make her a progressive thinking woman, who saw no problems with interracial engagements. I found witnesses, in fact if I could call myself to the stand I would, but I'd use my testimony in the closing arguments. The lone case my esteemed and prejudiced opponent hammered on was that a young black man had sexual relations with a rich young white woman. Unfortunately, that's all the proof needed in Louisiana.

The trial started with my opponent asking Isaac about the number of white women he slept with.

"I engaged in relations with three white girls before I met Ms. Delaroche. They all came on to me, and I took them back to my place. I never fell in love with any of them."

"So, you made a habit of luring these poor white students back to your apartment, to brutally rape them and have your way with them like a savage?"

"Objection." I hollered. "He is leading the defendant and his comments are conjecture."

"No, sir," he answered anyway. "I didn't lure them up. They came up on their own free will and spent the night with me."

I scowled at him. I could win this case, but I needed his help. My eyes pierced his soul, as he received a look that could kill. I went up and whispered. "Don't answer if I object, unless the judge allows his question.

The Klansman proceeded to interview one of Ms. Delaroche's predecessors regarding the extent of their relationship. The girl. also, a student at LSU, hailed from Shreveport society.

"Yes, sir. I went up to see the jazz band, and I spoke to Mr. Begnaud, and he did invite me to his apartment for a late dinner and a nightcap. I was unaware he wanted sexual relations with me. In fact, I remained a virgin, as I never, ever let a man touch me in that way. I saved myself for marriage."

"So, what happened?"

"Mr. Begnaud made me a po boy sandwich, and we shared it, and he also opened a bottle of wine which we shared. He kept refilling my glass, and I kept drinking. I admit the wine tasted good, but it made me feel funny. I told him I felt tired and went to lie down. He suggested I lay on his bed. Things became hazy because of the wine, but I remember he carried me to his room and laid me on his bed. That's about all I remember, but I woke up naked in his bed, with him next to me and also naked."

"So, this wasn't consensual?"

"No sir. He got me drunk on wine and I passed out, I'm pretty sure he took advantage of me, but I don't know. I didn't feel any different down there. I'm not sure if he took advantage of me or not. He told me he wanted to but saw me passed out, so I don't know."

I put my head in my hands. This wasn't an open and shut case, but I took this opportunity to cross examine the witness.

"You said you went to his place willingly. Maybe you downed a few drinks at the club, and it appeared to Mr. Begnaud that you seemed willing to give yourself to him. Now, as a woman, I know wanting to spend time with a man in the evening, does not mean I want to sleep with him. I know this for a fact. I also know that young men think that if a woman comes to your apartment after having a few drinks, he may expect some sort of relations. I'm not saying either of you were wrong. Though we, as women, must remain careful, when we make choices to visit a man alone in his apartment. My question is, what did you expect when you went to Isaac's apartment?"

"Ms. Barnum, I really don't know. I never reported it, since I wasn't sure if I was raped. I don't think I was, because I'm not sure if he touched me."

"So, you don't know if you two performed intercourse?"

"I don't know. I'm sure he did, I mean I passed out, and don't know."

"Now, Mary, I'm not sure if this was rape, as far as damaging his reputation. If he didn't touch you, didn't attempt intercourse with you, he was actually a gentleman. Maybe his intent was to seduce you, but when you passed out, a real man does not take advantage of a woman in situations like that. A real man may cover you up and sleep on the couch, or lay on his bed, and not touch you anymore. Personally, I think any sexual relations that aren't consensual are rape, however it sounds like in this incident, some bad choices were made by both parties. A man's indiscretions do not make him a rapist, like a women's bad choices regarding her sexual activities does not make her a whore."

"Ms. Barnum," the judge glared at me. I knew I did wrong, and I knew what was coming next, "language. Your language is inappropriate."

"I'm sorry your honor. I'm trying to make a point that we should not judge this incident. Two people made bad choices, most of us have. So, Mary made a mistake joining Isaac in this room, and Isaac made a mistake by allegedly taking advantage of a drunken woman, however there is no proof. Are we assuming because he's a black man, he has no will power? I bet a lot of these men in the jury or audience thought the same. Should I take advantage, or not?

It was time to call Jayne Delaroche and I figured I was gonna to make her sweat and cry.

"The first time I went to Isaac's apartment, it was the same as the previous witness. I watched Isaac perform on stage a few times before and I liked his music. He had a flair about him and the man's performances are charismatic, and sexual. I admit I was attracted to him, I guess it was his music, and the way he performed it. I wanted to get to know him better, so one night I introduced myself, and he invited me out for breakfast. I told him I can't. There isn't a place in town that would serve us. So, he invites me back to his apartment, and like the other witnesses, I said yes."

"Does going to a man's apartment at midnight mean having sex to you, Ms. Delaroche?" my opponent asked.

"No, it doesn't. I only wanted to get to know him better."

"No further questions."

It's my turn to cross-examine the plaintiff. "Ms. Delaroche, it's not a crime to engage in sexual relations with a black man. There's no shame in it. Some people may call it taboo, or forbidden, but it's not a crime, and there are many progressive people who find no shame for white people and Negroes to engage in sexual activity. The question you do not want to answer. Did you engage in sexual relations with Mr. Begnaud?"

"Yes, I did."

"Were they voluntary?"

"Yes, ma'am."

"Were you and Mr. Begnaud involved in a relationship?"

"Not really. I went up to see him in his apartment, but we weren't going steady."

"Did he tell you he loved you, and wanted more than weekend flings?"

"Yes, he said he wanted me to come home with him to meet his mama."

"What did you say?"

"I told him no."

"What did you say when he said I love you?"

"I told him I didn't love him."

"What did he do next?"

"He tried to hold me."

"What did you do?"

"I pushed him away, and tried to run, but he grabbed me and tried kissing me. I slapped him, and he got mad."

"Did he hit you back?"

"No, but he pushed me on his bed, and lay down on top of me. I slapped him again and I managed to escape out the door."

"So, at that time there was no rape. He did not penetrate you, or even hit you. The only violent move was nudging you towards the bed. Is that correct?"

"Yes, but he attempted sex with me, when I wasn't willing. To me, that's attempted rape."

"So, if a white man tried to kiss you, or if you're kissing him and he tries to have sex with you, and you turn down his advances, is he trying to rape you, or is he acting too fresh?"

"Objection. Irrelevant."

"Your honor, I'm trying to show that the plaintiff is charging the defendant with attempted rape, because of the color of his skin and not because of his actions. I find the question relevant."

"Objection overruled. Answer the question, Ms. Delaroche."

I sighed and looked at the plaintiff. She glared at me as I followed up my question with another. "Have you ever rejected a white man as he attempted to have more intimate relations?"

"Yes, I have." She started sobbing. She knew where I was going.

"Did you accuse him of rape?"

A loud no came from her mouth, in between the sobbing. "No, I did not, and I'm sorry." She stormed out the courthouse shamefaced, only to appear a few minutes later. "Excuse me, your honor. This is extremely hard on me."

"No further questions." I told the judge, and sat beside my client, who flashed an irresistible grin.

The trial continued. More witnesses were interviewed, cross-examined, and my opponent gave his closing statement. Soon it became my turn.

I turned and faced the all-white jury. "Ladies and gentlemen of the jury, this trial is not about rape, or attempted rape. This is about a woman who felt remorse over her involvement with a young Negro man or felt bad for rejecting the man, when in fact she fell in love with him." I glanced Jayne's way. She stared at her intertwined fingers and refused to look up. I strode around the court room and stopped in front of the jury. "My client owned a reputation for seducing women with his music, and has history to prove it, but does that make him a rapist? His morals will be questioned, but again does that make him a rapist?" I stared at Jayne, her family, and back again at her before continuing. "I'm ashamed that the esteemed Delaroche family even considered pressing charges on Mr. Begnaud. It's a shame Mr. Begnaud fell in love with the plaintiff. If he didn't fall in love with her, and they went their separate ways, I can guarantee you this case would not see the light of day. Men and women don't always react rationally when they feel they're in love and when rejected they often do crazy things. I'm sure we've all witnessed something. I know I have." I glanced at Jayne Delaroche. "I mean haven't we all done something foolish? Again, Mr. Begnaud fell in love with the plaintiff and engaged in premarital relations." I focused again on the jury. "Some of you believe that is a taboo, races shouldn't mix, and you have the right to think that. However, many of you might be curious, or maybe members in here who have been with a man, or woman of another race." I focused on man in the jury box in an ill-fitting suit, and at a woman whose breasts popped out of her blouse. They looked away, yet I kept at it and picked up a Bible. "According to this book here, sexual relations are a sin, unless you're married, and both the plaintiff and defendant are required to deal with the Lord above regarding their sin. Not the state of Louisiana. No crime was committed, and I'm sorry we wasted your time this week. In conclusion, I ask that you find the defendant, Isaac Begnaud, innocent of all charges. Thank you."

After exhaling all the oxygen in Baton Rouge, I shook my head, and my long black hair whipped back and forth, as I went to sit next to Isaac.

"You were great," he told me. "You think we got a chance."

I leaned over and whispered to him. "If we lose, I'm going to quit this lawyering stuff and become a blues singer."

"My dad's a blues guitarist, maybe you can join him."

The deliberation lasted for hours. The foreman read the verdict. "Not guilty on all charges." I got me a standing ovation from the black section of the courthouse, and Isaac's mother came up to hug me.

"Thank you." She strolled away. If that was my kid, or my kid brother and freed on all charges, I'd dance with joy. She could have remembered the young boys found hanging in trees for doing the same thing Isaac did, or rumored to do. Maybe she thought that my case a minor battle in an endless war that would go on and on for generations, or maybe, that's how I felt deep inside. On the outside, I flashed smiles, to the photographers, journalists and civil rights leaders of the NAACP. Most young attorneys fighting for civil rights would have thought the victory an ideal situation, but I didn't want to hang with them honchos. I wanted to hang with the people erroneously accused, the poor folks from the bayou, fighting against long standing repulsive mores. I wasn't the type of gal who could be bought or sold, even by representatives who fought the same battle as me. I had too much of my daddy in me.

Mr. Marshall asked me, "Do you want to work for the NAACP as an attorney?"

I rolled my eyes and smirked. I thought the darn fool crazy. "With all due respect sir, I think my work is here, helping these poor kids. They're the ones who need themselves a good public defender."

"With all due respect Ms. Barnum," he mimicked, "we need good, passionate young attorneys, ones who will take on these cases all over the country. We need tenacious lawyers, who aren't afraid to take on the establishment. We need attorneys who aren't afraid to kick society where it counts. I know you're one of these women. You possess fire and you exhume spunk." He reached out his right hand welcoming me aboard.

The next big case I became involved with was not my typical civil rights lawyering. I defended two members of the New Orleans mafia who did business in Baton Rouge. The second in charge, Mr. Carmine Marcello was charged with extortion, racketeering, and murder. His understudy and left-hand man was a man named Johnny Boulet. Normally, a public defender would not take a case like this, but as rising lawyer in Baton Rouge. I took the case. Besides Mr. Boulet's personal representatives made sure I did.

It was not an offer I could not refuse type of situation. The wise guys from New Orleans did not promise me anything for working with them. The state of Louisiana made sure my pockets remained full of cash for my services. The mob did not pay me, but somehow, I believe they did. I made sure the men were cleared and acquitted of all charges.

Part III

Chapter 6

Tomas Barnum 1952, Monroe, Louisiana

The full moon shone bright. Its pale glow sandwiched between two gray clouds that turned a shade of orange, while my partner, Odell Bourgeois, and me trolled through the vacant streets of Monroe. The older, balding fat man, hand-picked as my partner on the police force, scratched his arm, as if fur came out.

"Tomas? Are you a spic? Barnum ain't no spic name."

"I got a little mixed heritage from way back when," I stretched the truth.

He looked me over. "You don't look like a spic. Complexion too dark, but I figured you're Creole. Lots of white folks like me are Creole. They are a little darker. Not too dark, like them Niggers who run around, like them boys over there." He shined his flashlight towards the ESSO gas station that was closed for the evening. "Those little Nigger boys shouldn't run around at this hour. They up to something."

My stomach rumbled, like when my former crush, Miriam, cooked dinner for the family, every time he said Nigger. She was the best cook and always got me rumbling, but she wanted nothing to do with me. Anyway, I still hate that word, and the one-time Pa whipped me was when Miriam turned me down. I called her *a little n... bitch* and got my butt whipped.

"They are just roaming around. Hell, when I was a teenager..."

"They shouldn't roam around at all. Niggers need a curfew. We need to haul their black asses in."

"For what?" I peered at him in the dark.

"We'll think of something." He grabbed a wad of loose -leaf chewing tobacco out and stuffed a handful in his left cheek. "We'll think of something." He laughed the most irritating laugh I ever heard. It sounded like the mad scientist in those Monster movies I watched, but worse. "There's always something we can get them for."

"Kids probably shooting pool and running home. We don't know what they doing."

"Wipe that smirk off your face Barnum, or I'll do it for you."

My smile always got me in trouble with the ladies. I dated a lot of black women at Grambling, but I enjoyed my time hanging out at ULM. The gals always talked about my disarming smile, it opened my way into their hearts and other parts of their body.

My mouth clenched up tight and Odell backhanded me across his face. The stench of Beechnut tobacco filled my nostrils, since it draped all over my partner's hand. At this rate, my first night as a Monroe policeman was going to be fun. Maybe my last.

I quit the force that night, and like my father before me, I set off to fight the Klan until whenever death captures me. However, I received other offers, and playing the game is what I did best.

I accepted a job with the FBI. Soon I relocated to Virginia for training, and stationed in New Orleans, to work for civil rights. I had no idea I'd investigate the killing of my father, Bo Barnum. The key witness, my mother, Lydia Barnum.

"My ma witnessed it all, at least that it what she told my sister. Early Greene slashed his throat, while my uncle watched"

"Mr. Barnum, first that came from the testimony of an escaped convict. It wasn't Mr. Greene."

"How do you know?" I looked at him like a lost puppy, not sure what or who to trust anymore.

"Again, an escaped convict testified. We take what she says with a grain of salt."

"She's no escaped convict. That's my mother. She ain't guilty of nothing."

"Tomas, the woman who testified got captured escaping into the Huntsville State Prison. She's a felon and her words cannot be trusted. Early Greene had nothing to do with the murder of your father."

"My sister knows it was him."

"Because your mother told her so? Sara Barnum's your sister?"

"Yes, sir."

"Excuse me Mr. Barnum." He left the office to the back closet, where black file cabinets held overstuffed manila folders. The boss returned with three huge folders. "Your sister, Sara Barnum, you say?" He dropped three folders on my desk, all stuffed with papers that are falling out of them since they're packed full. "These are three of the files where we listed that she's a communist sympathizer, a union organizer and an agitator for civil rights. Also..."

"Sir I don't mean to interrupt, but that's why I joined the Fed. I'm here to seek justice against the Klan and bring that racist cult to its knees. Also, I want to seek justice from them small town, and big city police departments across the country, that feel it's easier to hang or beat an innocent colored boy, than to solve a crime. I've seen the corruption firsthand in Monroe."

"Is that why you quit on your first night?"

"Yes, sir." My Klan partner wanted me to go bust up some Negro kids, because they stayed out late and hung out in the white part of town. We had no evidence against them. That son of a bitch slapped me in the face. Sir, I want to know what happened to my family. I want to know the truth, but I don't trust anyone, except my sister, though sometimes I think she's a little off her rocker. I heard the case reopened, and even though it's my father's killer, I will act rationally at bringing the people to justice."

"Barnum, so far you obtained a good reputation in your months here." He put out that stanky cigar in the ash tray, his eyes on mine. "I will give you the files, and the ones on your sister. I want you to get out of here. All expenses are paid, and your first stop will be Huntsville, Texas to see your Mother."

The caddy was packed to the hilt and there wasn't any room in the trunk, so the extra suitcases were tossed in the back seat. I pulled out of The Big Easy in the morning and skedaddled west towards Vinton, Louisiana where I remembered my father stopped after we thought Mama got killed. I crossed the Sabine and headed towards Houston, and up to Huntsville. I packed for a week's visit. Interrogating Mama and discovering the truth about Pa's murder may face difficulties, but Mama always talked to me. Sara teased me about our relationship. Hell, she used to be Papi's little princessa.

A cheap motel sat near the state prison." Don't let strangers in your room", the clerk told me. "They might be escapees."

"What if I like escaped lady cons? They've been without for some time now. I might get me some action." I flashed a smile and gave the woman with an old wrinkled face and straight gray hair donned with unfashionable glasses a wink. I went on to find my room, turned the key, and let myself in. I tossed the briefcase on the bed. I hadn't seen Mama for months, and the last time I attempted a visit, the guards told me she was no longer detained. I knew they lied, since I circled around and went to the back of the farm. The location Sara always met her at, and she stood, kneeling over and picking flowers. She didn't acknowledge me, however she did, since I remember she spun like a carousel and rushed away.

I opened my briefcase and pulled out four files. The first one was for Early Greene. I glanced over the second one which contained the name S. Barnum on it and was the thickest. The third file was Mama's, the one required to read, and the fourth file, as thick as Sara's listed the name of B. Barnum. *What the hell were the feds after Pa for? Did they want him dead, too? Maybe Early was innocent, or maybe the folks he worked for paid to murder Pa.* Unsure if I even wanted to know the truth but speaking to Mama became essential. Since our appointment already scheduled at eleven the next morning, I opened her file and observed the name Lydia Fuentes Barnum Bourgeois, aka Lupe Benoit. I slammed the file down and peeked at Papi's folder. The manila envelope spoke to me, "*open me, and open me.*" I read it over and nothing damaging showed on the first few pages.

A hurried skim through, revealed another sealed envelope, but I couldn't see inside, but a classified seal appeared, "Only to open by the FBI." *Well hell, I'm the FBI. I always thought Papi was a straight shooter, even though he got into trouble every now and then.* I doubted this stuff in his file contained anything to do with bootlegging or pimping them women out years ago. I hesitated over opening it, but like a snoopy child on December 23, I grabbed my switch, and pressed it against the envelope, like I shaved someone with a straight edge. The knife tore through the paper right to left. Once getting to the end, I blew the top apart and removed sealed papers. They remained in a smaller envelope. I repeated the action, but this time took a swift left to right cut, with one backslash of my wrist. I pulled out the papers and unfolded them, scattering them across the bed. I read, "*Bo Barnum must die. He's a proven agitator since his arrival in Omaha, Nebraska and since stirred up racial integration in the south with his music and politics. He supports miscegenation with his Mexican wife, and their two children. The man's a danger to the Southern way of life. He cannot hide from us. Lydia Fuentes Barnum is his greatest weakness.*"

The letter dated in 1937, before Mama's kidnapping.

I read the briefing out loud. "Bo Barnum is involved with a former black hooker in his Zwolle home. He supports miscegenation and integration. He is not welcome in the South and he requires elimination". *I already knew that about my father. They weren't saying anything new about him. I wonder if Sara acquired knowledge of this.*

Of course, I couldn't wait to read my sister's file now. With Mama's file next to Sara's file on the bed, Sara's sat twice as thick as Mami's. My sister's laid on the left and Mami's sat adjacent. My head darted back and forth like I watched a tennis match, deciding which file required analyzing. Back and forth, my head went, while my neck creaked with each turn.

Sara's file called, so I picked it up and stretched the rubber band off it. It snapped across the motel room and hung on the lamp shade, that remained permanently attached to the lamp.

According to the file, she sympathized with communists, which I didn't believe. Sara's civil rights activities were widespread around Louisiana. The girl received fame and accomplished her lifelong dream. I became proud of her and heard she did well. The last I knew she departed for civil rights training in Tennessee. My damn big sister always got the recognition. She evolved into one of them who people sought out for advice. Daddy taught her how to play guitar and not me. Pa took her for a ride on freight train. He always took her. I mashed my fist against the table and stomped the floor. I tossed her folder across the room, like it was a plate of Pa's best china topped with her favorite crawfish pie which that bitch, Miriam Landry, made especially for her. The folder split open, and the papers skirted down the wall like blood stains. God Damn, Sara always showed me up. I'm a fucking fed now, working for the fucking FBI, and she's walking and training with this new pastor from Atlanta. Of course, she didn't write me telling me this, but I read it in the papers, and heard about it on the radio. At least she could have had the god damn nerve to tell me her kid brother that she's doing good.

In my duffle bag sat a small jug of Grandpa's shine, and I took a snort straight from the bottle. The crap burnt my throat, but an evil grin splashed on my face. I wasn't sure if I smirked with evil intentions, or my normal smile, that would bed a girl of my choice. I took another snort, and the grin spread. Lighting a cigarette, and I paced circles around the room, grinding tracks into the beaded rug. *'Fucking Sara Barnum, making it big, getting headlines for saving Negro boys from a life of jail, or worse. My dyke sister running off with my little crush, and I spied on them. She played with her, got her naked and the little slut who I crushed on was lezzing out with my sister. The woman that Pa banged, fucked my sister. I didn't get shit from Miriam but a cold shoulder. Hell, I'm a man. I want to know how Miriam screwed. I wanted to look at that body. Everyone else in my family screwed her, I wanted some of that brown sugar, too.'*

Another snort of whiskey went down my throat, followed by another cigarette. All riled up, I admired my reflection in the mirror. Figuring I looked good, I departed the motel, and walked down Main Street, hoping to catch some blues music and brown sugar. I desired someone who reminded me of Miriam. I wasn't going to treat her right but would mistreat the little chica. I found a little club on the corner of Main near campus and I assumed a bunch of two-bit hipster beatniks hung out there. Not my type of crowd, but I wasn't a fan of the hipster commie crowd, especially when those boys moved in on my action. Hell, I carried guns and a badge. If those commie hipsters attempted to pick up what I want, I will send them straight to the farm. Hell, I'd do the same if my brown sugar resisted my advances.

I walked in feeling like a fed. I was in charge and felt taller than 5' 9". Grandpa's shine aided the effect, as I bumped into a few old black men at the bar. I'd fucking take them in also if they gave me any shit. Onstage an old Negro sang the blues and that's what I wanted to hear. That old fucker passed through Pa's place some time ago. He sliced the strings on his guitar, but my attention turned to his accompanist, who must have been his granddaughter. She looked no older than 16, but I hoped to hell she'd turned eighteen. That girl was going to be mine tonight. I watched her pick the strings with precision, flat picking them, like a good ol country girl, and she ripped that broken whiskey bottle across the strings, like she flashed a blade on them, and called out the gators from the swamps back home. I no longer heard that ol black man, as my attention focused on the girl. She looked up and caught me staring. I turned on that smile the ladies loved, and it seemed she missed a beat or two. She regained composure and ripped her solos, and flat-picked to her heart's content. She did no singing but ripped her instrument like no woman I ever heard, and I heard my sister and Miriam play, and they're damn good musicians.

Their first set ended with a long song, and several solos. The old man shook it up, danced and played the guitar behind his head, showing off to the Negro crowd. They hooted and hollered, and then stood and danced. The big butt ladies shook their bottoms to the rhythms the band hit, and I thought about what I'd do with the rhythms of that lil guitar player. I did not care if she was married, I did not care if she already popped seven kids, and I cared less about how old she was.

The combo took a break and I made my move. "Damn girl, they don't let you sing none?" I tipped my hat towards her. "You can wheel a mighty axe there, like ol John Henry himself."

"I'm sorry, sir. I don't talk to any hipster white boys who come here. Besides my Daddy, Lightning Wilson, would kill da man."

"Do I look like one of them hipsters?" Besides, I ain't white. I got me part Negro and Mexican in me. I pointed over to the corner where there stood a bunch of college students with glasses, fedoras, and goatees. I'm here on business and need a night out. I ain't afraid of your daddy either. I'd rather die trying to go out with ya, than to sit back and watch you walk away and do nothing. Hey, pretty lady, I grew up with the Blues, across the river. My ol man ran a juke joint on the Sabine. Your Daddy probably came across and played there."

"He might have, I don't know. I've been playing with him since I turned sixteen."

"You've been playing with him for about two years?"

"Nah a year. I'm seventeen."

I exhaled, grabbed my flask, and took a snort. "Do you want a shot of my grandpa's best? Best shit in five states." I needed to get my mojo going and that started with my smile. I winked, closed my left eye a few times, and started that smile that would weaken her resistance.

She looked around for her father. Neither of us saw him. She opened the flask and took a snort. She smiled. "Damn, boy. I like your smile. I'm Ruby Wilson, best picker in Texas."

"I'm Tomas." Even drunk I resisted using my last name. Barnum's obtained a reputation in these parts. "I can't play a lick of guitar, even though my pa and my sis shred. They made me do the washboards." I smiled back at her.

Her laugh was cute and sexy as was her smile. She didn't laugh loud, sort of a snort and giggle. Her teeth protruded crooked, and she missed one, but they glowed in the smoky atmosphere of the club. "Washboards take a certain skill too. Plus, you can wash your sissy's clothes afterwards." She walked away from me, flipping that long curly hair away. She reminded me of a younger Miriam Landry. I guess if I couldn't lay Miriam, this little thing would do.

"Hey, hey, hey where you going? I want to get to know you better."

"We are playing till three. We can talk later."

"I'll wait for ya." I sipped Gramps finest out of the flask, no more big snorts; enough to keep me occupied, while inhaling some tobacco, and enjoying the show. Plenty of other Negro ladies shook their bottoms at me. I leaned my back against the wall, loving this performance, and relaxed and waited until three. I liked this gal who shredded the guitar. A couple of times, while playing, she took her eyes off the strings; stared at me and smiled. I smiled back, every time.

The great show ended, and she ran up to me. "Tomas, we got us a room near the prison. It's a Negro motel."

"I'm at the Starlight, room 14. I think that place sits right across the street. You should come over."

"I want to; I'll need to sneak away from my daddy. Luckily we ain't sharing a room."

"I walked down here. Do you mind giving me a lift? I ain't seeing that good. Took too many snorts of this stuff." I pointed to the flask and turned it upside down, showing her my empty hooch jug.

"I need me a shot or two."

"I got more back in the room. I never leave home without it."

"I'll sneak over. I think we can give you a lift, Tomas."

The family did give me a lift back to the motel. I tried my best not to flirt with little Ruby, since her father stared me down as I stretched out in the back seat, next to some gear. They dropped me off, and I crossed the parking lot. I freshened up, got me smelling good, and lay on the spinning bed. I pressed my hand against the wall to stop the bed from rotating. It didn't work and soon that girl knocked on my door.

I woke up to a naked girl slapping my face. "Damn, you drank way too much whiskey. I'm calling you whiskey dick. You didn't give me nothing last night." She looked fantastic, even while slapping me.

"What time is it? Quit the slaps, babe. I'll make it up to you sometime soon. I need a shower. Come join me."

"It's 9:30am. I'm getting ready to take one Tomas."

"Call me Tommy. So, we didn't screw?"

"Oh, you tried, but passed out on me."

"Well I'm roaring to go. Hope you are too."

We dragged our naked bodies into the shower and took pleasure in washing each other off. She grabbed the shampoo and massaged it into my hair, while washing every part of my body. We proceeded to the bed, and took in some good loving, the best I ever had, and I played football at Grambling. Laying there sharing a smoke, I asked her again what time it was?

"It's one o'clock."

"Fuck. I was supposed to meet my mom at eleven." I relaxed. "But sex with you was better."

"Where you are meeting her at?"

"The damn farm."

"She's in jail?"

"Hell yeah. She says she was framed, but ain't in no hurry to get out. Hell, my pa and sister busted her out when I was younger, but she escaped back. That's the day Papi got killed. That's why I'm here. They figured I'm the person she'll talk to."

She looked at me, like I revealed too much. Her eyes brightened. "You ain't a Barnum are ya?"

My head felt like someone went bowling in it, and my throat craved water. I pressed my throbbing head into my palm, realizing I said too much to her. The reaction I gave answered her question.

"My Daddy and your daddy were friends. Played over there in Zwolle many times. He also played up at your Grandpa's. Can I steal some of your shine? That's why daddy liked playing shows at your family's place."

"Yeah, take a flask. The problem with growing up a Barnum is you can't trust no one. I don't want to reveal my name. I don't want anyone to know I'm a Barnum."

"Your secret's safe with me." She kissed my lips, and licked and nibbled my forehead, and her lips and tongue returned to smooch my mouth. Them kisses set my mind and other things roaring, and she went for pay dirt and kissed my pecker. Mami could wait since she's in jail and not going anywhere.

My hands could not keep still, as I felt like a person with bad equilibrium. Nervous, hungover, but full of bliss, with a double session of Ruby Wilson on my belt. I liked the gal, I wasn't sure if she's everything I ever wanted, but I wanted a singer of my own. I grew up with blues music playing in the parlor, the living room, the back yard, or in an adjacent bedroom, it felt like family. I planned on marrying this girl.

The red brick walls of Huntsville Prison awaited me. The building looked like Shreveport Central, except much bigger and with guard towers watching my every move. I hadn't talked to Mami for a while; though, we wrote often. Today would be official government business. I reached for my briefcase, but in my euphoria and drunken stupor, I failed to read Mami's file, and it sat scattered across my motel room. I was also about six hours late for my appointment.

"Lydia Barnum?" I asked the snot faced guard as I walked in the door, passing three levels of security.

"Who can I say is calling?"

"Tomas."

He went through the file, skimmed his way through like he shuffled a deck of cards.

"Sorry, no Lydia Barnum here."

"Lydia Fuentes?" He went back through the file, speeding his way through it.

"Lydia Bourgeois? This is official business," I flashed my identification.

The man wiped the snot off his nose with his uniform sleeve and rubbed his hand on his desk, before reaching for my I.D. I didn't hand it to him but shoved it in the glass that separated us.

"I'm with the FBI. I demand to see her."

He repeated his snot action, this time with his left sleeve. "Mrs. Bourgeois checked out at noon; she's no longer a prisoner here at Huntsville."

"Where the hell did she go? I had an appointment with her earlier today?"

"Agent Barnum, you were late for your appointment. She was released right after that."

"I need to know to whom she was released to, and where was she going?" I shoved my badge back into the safety glass.

The guard, sighed for an eternity, and rose to his feet. Thy guy was a puny 5'7" on stilts. "My notes here indicate you were properly briefed. She is no longer at the prison. Agent Barnum, if you do not leave the premises you will be staying much longer than intended. Much longer." He reached down for the phone to make a call.

I skedaddled out of there like my sister busted me out. I walked back to my room and observed Ruby peeking through the manila envelopes. "Watcha you doing with those? They're classified. You know something that I don't?"

"I'm picking them up. Of course, I couldn't help looking."

"Hand them over." I stretched out my hand. She stacked them against the desk and put them in my palms. Is that all the papers? Ain't nothing scattered about, is there?"

"That's all I saw. I didn't see nothing else. I didn't see nothing important either."

"I think you did, that's why you're still here."

"Okay, I know something. We got a show in San Antonio tomorrow night. You need to come to it. That wasn't in any of the files though. Something I already knew."

"So, she's heading to San Anton?" I stared her down, my eyes locked on her pretty ebony face.

"It said she's off to Mexico. She needs to meet a Mr. Greene in San Antonio on Friday."

"Where is that?"

"It's in your mama's file. If you would have read it instead of getting drunk and fucking me, then you would have known." She smiled when she said fuck. I craved more. I'd see Mami tomorrow.

Ruby and I split from the motel, following her father on the road to San Antonio. He drove like a bat out of hell and we became distracted and lost her daddy. It was time for me to get to know this girl, and that would be on a five-hour car ride. So, it became interrogation time. Glad the Feds taught me.

"Tell me about your Mama?"

"Mama's Creole. She lived down by your daddy's place. I think she even worked there as a whore. Daddy met her there when he was playing, and she be whoring."

"You ain't no whore are ya?"

"Nah. I'll whore out for only you." She kissed and licked my ear for a good long minute. She stopped the delicious torture, smiled at me and pushed her hair back. "There's just a couple of ways for a black girl to make it out of the swamp. First is to whore yourself. Second is to get a job as a maid to a rich white man and whore yourself out to him, and third is to be a blues player. That's why I learned the guitar. I ain't no whore, but I'm willing to be yours." She gleamed into my eyes, as I drove down highway 30 in Texas. I smiled back at her. "Damn Tomas that smile of yours makes me melt."

I kept grinning, as I returned my attention to the road ahead, and peeked back at Ruby, who licked her lips and rubbed her leg. "I know you ain't no whore, but you can be my gal."

She took her left hand, the one she caressed herself with and stroked my bicep. "Oh Tomas, I want to be your gal. A strong man like you will protect me from the Klan. I know you Feds got it in for them bad boys. We're going to find your mama." My new lady friend leaned over, and I smooched her lips. "Tomas Barnum, I didn't tell you earlier, but my Mama knows your Mami. In fact, they worked together."

"Ruby Wilson Barnum, I'm checking if you like the ring of that. I ain't asking, but my Mami been in jail for some fifteen years or so for attempted murder."

"My future husband. You don't know diddly squat about your Mami. She was never arrested for no attempted murder. She ain't never arrested at all. They tossed her in jail to keep your daddy from finding her. That little bitch, Miriam Landry got her scrawny ass tossed in the farm. Mama always hated that little skank."

"Why did your Mama hate Miriam?"

"Well that little bitch never whored herself, and all she did was cook and take care of you kids. Plus, she started bopping your poppa, and my Momma wanted your daddy to bang her."

"I don't want to hear that about daddy. I don't want to hear about him bonking some whores. I knew about Miriam, but she was the only lady after Mami."

"Mama told me about your family Senor Tomas Barnum, or is it Terrance Bourgeois? You see, there are Barnum's and Bourgeois and maybe even Greene's. What's your real name? Tomas or Terrance?"

"I don't know no Terrance Bourgeois. I'm Tomas Roberto Barnum. I'm as mixed as a cocktail."

"Take a left here. This is where they use to work; it's called the Chicken Ranch. My Mama and your Mami both worked there, and they might be there now. But then again, they may be getting too old to whore out. Besides, my mama does not whore herself out there. She's a cook in the back, so them Aggie frat boys don't see her. The place is supposed to be classy."

I made the quick left turn and turned to look at her. "Mami ain't no whore. She'd never whore herself out."

She shrugged. "You don't believe me, Senor Barnum, my future husband. I bet she's there right now. Some guys like older women. My mama still taking care of clients still, but at a different whore house. They got white women there, besides your Mami. She makes a bunch of money. Wanna make a friendly bet? A real friendly bet wager?" She winked at me and flashed her pretty smile. "It will be a win, win wager."

"What are we betting?"

"Whoever loses undresses the other tonight and pampers them to their hearts content. So, if Mrs. Bourgeois is there, you must wait on me, and pamper me, until I'm silly, and if your Mami ain't there, I'll do whatever you ask, hubbie."

"This damn Fed car probably shouldn't be used to make a run up to a whorehouse."

"Don't call it a whorehouse. This is where our Mama's work. You said yourself; your Mami's no whore, so this can't be a whorehouse."

"Still, I can't be driving a fed car up here, unless I'm hauling some fine asses in."

"They don't know you're a Fed."

"Mami knows."

"You're off duty."

I pulled up to a decent sized white house surrounded by a white picket fence, adjacent to the Colorado River that runs across the outskirts of La Grange Texas. We parked the car, and Ruby hauled out of there, carrying her Stella guitar, the same kind my sister plays. I followed her like a good federal agent tails his prey.

"Little Ruby Wilson, is that you?" the warm-looking woman asked. She saw me and continued. "Who is this fine strapping young lad? He looks familiar." I tipped my hat to her and smiled. "What a beautiful smile on that boy, too"

"This is Tommy, and he's my man. We gonna marry someday. Tomas, hang tight, I need to talk with the madam here for a couple of minutes." Ruby dashed out the door, abandoning me in a waiting room with some white frat kids. Them frat boys drank up a storm, and drank factory liquor, not the good stuff, plus they yelled profanities I ain't repeating.

"I hope I get that old Mexican lady again. She sings so purdy right before she goes down on me," one pimply face, goofy looking dude said. "She gives the best blow jobs."

There must be some other older Mexican lady here who sings as sweet as molasses. Still, I ripped down a wall of books which sat on the bookshelf and came close to kicking a hole in the wall. I plopped down on the luxurious sofa, crossed and uncrossed my legs as I waited in the lounge.

There she came. I hadn't seen Mami in a long time, and that was a short meeting. Her eyes caught mine, and she turned to run out the door, but using my speed that made me a reserve defensive back at Grambling, I caught her as we approached the river that flows towards the back of the ranch. She sat down on the bank and tossed a small stone in the Colorado.

"Mami? What the hell you doing here? This is a whorehouse."

"It's not what you think baby."

I stared right at her, and I wasn't smiling. "Mami, I'm sorry I didn't meet you at the prison," My voice perorated quieter than normal. "I was busy, but I met someone who knows you. She says you and her mother are friends."

She put her hands together like she prayed; rested her face in her hands and spoke into her hands. "Tomas, my son. It was all a lie. What I told your sister, and what I told your father."

"Look at me Mami. I need to know what happened. I need to know you're telling the truth."

She raised her head up from her hands and I counted the gray hairs that formed on her head. I noted her weathered brown eyes, and the moisture that formed around them, as a small drop crawled down her left cheek. Her head bobbed a few times, hiding her eyes from me, where I noticed the tears flowing when she stared at me.

"Tomas, like I said, it's all a lie. A total lie. I was never kidnapped. I left on my own. I wanted to sing so bad with those guys, but they took me to a house in San Antonio. I never got a chance to sing with them." She lowered her head into her chest. "Tommy, I killed that creep Torreon, when he tried to rape me, and got arrested and sent to the farm."

"Why are you whoring yourself?"

"Tommy, I need to work. There's not many jobs for a Mexican girl who's done time in the farm."

"You're lying!" I snapped, struggling to hold my temper in check. "Tell me the truth."

"Tomas Roberto Barnum. I'm still your mother. You need to respect me."

"So, you can lie to me?"

"You sound like your sister. I thought you were different."

"I am different, but I also want the truth. There's a lot more that you're not telling me. What about Warden Bourgeois? I heard you married him. You know Bourgeois are a white version of Barnum. They're the ones who joined the Klan and I know you married him."

She leaned up to me. "Tommy, I know all about it. One thing is I enjoy the prison life. I can sing, I'm the star, but I'm there when we play shows. Your Papi and I would never be free. There's no one looking for me or chasing me down here. I can drive from here to Huntsville, not in fear. At last I found freedom here in prison."

I whispered. "So that's why you're in and out of prison? Aren't you married to the warden?"

"Only to get a pardon," she whispered back. "I'm still married to him, but he's also with his wife, and won't give me money. He sees me when I perform."

I took a deep breath; I needed to ask her the question I didn't want to hear the answer to. "What do you know about Daddy's death? I want the truth."

She walked to the river. It flowed with a force as she took three steps into the water and dove in headfirst. She reached down and splashed her face with the clear stream water. She grabbed a few more handfuls and soaked her hair with it, pointed her finger at me and then wiggled it towards, her inviting me towards the water's edge. "Tomas Barnum, you're the sole person I trust. I know you work for the FBI; I know your sister became a lawyer, and I don't trust Sara with what I'm required to say. You can't even tell her." Tears ran down her face before she dove into the river again. I went after her and pulled her ashore.

"Tell me."

"That night I escaped; it was a set up. The judge and warden arranged it for me. I did my part, but I didn't think they'd kill him."

"It wasn't Early?"

"No, but he might have been involved somehow. He always seems to stick his nose in everyone's business."

"Okay who did it? You were there. Remember we chased Papi to the freight." I wasn't going to let her absolve herself from blame.

"That deputy who lived by you guys. Deputy Bourgeois. He's the son of the judge and Zeke also was there. They required me running towards the train, and I knew the exact time it passed, plus I knew Zeke and the deputy hopped the train. I also knew your Papi would chase me all the way."

"Why did you run? Why couldn't we have our family?"

"Tommy, I needed freedom. I wanted to sing, and I could never have my independence married to your father. Like me, too many people chased him, and it reminded me of my parents."

"So, you had him killed?"

She shook her head. "No, the warden and judge did, and the deputy and your Uncle Zeke killed him. Now you know the truth. I needed to tell someone."

"Mami, you're as responsible as Zeke, and you know that. I won't arrest you, even though I have the full authority. I also possess the authority to let you walk, but you must come with me. I got me a houseboat up by Monroe, on a bayou. I use it for hunting ducks. You can stay there until you're required to testify against the deputy."

She leaned towards me on the riverbank. The water gushed by us, meandering towards the gulf. "Tomas, do you know that if any of the Bourgeois Klan ever found out all hell would break loose for the Barnums? The judge would make sure Sara, you and the rest of the proud Barnums will be executed."

"Mami, I know all of this, but aren't we raised to fight the system?"

"Tommy, I'm tired of fighting. I'm tired of running," She said with passion. "I like my life. I'm doing what I want to do. I'm singing and making good money."

"You're a prostitute. A high-class whore, who sings in a prison band. You do not want to rent your body out to some fat ass politicians, or nerdy college students. Tell me, who's that friend of yours?"

"Her name's Lonnie Mae. She works here as a maid, and sometimes she goes down to work at a house downtown."

"Do you trust her with her life?"

"Of course, dear."

"Do you trust her with Sara's?" I needed to be sure how far she was willing to trust this woman.

"Yeah." She rolled her eyes a bit. I knew she fibbed.

"What about mine?" I insisted

She took a deep breath, looked up and down the river, like she waited for a train, still avoiding my glaze. "Why are you asking dear?"

"That houseboat is hidden; you and Lonnie Mae can live there."

"Tommy," she looked at me then. "I won't go in hiding. That's the same as running. I will always be on the lookout. Here, I don't have to worry about a thing."

I threw a flat rock underhand like Papi taught us. It skipped eight times across the river. I still couldn't beat Sara's record. I kicked the dirt in disgust. "I ain't going to arrest you, but I can get you to talk. If anyone can, it will be me."

A sad look shadows her eyes. "Tommy, I need to go back since they need me here anyway. I've got one more secret to tell you before I go. The judge wants to shut this place down and I'm gathering information. Sheriff Jim watches me like a hawk, and always asks for me when he does his rounds. When we get back, I want you to check for him. You will recognize him right away. He's a tall man and wears a cowboy hat. He parades around the place like a prize pony. I didn't see him when we ran out, but that's because I saw you."

"If Ruby's around, I might leave with her. Maybe I'll get a motel and sneak her in."

"You and Lonnie Mae's daughter are seeing each other?"

"I met her two nights ago and we've been together ever since. I think I love her."

"She's a little crazy, but you've got my blessings, if you want to make her your wife. Remember folks don't like this sort of thing down here."

"You know a judge don't you. He'd marry us after all this is done and I'll arrest him for the murder of my father and your husband. You and Lonnie Mae can live with me and Ruby. We will cruise the river."

"Tommy I can't...."

"You will. There's plenty of plans up my sleeve. Let's get back. I'll be here next week."

"Okay, let's walk back together."

We took the long walk up the hill past the white picket fence that surrounds the large white house. We walked around the back towards the servants' entrance where Ruby and her mother waited for us.

"Ma, this here is Tomas Barnum. We gonna marry."

"Over my dead body. Barnum's are evil." She made the word evil about four syllables, with extra emphasis on the e.

"No offense, ma'am, but my daddy never hurt no one. He fought for equal rights and got bopped doing so. All he did wrong was loving someone too much. C'mon Ruby. let's find a place to stay."

I hugged Mami goodbye and we took off to find a little motel where I could sneak my gal in.

Chapter 7

The following morning while we slept naked next to each other, we awoke to a loud bang that sounded like gunfire. At least, that was what we thought at first. The pounding got so loud that I figured someone better be dead. The noise came from outside our front door.

"Open up! I know there's a nigger bitch in there," came the voice in a deep Texan drawl.

The chain stretched out across the door. I checked the peephole and a tall man, wearing a cowboy hat stood at attention. I didn't see any rifle or pistol in his hand, and the man looked like Mami's description of Sherriff Jim.

"You hoarding a nigger in there?"

"No, sir. I'm here with my gal. We're heading to California and I ain't paying for two rooms. We're trying to make it in the music business out there."

"Niggers can't be seen with white folks in this town. It's against the law and I'm going to haul your ass in." He talked slow like he got himself stuck in a jar of molasses.

"So, married sheriffs can get blow jobs from Mexican prostitutes? While you have a problem with an FBI agent bonking his gal. Honey, grab my badge." I looked back and Ruby tossed the blanket over her naked body, as she came over carrying my identification. She handed it to me and nabbed some clothes and retreated to the bathroom. "I dare you to knock me back to Louisiana with that billy club, officer. I'm a Federal Agent and former defensive back. I also know who the real law is down here and it ain't you. Maybe sheriff, we can work together and expose the real law as a murderous clan."

The ogre man's hand remained clutched to the nightstick he intended to use for clubbing a young mixed breed Federal agent. This fed fornicated in motel rooms in La Grange, Texas's seedy side of town with his sexy dark-skinned Creole honey. The sheriff's hand gripped the club, attempting to squeeze the timber out of it, and his right arm sat cocked and ready to wail on the son of Bo Barnum's head. Daddy told me stories of how he got his head beaten in by railyard bulls. My first experience came in seconds.

I glared at him as his eyes darted from me to my once-naked girlfriend. He looked at her as though she attempted walking out with a lamp or a cheap painted picture, or if he might catch a quick glimpse of her ass or boobs.

"Looking for something old man?" I thought he wasn't gonna do nothing. His body language gave him away, and by his gyrations, he wasn't the big cheese in town. Judge Bourgeois ran this whole area. But I thought wrong.

I'm not sure what time I came to, but Ruby wasn't in the room and the bathroom door was locked tighter than a bull's ass at fly time. Stuck in porcelain hell, my head pounded as if I drank a full flask of Grandpa's shine. I did my best football moves on the bathroom door and broke the lock on the third attempt, went shoulder first through the door and stumbled on the floor. I checked the pocket watch Grandpa Cecil gave me, and figured I passed out at least one hour. I knew they couldn't be too far. I staggered to get my car which wasn't in its spot since someone stole it. Stealing a federal agent's car is never a good thing, not even for a small-time county sheriff. Jim needed busted, even if I teamed up with the Judge.

I hitched my way back to the Chicken Ranch and knocked on the door. The nice woman who introduced herself as Edna said. "There's no Lydia Bourgeois working here."

"I'm her son. I spoke to her yesterday."

"That's impossible young man."

Before I could whip out my id, the door slammed in my face. No car, no money, I needed to think like my sister. What would Sara do? Luckily for me, I already headed east towards Huntsville. I crossed the highway and found the train tracks which I followed out of town. I hiked my way east until I heard that lonesome train whistle. Unlike my big sis, I ain't never hopped freight before, since daddy never took me for a ride. I was a train-hopping virgin, just like I was still a virgin when I went to Grambling, since Miriam Landry never fucked me, even though she fucked my entire family. I hoped I judged the speed right. I walked several miles, noticed the sky turning gray as steam rose from the southwest sky and wondered if this was the same train Sara took from Huntsville to Zwolle. I dodged into the forest and waited. The train roared past me, shaking the trees and spitting up rocks and gravel like a twister. I ran beside it, pulled myself in, and became prison bound.

The Judge welcomed me into his office where Civil War paintings, artist's renderings of Indians slaughtering the white man, and paintings of Mexican peasants revolting against the landowners all hung perfect on the tan walls. I studied the signatures and noticed several of the oil paintings were all signed by Reyes, and that was Mami's mother's maiden name, and her mother worked as an artist in the revolution. I pondered my grandmother's work until the powerful man distracted me.

"Welcome to Huntsville, Texas Terrance." The stout man didn't bother shaking my hand but remained seated. He removed his Stetson, and I noticed thinning silver hair, pressed down from the cowboy hat. A red bandana handkerchief and carnation rested in his pocket. In one eye rested a monocle, which he took out, spun it around like a coin, and set it down next to a fountain pen. I plopped in a leather chair across the mahogany desk from him.

He continued. "You want your girlfriend and your mother back." His voice boomed like a radio announcer spinning the hip new songs or broadcasting a baseball game. The rhythm of his speech, methodical at best, he made sure I heard every inflection and syllable.

"Yes, judge. I want them back. I'm sure that big old hick, Sheriff Jim took them."

"Yes, he did, and I can take care of it." The inflection in his voice never changed.

"What's required of me?"

"Well, Terrance." The name Terrance had no effect on me since Ruby assumed that was my name. "As I'm sure, you know about the Barnum and Bourgeois feud that happened for decades."

I looked at him as if he taught at Grambling.

"I do know that most of the Bourgeois' are Klan, and that's why I'm here. That and the unsolved murder of my father."

"The murder is easy. Your mother witnessed everything, that fiddle player, Early Greene slash your father on the train. For the Klan, there are no organized ties to the organization. I can't control what a Bourgeois does or doesn't do." He took a pull off his cigar, and tilted his head back, exhaling the smoke towards the Casablanca fan which circulated the air.

"I understand that, but as far as the feud goes, why the hell are Bourgeois trying to kill the Barnums. It seems like the Bourgeois family possesses the clout, while the Barnums struggle for everything they believe in."

"Barnums have one thing the Bourgeois require, and they're not giving it up. Plus, they're terrorists and won't stop. They will die trying. I saw that in your father, and I see it in your sister. They never know when they're defeated. Barnum's are nothing but fools. He let out evil laughter like a mad scientist, as he put out the cigar, in the ashtray. "Now in you Terrance, I see someone who wants to play the game, someone who wants more than idealistic success. I see someone who wants to own the world. Am I right, or wrong?"

I wanted to display my best poker face, but bluffing and me, well let's say it's not my strong suit. I tried to lie, but the words did not come out. I stuttered a little, wondering how he knew all about me. "Yeah, what's wrong with that?"

"Nothing Terrance. You are unable to do it as a Barnum, which is why I'm calling you by your real name, and not your given name. You're Terrance Richard Bourgeois; your heritage stripped from the Negroid race."

"Before I go through with this and commit, can you do something about Ruby, and my mother?"

"Of course, you will live a normal life after you commit to the Bourgeois name."

"What about my sister? I see her as a Barnum for life. Can we protect her?"

"Her life will be spared. She's the sole Barnum causing trouble out there, since the unfortunate death of Isiah and his daughter in a fire…"he smiled as he blew out the match that lit another cigar, "in their Austin diner."

"So, all I must do is say I'm Terrance Richard Bourgeois, and I will see Mami, and Ruby again, and Sara will survive? Do I tell Sara that my name is Terrance and no longer Tomas?"

The fat man took a deep pull on his cigar. He blew a ring with the foul- smelling smoke. "You can do whatever you want, your sister will keep her life, but that's up to you. It depends on what you decide to tell her. She may lead a productive life, or she may end up behind bars, or on the run. Terrence, it's up to you."

I loved my sister, but I did not want Mami living her life as a Bourgeois. She's born a Barnum, the same as me. Sara, true blooded, with skin as thick as a turtle. Sassy and smart, she helped me a little through college, took adventures, thanks to my father, who took her on a freight train at the tender age of four. She learned to fish and hunt gator. He taught her the guitar and harmonica. I can't remember him teaching me nothing.

The tapping of my fingers became louder as I stared down the Judge. My eyes shot right at him, while he returned the stare. He glanced down for a minute as the sound of my fingers rapping on his desk bothered the old man. His face scrunched up, and the usual poker face of the judge showed his ire.

"What's it going to be Barnum? Lydia will no longer be my brother's wife, and she will remain comfortable. You're free to make Ruby your wife, and Sara's life will remain intact. The quality of her life may be in question as she may be in exile, or behind bars, and believe me, it can be arranged. I know there are issues between the two of you, so this is your call."

"No, it's your call Judge Bourgeois. Call me Terrance." I shook the devil's hand, and the scaled skin ripped through my hands. Tired of running, I made the deal.

"Terrance, you're required to capture Early Greene. He's a professional and I'll allow you six months to kill him. After that you'll be set up for life. Your sister is convinced he's the murderer, and Lydia informed her. You'll set a trap for two people, Early Greene and your sister. The man killed more innocent people than you and I know about. The other person you'd set a trap for is Sara. She's going to do the extermination of good Ol' Early Greene." He flicked ashes from his cigar on the back of my hand, and I cringed. "Get the fuck out of here, the last of the Barnum's."

I sat there motionless, aware the deal with the devil was completed. I did not want to see my sister on the run, even though she liked life that way. I wanted my mother back in my life, and the love I felt for Ruby already meant that soon she'd become Ruby Barnum, or Bourgeois. That little girl treated me like none of those coeds at Grambling did. I wanted a normal life. I wanted kids, I wanted to run a business and Grandpa Cecil made sure the whiskey business would be mine. I knew the ropes, the ins and outs, and soon the hooch would be legit. The world laid waiting for me as I stayed seated in the plush chair, enjoying its comforts.

"Barnum, get the fuck out of my office. You will meet your mother, and nigger girlfriend further south. The lone clue I will give you is, it's your Mother's hometown. Maybe you will realize why this is all happening."

He put the cigar out on my hand. My eyes clenched as that thing burned, and the smell of burnt hair drowned out the cigar stench. A dime size burn mark sat on the back of my hand as I rose and departed the office. His aide showed me out and, still without my vehicle, I needed to hop a Mexican bound freight. My adventure waited.

Part IV

Chapter 8

Sara Barnum: Monteagle, Tennessee

I rode the bus towards The Highlander Folk school. Rosa and Martin trained there and the rising attorney, Sara Barnum, one day would join their legacy of the names that passed through the training center. The Trailways bus meandered along the Southern Tennessee Mountains, and it swerved down route 41 in the Cumberland Mountains. Daddy taught me how to play the song Cumberland Gap, and I wailed the tune on my harp, to the rhythms of the road, as I stretched out in the back of the bus, next to the people who headed further up the road.

Some of my Negro traveling companions clapped along to the beat, and others looked at me with a side eye. I listened to them whisper to their companions and witnessed the little glares they gave me. I wished they let me play my guitar, since the jig became one of my favorite songs that wasn't zydeco or the blues. The Stella sat stowed away in the belly of the bus, packed away, and I hoped my guitar made it to Tennessee in one piece.

The bus made its descent into town. A city surrounded by the Appalachian Mountains, as the town nestled into the valley. Tennessee never brought me much luck, and I wondered if that commie squirrel Robert Greene attended. I hoped he wasn't, but we worked for the same cause, and that thought made my legs shake.

The motor carrier stopped at a make-shift bus stop. The driver told me the old depot burned to a crisp in a fire a few years back, and this temporary station lost the ambience of an old southern bus depot.   Though the colored water fountains which spouted rust-colored water, and the Negro toilets remained.

Standing on the corner, I looked around for the man scheduled to pick me up. Holding my suitcase in one hand, and Stella in the other, I soon noticed the man, with a Fedora hat, horned rimmed glasses, and an uneven goatee. His whiskers were uneven, the hat bent crooked, while his glasses hung over his nose too far. I started to walk back to the station.

Aware of my arrival time, he yelled. "Sweet Sassy Sara. I've missed you my little gal. I'm your trainer. Hop in my sexy, sassy lady."

"*Fuck*," I murmured. "*It's goddamn Cisco; and the last damn person I damn want to see.*" I needed the training and becoming an activist for civil rights became my goal and birthright. The training I'd receive here only accelerated my drive. Being a professional, and ignoring any past feelings I shared with Cisco Greene, the commie, orgy partaker, I grabbed my bags and strolled towards him. I'm glad Miriam wasn't with me; otherwise she'd want to partake in a rendezvous, take him for herself, or kick him in the groin. I considered kicking him in the balls, but I came recommended to be taught non-violence, like Mahatma Ghandi. With Cisco Greene as my trainer, this would not be an easy learn. I wanted to plant my heels on his forehead again.

"Hey, Cisco," I called, and he sprinted towards me, arms waving in the wind. He arrived in a second and grabbed my suitcase. He knew better than to touch Stella, as the weakling carried my suitcase. The young Mr. Greene tried to impress me with his strength. He tried to lift the oversized bag with one hand and balance it on his head but lacked the arm strength to lift it. He tried with both hands, but still struggled. Arm strength doesn't impress me, passion and intelligence always got me, and he obtained these traits. I hated his morals and sleaziness.

He came to his senses and used both hands to carry the bag, while he dragged the suitcase at his side. A few times the luggage bounced along the sidewalk.

"We made it to my car, Sassy Sara. Let's hit the Highlander." I threw Stella and my suitcase in the front. I climbed in the back seat, praying I didn't invite him to accompany me. We took the car out of town a little bit, winding up at the place where two large buildings lay nestled in the woods and mountains, surrounded by several cabins.

The main building resembled an enormous house that I spotted on the plantations back home, brown in color, and made of wood. That little rat, Cisco, tried to grab my bags again to take me up front to register. He struggled with the bags, but I shoved him to the ground; grabbed my guitar and suitcase and marched my ass towards the main entrance.

"Oh, sassy Sara, such a sweet and sexy, sassy Sara. You need to learn non-violence; I'm going to teach it to you."

I turned around and the weasel attempted to stand. He leaned on his left arm, pushed up, and the rat tripped over his feet and splat on his face when he made a run after me. I turned to help him, but splat on the ground myself. I tripped on a log that fell from one of the large Dogwood trees around the area. I laughed hysterically as tears gushed from my eyes, since I busted a gut laughing so hard at him. At last, I stood upright, wiped the tears and smirk from my face, and walked back to help the poor kid. I grabbed his hand and pulled him upright, while I blocked the urge to trip him. He held my hand tight, stronger than a former lover and my future trainer should, as he stumbled to get his balance from the force of my tug. He put his Fedora back on his head, covered up the prematurely balding head, and tipped it to me.

"Thank you, my sweet, sassy, and sexy Sara. Thank you very much."

"Knock it off with that shit. I saw you struggling. I'm helping ya."

"You're so sexy and sassy. The woman of my dreams. Let's forget about the past."

"Oh, I'm trying to forget. Let's get up there and get started."

He smiled at me and held onto my hand. He leaned over to kiss me but I turned my face at first, then in a flash I forgot how I hated the weasel and all I could think of what attracted me to him in the first place. My lips pressed against his for a second. Each peck a little longer, stronger, and passionate than the previous. He broke off the kiss. That fool screwed up again. Realizing why I hated this young man. I wiped my lips off, enjoying the kiss but hated the man who gave it to me. We walked up towards the center, with him to the left of me, and me carrying Stella and my suitcase. My better judgment took hold, and we stopped the kissing, but I knew Cisco's the type to leave a woman wanting more. That doesn't always work for an old lover who cannot stand her sole ex.

He escorted me to the women's dorm. As a trainer, the man obtained full access to the place. My roommate had not arrived yet.

"Diane won't arrive in for a few hours." He looked at me, the passion in his eyes fired holes at my defense. "Let me see Stella. I want to play a song for you." He played an old Gospel song *"We Shall Overcome."* "The song doesn't have to be about Civil Rights, or Jesus. People overcome lots of strife." He walked over and kissed me again. This time, he didn't stop, and the earth still didn't move.

"Cisco, we can't do this anymore. There's way too much family history, plus we're here to learn, to make a better world."

He laid back on my bed, naked as the day that he came into this world. "Yeah, but we can enjoy ourselves at the same time. Do you want some reefer?"

"No. I don't do drugs. I like to stay in control."

He stared and smiled. His grin got bigger. "So, you let me fuck you again on your own, with no chemical seduction. I must be damn sexy, sweet, sassy sexy Sara." He kissed my forehead, gathered up his clothes, and left to get my roommate. What his intentions were with this woman, I did not know.

I met Diane a few hours later. A professional looking young Negro woman, similar in age to me. "I'm a lawyer in Greensboro. We're trying to start something here and I hope we can do sit ins, where us African American's can protest without violence. We can go into Woolworths, and sit at the lunch counters, not order anything, and keep the white people from eating."

"Diane, I'm Sara, and I'se also a lawyer from Baton Rouge. I defended a dark-skinned Creole musician from the peninsula for raping a white girl when it was consensual screwing. Da big folks down in Narleans figured I'm going to be some sort of mover and shaker in the scene."

Diane strolled over and shook my hand. She rolled her eyes at me.

"It's nice to meet you Sara." I reached out to hug her, but she turned and walked back to her bed, and threw her bags on it. She walked like a white woman, all prim and proper back to the bathroom, where she washed her right hand; the hand she used to shake mine. In the bathroom she sniffed the towels to make sure I didn't get my greasy swamp paws on them and wiped her hand dry.

"I'm going out to get dinner. I'm starving." She returned and walked past me while I used my blade to create the swampy sounding slides on Stella. "You know Sara you're playing the devil's music. This organization is about religion and overcoming strife. The only devil we have is the people we are fighting against, and that's the white man." She shook her head to the left, and her sprayed hair refused movement.

"Snooty bitch." I muttered under my breath. At least I hoped my comment fell on deaf ears.

She turned and glared at me. "What did you call me?"

"I called you a snooty bitch. Damn uppity negroes. I was raised in the swamps. I'm a swamp girl. This dress I'm wearing is the only one I brought, cause it's the only one I got, and it's stained already. I may not look it, but I gots me more morals and values than the most refined Christian uppity Negro bitches. You know the type."

"The trainer, Cisco Greene bragged about sleeping with you."

"He's my first and only, I bet you even skank up with some of them leaders. That's why you're here. I'm here cause I'm one of the few lawyers that got an innocent man off from banging a white woman."

"Listen you backwoods country woman. I never did judge you; I grew up in the city and received a wonderful education. I'm not going to put up with your attitude. You know what your problem is? You think people look down on you because of your mixed race."

"You don't know me. Go get some food, and I'll get mine when you get back. Let me see about getting a private room. Dat way you can bang dem leaders who helped you get here."

The door slammed shut and she split. I played some blues and got my stuff ready to move out. I didn't want to room with no one, especially a high-class religious whore.

An hour later, I heard voices outside our little cottage. Already packed and ready to go, Diane opened the door. Two men in dark blue suits, who I didn't recognize glowered at me.

"Ms. Barnum, you need to leave. We've arranged a private room for you." They pointed in the direction of the dining hall, and I fled. I turned and smiled at Diane, I got what I wanted, and she received the privacy or the company she desired.

I met Cisco in the dining hall. He waited for me and tapped his fingers on the dining table. "So sassy Sara, I heard your sass was a little crass. You will get that fine little ass thrown out in the grass. Don't worry though Cisco will take care of you. I'm working on getting you a private room." He tried to kiss my hand, but I pulled away, and his weasel paws roamed over me.

"I already got me a private room, and don't touch me. I need to get some food. Do they got Crawfish pie?"

"Nope, but they got some mighty fine Carolina barbeque."

"There better be some red beans and rice at least."

"Some good ol' BBQ and beans and rice. Let's go get some."

Around thirty other folks sat in the cafeteria when Cisco, Stella, and I arrived. The food tasted good, not Louisiana good, but still okay. After dinner, I got up and sat on the table, with my feet planted squarely on the bench, whipped my blade out first and flashed the shining steel at all the non-violent trainees and trainers. I made sure they received a grand view from the reflection coming from the overhead electric lights. Cisco sat next to me smiling. As I put the blade back in, I saw an empty cola bottle sitting on an adjacent table. Stella came out of her case, and I crashed the soda bottle on the floor which got the folks attention. Stella tuned in open g, and I put the end of the bottleneck on my ring finger like I married it. I played, the shuffle and screeched the bottle neck on the strings. I sang the most gut-wrenching song I made up on the spot.

"I seen my Mama taken away
I saw my Mami walking away
Don't know why, not even today.

I saw my daddy thrown from the train
I saw Papi falling from a train
My tears fell like Louisiana Rain.

Dark skinned men, hanging from a tree.
Dark skinned girls, hanging from a tree
Their spirits will never be free.

I ain't you and you ain't me
I ain't you and you ain't me.
Ununited, we will never be free."

I got a good ovation from the crowd that consisted of uppity Negroes, and northern hipsters. During their clapping, I grabbed a broom and cleaned up the broken glass, grabbed my suitcase and Stella, and headed out the door to my new room. Cisco Greene remained hot on my tail like a lost puppy. He wouldn't leave until morning.

Training consisted of taking all kinds of crap from your trainer. Of course, my trainer was Cisco.

"Hey, you little nigger bitch, who's your daddy?" He slapped me. I was required to not fight back, I attempted to turn the other cheek. "C'mon darkie, I know you niggers like it rough."

He tossed me out of his chair and pushed me on all fours, grabbed my ass and slapped it. I turned around and saw the mama's boy weasel I detested. His tongue hung out like a dog, and the bulge in his pants was inches away from me. It looked like he enjoyed this too much, so I shot up to my feet, pushed him over, stepped on his face like a few times before, and headed back to my room, to grab my belongings.

"Screw the bus," I mutter to myself. "I need to hop me a freight."

I stroll towards the edge of town and sat by the railroad tracks hoping a westbound chugged by soon. Being degraded and not fighting back were issues I struggled with. An uneventful ride home followed. I rolled off in the Jackson yard, where I searched for a Southbound to carry me home.

Chapter 9

Baton Rouge, June 1953

When I returned to Baton Rouge, impressive and distinguished African American men in dark blue suits and shiny red ties sat in my office waiting. Scowls spread across their faces, and I knew I did wrong, I don't like no jack-assing around, and that's what happened in Tennessee. My sole picture of my father rested on the wall above them, next to a framed picture of a freight train.

"Ms. Barnum," Mr. Marshall began, "we're disappointed in your actions at the Highlander. We went through great expense to get you in there."

The man to his left, who did not look as dignified as Mr. Marshall or my pastor Reverend Jemison, spoke up. "Now Sara, we have high hopes for you on the courts. An intelligent, pretty woman like you can do wonders for the movement. As a gorgeous, light skinned Creole woman, you'll have no problem switching a juror over, or even a Senator or Congressman." The man smiled at me, acting smooth as silk. My Pastor and the distinguished Mr. Marshall cringed, and shrugged their shoulders.

"Excuse me! Oh, and it's Ms. Barnum to those I do not know. I ain't going out and whoring myself to fat old Congressmen to get them to vote on civil rights, and I ain't screwing no jurors either."

"Now, Sara...I mean Ms. Barnum; I'm not asking you to sleep with anyone. What I'm asking you is don't be afraid to expose some cleavage or display some leg. It can't hurt the cause."

I sweat like a whore in church, and I spurted out, "Mr. Marshall, Pastor, can you please show this guy the door? I can't believe he's asking me to do this. You're lucky I don't press charges on you."

Mr. Marshall whispered something to the creepy, younger black guy. He put his hand on the younger man's shoulders, nudging him out of the office.

The distinguished man came back in and put his arm around my shoulder. "Sara, I apologize for Mr. Watson. What he said, came out wrong. He told me he's sorry, but we also won't use him on anymore recruiting trips. You're a rising star here in the movement. You have passion and desire, you crave taking down the powers to be, making them sweat and squirm. The movement needs you."

"I don't want to be a player. My grandparents, the ones I never knew, well they played a major role in the Mexican revolution, and they were assassinated. My daddy wasn't a player, sought justice before his time, but he got chased down everywhere he went. He finally got killed. My mama, she's walking around the Texas State Penn, like a drunken old coon and she's happy there and feels free because she's not chased." My eyes danced back and forth between my Reverend and Mr. Marshall, and back to my pastor. Pastor's soft brown eyes stared direct at mine. I took a soft breath, but exhaled loud enough that he heard me. He glanced at my mouth.

"You know why I don't want to be a player? I want to survive."

"We have work to do here, there are things you can do from behind the scenes. But tell me, Sara, and can you honestly say you'd be comfortable working behind the scenes?"

"If it's for a just cause, I'd take the trash to the landfill, and scrub the floors."

"Sara, remember I'm your pastor." His smile turns warm, like the one Papi used to give me, and a soft laugh bellowed from him. "You can't lie to me." He brushed my hair away from my eyes. He searched my face for my honest reaction, which can be told from the soul, and the eyes are the gateway. "Did you hear they're raising the price of bus tickets?"

"Yeah, I heard that."

"Don't you think we should get involved? After all, we ride the bus at an alarming eighty percent rate more than white folks. This is another way us folks give the white man more of our money."

I looked at him, my eyes brightened, and a big smile ran across my face. "Let's boycott the buses."

He smiled back. "I like you're thinking Sara. Start planning."

I never staged a boycott in my life. I guess gathering the black folks who rode the bus to and from their slave labor jobs and arranging alternate transportation for them. The task was not an easy one, but most black folks in town hated the bus company and hated riding in the back. Not this swamp girl, I strutted to the back and mingled with the folks. I sat in front if I wanted since I passed for Creole, and Creoles at times got a free pass, depending if they're light or dark-skinned. No one assumed my Hispanic heritage, which was a good thing, because I heard the Klan folks down here hated the Mexicans as much as Negroes.

One of our church secretaries made fliers, and my job was distributing the pamphlets on the bus. I boarded public transportation with a hundred or so fliers from the front and pranced my way down the aisle in my torn swamp girl overalls. I gallivanted past the white folk whom, of course took their seats up front, and sat in back where I distributed the literature. Of course, them white folks, glared at me like I am some crazy woman, as they stared me down. I heard little rumblings about my attire. Most of the Caucasian riders, older white women, oblivious to my identity ignored my shenanigans. Most of the Negros knew me or, at least, acquired knowledge of my cause, so they read it with eyes wide open.

"How you gonna do it? I ain't got no other way to work. If I don't work, I don't get paid and can't feed my children."

"I got a car that sits six, and I've driven since I turned fourteen. If you folks need a ride to work, I'll be your chauffeur. I can guarantee you will get a seat. I can't believe we have to stand when there are plenty of seats up front amongst them white folks."

"Ain't you white ma'am?"

"I'm whatever I want to be, and whatever you want me to be. I got a lot of different blood in me, including runaway slave blood, so if you want me to be a Negro, I'm a Negro. I got kicked out of LSU, because of my heritage, and ended up getting my education at Grambling, and my law degree at Xavier, so I'm one of you folks."

"Well, ma'am I've seen you sitting up front, you can pass for a cracker girl!"

I ain't no cracker girl. I'm a swamp girl, raised in Western Louisiana. I've studied civil rights and seen a lot of senseless acts. I'm here to fight for y'all."

The lady opened her flyer and reread it.

"Mmm. Say ain't you the lawyer who got that boy freed."

"Yes, Ma'am. That's me."

"Girl, you don't look like a lawyer, I mean you should wear a fancy dress, instead of those torn up overalls."

I leaned over and whispered, "this is my work. Getting you folks to stop riding these white owned buses and getting some other folks to taxi you around. That's my job, so I can dress and be a swamp girl, instead of a stuffy lawyer. You ladies like me better as a bayou dolly anyway. Are you ladies in?"

Nine of the ten ladies agreed. I walked into Mt. Zion and changed into my lawyer outfit, the long dress that went down by my ankles and a matching long-sleeved top. My hair tied up into a bun, instead of dangling way past my shoulders, and the straw hat tossed in the restroom, replaced with a more fashionable style hat for an attorney. I hated dressing like this in the scalding summers of Louisiana. I'd rather walk around barefooted as a yard dog.

The bus picked me up and as I went uptown. I delivered additional flyers to the Negro population of Baton Rouge. Riding back to Mt. Zion, I received the same driver who took me up to the chemical companies uptown.

"Ma'am. You look like a troublemaker. Now, skedaddle off my bus, young lady."

"I paid my fare. I got every right to sit on this bus."

"Ma'am, I got the final say on who rides on my bus, and I'm telling you, that you're not riding on my bus."

"Sir, I paid my quarter. Get me back to Old South. I know this bus takes me there."

"I ain't moving this bus with you on it. If you ain't out of this vehicle, I'll have the police down here in two shakes of a tail."

I didn't move a muscle. I sat motionless, like a gator in the Sabine, stalking its prey. The driver walked back, and the man was uglier than homemade sin. I swear that man, spawned from one set of grandparents. He got closer to me, and I smelled the stench that came from his inbred body. I still wasn't leaving, but them legs of mine shook like they're ready to detach. My legs squeezed together, protecting my privates, cause this man looked crazy enough to take me out to the Mississippi River, and do unprintables to me, and toss me in the river. "Call the police, or I will."

"No, sugar. I ain't calling the police. You as sweet as the sweetest tea. You are coming with me, young lady."

"Arrest me. Throw me in jail. I ain't going with you, you inbred."

"Oh, sugar." He stared at me, like he ain't never seen a woman before. "There's a nigger in the woodpile somewhere sugar ain't there. I like them Mulatto women. I bet you Creole, aren't ya sugar. Creole women taste even better than mulattos." He licked his lips and did a disgusting thing with his tongue. He pulled up his shirt and adjusted his pants. "Sugar, since you didn't get off the bus when I asked you polite like, I'm going to take full advantage." He rearranged his pants, and I saw that little thang of his poking out his trousers. The man was bigger than me, much larger and fatter. I figured the slob planned on becoming the main attraction at a pig roast, marinated in butter, and seasoned with red pepper, spinning on a spit over an open fire.

"I'll arrest you after I love you up there, little sugar. I know you commie girls want arrested. It gives you more for your nigger, commie loving causes." His thing poked out of his trousers, the thought of raping a woman excited the man.

Studied in non-violence, I can't remember what it said about attempted rape. The stench got worse as he hovered over me, and I figured the time was right to kiss all the non-violence stuff good-bye. I cocked my right leg and kicked him right in the exposed part of his uniform trousers, and he fell onto the floor. Still wearing my one-inch heels, I stepped hard on his face and his fat body, running out the back door of the bus. I kicked the shoes and ran barefoot as a yard dog down the Baton Rouge sidewalks and headed towards the nearest anything. The fat bus driver drove me to the developing end of town, and there weren't no stores or nothing, only an endless cotton field. I cut across the swamps and fields, knowing he couldn't catch me. Back in the city, I found me a pay phone and called Reverend Jemison.

Panting like a puppy dog, I sprinted about three miles in my good duds, and I sweated like a whore in church. Perspiration seeped out of my skin, and I spied the water fountains. Whites and colored they said, while the fancy clean-looking silver one waited for the whites, the coloreds used the raunchy, dirty, rusty old thing that looked like rats climbed through the drain and refused the water. There weren't no one around so I took a chance, a chance that changed my life.

I drank from the white folk's water fountain, and ain't nothing bad happened to the water fountain, and ain't nothing happened to me. I stood behind the building, and some white kids came up and took a drink from that same water fountain, and their skin didn't change colors. I figured I'd start protesting water fountains and toilets too.

"I've lived in Louisiana for nine years, Pastor. I still can't believe colored people have to drink out of rust buckets and use them stanky toilets."

"Sara, when the laws get passed, there won't be any colored water fountains and there won't any white only toilets, and you'll be able to eat lunch at that café over there. Let's get you home so you can change clothes. Do you feel like working some more?"

"Of course. I'm not stopping until all this ends."

"Pace yourself Ms. Barnum. Pace yourself. This fight may never end. If it does, probably not in our lifetime."

In Baton Rouge, they passed a law stating that coloreds must board the bus from the back, while whites board the bus from the front. The new law that came out opened the seats for everyone. Colored folks were still unable to sit in front of white folks or share a bench seat with a Caucasian. Well, them fat white bus drivers still made some folks sit in the back, or go to the back and stand, or when I attempted to board, they threw me off the bus with the help of the police. Even the good Pastor got involved and refused to give up his seat, and was taken to the police station. The cops sided with my Pastor. I often challenged the drivers, and gained a reputation throughout town as a troublemaker. I knew Papi looked down and felt proud, as well as my grandparents who I never met.

The drivers were furious about the new law, which made no sense to me, why they tore up a Jake about it. A few days later, they went on strike, and this damn state's attorney general declared the new law as unconstitutional, forcing all of them folks with color to the back of the bus. The fat Klan bus drivers all went back to work.

On June 19, 1953 we announced on the radio that the next time the sun rose, none of us colored folks will board a bus, and we planned a boycott. People walked or received rides. I volunteered to drive my brothers and sisters to work, their homes, to the stores, or wherever they needed to go. Five people fit in my Buick Woodie station wagon, and I took the ladies and gentlemen to work, and picked them up. I took people downtown to do their shopping and picked up folks after work to take them home.

The boycott worked, and I stood front and center of it. The top brass of the Red Stick town got together and worked out a compromise, and the boycott ended after two short weeks. I wanted to keep it going and raised cain about it, but in the end the brass won out. More cases came and went, and I traveled to places I didn't desire on going.

The main case on my agenda as scheduled in Topeka, Kansas remained the movement to integrate the schools. I wanted school integration, like I wanted crawfish pie. This was a law that needed passed, and a bill I believed in. As a girl, who went to a white high schools and Negro schools, white colleges and black colleges, I noticed the difference with the facilities and teachers. I believed all folks deserved the same opportunity for education.

Part V

Chapter 10

Tomas Barnum
San Antonio, Tx. 1954

I hitched a ride from Huntsville down to San Antonio. The Texan heat took a toll on me, sweat seeped from my head and dripped down my body. I was used to it, since I played football at Grambling, and I needed to keep hydrated. I stole one of my sister's favorite expressions, I sweat like a whore in church, as I braved the 100 plus degree temperatures. The Hispanic gentlemen dropped me off a few blocks from the train station.

"Hey, gringo, do you want to make a few dollars?"

Stomach growling, with a dry mouth and no money, and raised in Louisiana, I needed money or food, and a nice beverage since us Louisiana boys need food. "Yeah I need money. What do you need?"

"You're not a federali are you?"

"Not now. I'm off duty. Don't worry, I'm heading to Mexico."

He took out a revolver, twirled it around on his pointer finger. It circled thrice and pointed it at me. I found myself staring straight into the wrong end of a pistol.

"Don't worry. I'm not going to shoot you, Senor Barnum. I know who you are, and they said you'll be heading this way."

"Who's they?"

"Los Choco's. They're the toughest gang from here to Saltillo. I know that's where you're going, senor since you're chasing tu madre.

My mouth dropped open. I stood alone in a city I hadn't visited since I was a young kid. I didn't know anyone here, but this first guy I saw on a street corner knew me. I paced with a purpose up towards him and glared at the man. "Senor, would it matter to me if my name was Bourgeois instead of Barnum?"

"If it was Bourgeois, you'd be shot. Los Choco's don't play with the judge. He thinks he's the law down here, too, but Los Choco's runs this town.

"I'm still a Barnum."

"I heard you sold your soul to the Judge, Senor. If you try to fuck with the Judge and any of the other Bourgeois Klan, you're a dead man, and your family is, too. I've got secrets for you Terrance, or may I call you Tomas?"

Sweat poured from my head. With a soaked hand, I pushed the dripping perspiration from my eyes to stop the burning sensation. I knew I was fucked. This man wasn't trustworthy, but I needed a strong faith in God, my guts and brain. I concentrated on the Mexican man, thirty years my senior, hoping to burn a hole in his defense.

"Como se llama?"

"Me llamo Paulo Torreon. Su Madre mato a mi amigo. El esuniqo que la sequestro, y la viola una y otro. I'm glad your mother killed him. The judge and him we're partners. I wanted nothing to do with their deals. I joined Los Choco's to rid San Antonio of the Bourgeois Klan."

"Donde esta mi madre?"

"Ella esta in Saltillo."

"Y Senorita Wilson?"

"Si."

"Take me to them. Are they together?"

"Hay que un tren de carga."

"Por que?"

"It's the only way to bring her back across the country. Senor Barnum, the feud has gone on since before your Civil War. Barnum's and Fuentes have been at odds. No se suponía que de Barnum y Fuentes para casarse."

"My mother and father were not supposed to get together?"

"Si. I'm sure your father and Lydia did not even know this. I liked your father; he was a good man and musician. He loved your mother, but my partner received orders from Los Chocos. They were to take your mother, and to eradicate the Barnum name."

"No comprendo, Senor Torreon."

"Tu entenderás, Senor Barnum. See that train over there?" He pointed to a long line of boxcars that looked ready to roll. "Stay low, so the bulls here don't bust you up, and let's sneak on. Follow me, Tomas."

There wasn't a choice, Mami and Ruby needed rescued, and this family history got interesting, and only I knew about it. I smiled, knowing Sara had no clue about this and Papi didn't know and neither did Grandpa Cecil.

I followed Senor Torreon around the San Antonio railyard. We searched the bulls like we were in Asia spying for North Korean soldiers. He found the car we needed to get on, helped me on by shoving me inside. I stretched out my right hand to help him up. That son of a bitch pointed his revolver at me again. "Sorry Senor Bourgeois, you're on your own." The gun still aimed at my face, as I stared down that same barrel. His trigger finger got itchy, as it shook around the trigger. The Mexican man adjusted the gun, aimed it to his right and pulled the trigger. I smelled the powder as the bullet whizzed past my left ear. He vanished in the yard somewhere, and I sat in a vacant freight car, hoping its destination was Monterrey, or Laredo.

It seemed like three hours of travel. I sat in the back of the boxcar with my legs bent, and hands folded over my knees for the duration. The train jolted to a stop. I hoped we made it to Monterrey, but I sat clueless and motionless. Minutes passed and I did not budge a muscle. I eavesdropped on the Spanish-accented men speaking English in the railyard.

"This is the car he's on."

"Are you sure?"

"Yes. Paulo radioed me. Get your sword ready. I think he's tied in with the Bourgeois group. He's also FBI."

"I got it, plus the pistols are loaded."

I crawled out the door, smelling as if I'd gagged a maggot. "Are we in Monterrey?" I asked the two conspicuous shadows that hung by the boxcar.

"Senor Barnum, of course not. We must cross the border. That's why we're here. We need to get you on the Mexican train. Feds inspect every car to make sure nobody crosses, but they do take bribes. We understand Judge Bourgeois stole your money, so we will take care of you."

"The judge didn't take my money. That Sherriff Jim, up in La Grange, did."

The shadow crept along the gravel, adjacent to a train parked on another track. My eyes followed it, as it seemed to close in on me. I spied a shadow of a long blade creeping closer. I dove for where I though the shadow appeared, and I made contact. Playing college football did me well, as I took both out, and the sword fell harmless to the ground, as well as a pistol. I grabbed the sword, and the revolver and pointed them at both men."

"I'm not a Bourgeois. I'm here to rescue Lydia Barnum, my mother." The revolver fit perfectly in my hand, and I aimed at one of the men, while the sword nestled blade down against the other's neck. I increased pressure.

"You've signed with the judge. I know it, you admitted it."

"I'm undercover. I'm trying to get my mother back, and whoever too her also kidnapped my fiancé. If I were a Bourgeois, would I marry a black girl? Help me get them, or I swear this sword will go down quicker than a hot knife through butter." I added pressure on the sword, I saw a little blood splatter, and heard skin tearing.

"Don't kill my brother," the other man said. "We will help you."

Too late, the adrenaline pumping through my body exhumed too much pressure on the sword, cutting his partner's jugular. Blood spouted out from him like a Yellowstone geyser. Law enforcement training did me good, since I eliminated the sole witness with one shot, and crossed the border through Nuevo Laredo. With sword and pistol in hand, I hijacked an old man who drove his Desoto towards Monterrey.

"I'm a US Federal agent. Take me to Saltillo now."

"No comprendo, senor."

I cocked the pistol and pointed it at him. "Sun un agente federal. Llevame a Saltillo ahora!"

"Si, senor."

We traveled down a semi paved cart path. I bounced like a basketball as we drove down Mexican Highway 85. It cut through mountains that surrounded the area and zig zagged its way south. Once we got out of the mountains that besieged the border town, the road levelled off. The hijacked man drove like a bat out of hell, while I kept the pistol aimed at him. My right hand grasped the door handle as if I attempted strangling its life. The man made it to Monterrey in two hours. "Sir, I cannot take you to Saltillo. My wife is expecting me. She will divorce me if I'm not home by midnight. I will show you where you can catch a freight train to Saltillo," he said in perfect English.

"I thought you couldn't speak English." The revolver clicked once.

"Oh, no, sir. I'm so sorry. I wanted to see if you spoke Spanish. Many Gringos' passed this way and they've sought trouble. I see you're fluent with the language, so I trust you."

"Mi Madre es una Mexicana. I come for her."

"I will drop you off at the train station. It's an hour ride."

My finger let off the trigger. "Gracias, Senor. This one looks like it's going west."

"Si. I take that train to Saltillo all the time. I see my chica in Saltillo. Mi esposa, does not know."

I felt bad for pointing the gun at the man for two hours, but I needed to get my mother and my gal from whoever kidnapped them, if they were kidnapped. Hell, this trip and my killings might not have been necessary, but I cared less. I climbed in the railcar and sat with my legs up against my chin, toes tapping the floor of the box car, waiting for the movement that would wake me from my slumber. I did not feel the train moving, but something else made me rise. Dos pistoleros stared me down.

"Senor Bourgeois, you're under arrest for the murders of Juan Castellano, and Esteben Fuentes."

"Fuentes?" I questioned the man. "I do not know either one of those."

Si. Senor Fuentes was an undercover policeman, working both sides of the border. Mr. Bourgeois, you're in big trouble."

"No soy el Senor Bourgeois. Me llamo Tomas."

"Come with me Tomas, so you can meet your family."

In the prison cell, I saw my mother and Ruby, the two women I loved more than anything in the world. Both wore dirty rags for clothes, the bags under the two women's eyes reminded me of the raccoons hanging outside Papi's old place, and I noticed purple bruises on their exposed flesh. Peering into the jail cell, I was clueless if I needed to rescue them, or get tossed into the prison cell and spend my life locked up with my mother and fiancé. This was a Sara-styled adventure where I spent a short vacation in the Saltillo jail cell.

Mami came up and hugged me. She squeezed hard. I wanted the same from Ruby, but she sat motionless on the bench, hands locked and shackled behind her. I noticed the chains around her feet, too. I broke off the hug with my mother and walked up to my lady and kissed her forehead.

She shuddered and clutched me tight.

"Tomas, I'm glad you're here. We'll be free soon. All we need to do is go before the police and the judge and state why we're here." Mami stated.

"Mami, I have no idea why I'm here, except to talk to you."

"Tomas, I know I told Sara, but this is the land where my father grew up."

I shook my head thinking Sara knows about this too, and refocused.

Mami gave me a sad smile. "My grandfather was an influential man here. The Fuentes' owned land and became powerful people. After the revolution, they lost everything, but a faction remained loyal to our family, and they still rule in the area."

"Was one of them Esteben Fuentes?"

"I don't know. Why do you ask, Tomas?"

I whispered. "I killed him, I put a little too much pressure on his neck with his sword and shot his partner. I might have to stay in Mexico for a while."

Mami looked down at the floor as if in deep thought. She glanced up with bright eyes. "Esteben Fuentes was a cousin of mine. He tried to steal from the family and got exiled from Saltillo. He's a bum, and works as a thief around the border, stealing money from rich expatriates trying to sneak in and out of Mexico. The family wanted him dead anyway."

"I did a good thing then, I guess." I smiled at both ladies. They smiled back.

"We must denounce the Bourgeois family; we do not want this life. Tomas, you will hear the truth, the real truth. Not the truth I told you earlier."

My eyes rolled. I shook my head. "Mami, do you know the truth?"

"Tomas Barnum!" she snapped, as her eyes pierced right through my soul. "Don't talk to me that way. I know the entire truth and so will you. Your father and I taught you kids to speak the truth, to stand for your convictions, and I'm sure this is the reason why you're enforcing the law, and Sara defends the innocent. I wanted to live a peaceful and normal life and ended up betraying everything that you were taught. We're meeting my cousin, Gilberto Jorge Fuentes, tomorrow. I need to tell him everything. After that, you and Ruby will go free, and I must return to Huntsville. Sara has no idea of any of this, and it must remain that way. If she finds out, she must be killed. Do you understand, son?"

I rested my hand on my chin. My eyes swirled around the room trying to decipher what she said. Then I lied to her. "Yes Mami."

The sun beat down on the Saltillo courtroom. The temperature already pushed eighty and the clock in the bell tower chimed eight times. The building reminded me of any other courthouse in the States, with Greek or Roman style pillars, with two sets of steep steps to climb. I ascended the steps solo, as Mami and Ruby already made the climb and nestled comfortable in their seats. My mother protected her for the time, since I wasn't trustworthy. The guard advised me of that fact the previous night.

The court room was divided in half, one section reserved for non-violent offenders and, in shackles, I received assistance to the other side, the south side of the building. This section was reserved for rapists, armed robbers, and murderers and I never raped or robbed anyone. Not cuffed or chained, there stood a chance of running, but I'm sure Ruby and Mami may get shot or chopped up, and I wasn't going to let that happen. They led me to a hard-wooden chair. I twisted and turned, and figured becoming comfortable would not happen, so I sat and waited. The rumblings in my stomach sounded like folks bowling, and my red eyes stayed shut. My mother walked in at a pace that exuded confidence. Head held high, and her stride elongated. It looked like she strolled forward purposefully.

The judge spoke first. "Como se llama por favor?"

"I will speak in English, so my family will understand. What I say they must know and not have any confusion. My name is Lydia Fuentes Barnum Bourgeois. I'm the granddaughter of Don Gilberto Fuentes, and the daughter of Jorge Fuentes. My husband's name was Bo Barnum, and I'm married to Warden James Bourgeois in Huntsville, Texas. My children are Tomas, who is present, and Sara who is not here, and must not know anything about the conspiracy." She raised her chin. "I met my husband, Bo, in Nebraska where we knew nothing about a feud. We married for the love Bo and I shared, and Sara and Tomas," she pointed and looked at me straight in the eyes, "are the wonderful legacy of our love. The children should not be harmed and must be free to live their lives as Barnums. As I understand, and I want Tomas to know, this rivalry started before our revolution, and before their civil war." She pointed over to me again. "This young man and his sister, like their father, had nothing to do with the feud. Please, let them live free. Please, let Tomas and his young girlfriend over there live free in the states and live their life. Let them multiply, let me become a grandmother. I did not mean to get them involved."

My eyes remained on Mami, but glanced at the judge, shuffling back and forth between them as if I watched tennis. The judge looked like he played a game of poker in a saloon, since he showed no emotion in his face, while Mami retained a more dramatic countenance.

Mami continued. "My cousin and Judge Fuentes. Again, I must speak in English. We cannot hold things against us that our parents did, or even those committed by our grandparents. After my parent's murder, I met with and told your family that Bo Barnum would become my husband. You approved of the relationship, approved of me going back to Nebraska so I could marry him, and live my life there with him. All we wanted was a simple life, and to raise that handsome young man over there and his older sister." Again, she stared me down, at pointed at me. "Please, we need your help to end the feud between the Bourgeois' and the Barnums. I understand that a young Josiah Barnum shot in cold blood an Eduardo Fuentes on their trek to Vera Cruz, but you need to understand that it has nothing to do with us. Those boys were heroes for taking the slaves across Texas. Instead, both the Mexican and US Government wanted them dead. My parents' murder still remains unsolved, and they need brought to justice, and from my understanding, the culprits are the brother of my former husband, along with his partner, Early Greene. Also, going by my knowledge of what happened, my late husband was hand-picked to kill my parents, but Early Greene picked the wrong Barnum brother. I know Bo loved my family, and I know he loved me."

My eyes widened, following Mami wherever she went. She paced across the courtroom, leaving dusty prints on the floor. She shuffled her feet along the dust, slid, and she grabbed a hold of the post to keep her balance. She looked up at her cousin, the Mexican judge, and continued her speech.

"My children need to live free. They were raised without any knowledge of the past. The children, totally unaware of any Barnum-Fuentes feud, and any Barnum-Bourgeois feud. I will retire to my Huntsville prison cell for the rest of my life, as the one who took Judge Bourgeois and my ex-husband the warden Bourgeois down. I will not do the killing. I'm sure there's someone you know who can do the killing. I just want my babies to go free. I want them protected from this mess."

Mami repeated herself in Spanish. I've always been fluent in Spanish, but was unable to keep pace with her. It sounded like she repeated herself, but I wasn't one-hundred percent sure. Ruby sat there staring at my mother and the Mexican judge. When mi madre finished her solo, she took deep breaths and then collapsed into her chair. She leaned over, head-first, and gasped. She turned and motioned me forward.

I came up and she hugged me, and quickly whispered. "Tomas, now you know everything that your father did not know, and your sister will never know. It was Grandpa Cecil who told me one night, while your father played blues to some colored kids. I confirmed it with my family."

I looked up at her sharp, angular face admiring her courage. Tired, hungry, and barely eaten or slept for three days, a rush of energy shot through me. "Mama, you will die in prison, or someone in the Bourgeois Klan will get you before these gangs will get them."

"Tommy." She stroked my face with her pointer finger. "Make sure you do no deals with the Judge." She glared at me, and her eyes narrowed. "You haven't, have you?"

"No, mother. I didn't. I know they killed Pa, and I won't deal with no one that took out my father," I lied.

"Whatever you do, do not become a Bourgeois, even if it's to infiltrate them." She leaned over to my right ear and whispered. "You know the story of Cletus Barnum. Josiah's brother who stole the slaves. He was a wanted man, changed his name to Clarence Bourgeois, and moved to Texas where he turned into and remained an outlaw with an alias. You can blame all of this on him. I discovered the truth down here, when I went back for my parents' funeral, that was before you and your sister were born, and right before Bo and I married. I wanted a normal family, but I knew I couldn't, so I tried to escape here to save everyone." She sighed and shook her head. "I fell into their trap."

My cousin returned with his entourage that consisted of six other men. We all stood up; and then took our seats when he banged the gavel on his desk.

"Senora Fuentes Barnum, we agreed to your offer. The offer is pending due to any arrangements your son might have made to Judge Bourgeois."

"Your honor. Tomas confided in me that he has not approached the judge."

I sweated like a whore in church, or a fucking liar in a courtroom. I buried my head in my hands to hide the perspiration. Ruby stared at me; aware I made a deal with the devil. There were two options, and the first was crossing the Rio Bravo, get back to Huntsville and do the job myself, or hire a hit man and I knew the right man for the job. I knew the man's reputation for killing anyone for hire. That man, the gringo, who the family assumed killed our father. The gentleman's name was none other than Early Greene.

Chapter 11

Mami and Ruby returned to the hotel room, better known as the Saltillo jail. They prepared for the arranged escape, while I sat in an office talking to Senor Fuentes, my second cousin.

I made myself comfortable, relaxed in a plush chair which I fell into, and the cushions surrounded my butt. I scarfed some tacos, and sipped tequila, listening to my second cousin speak. Behind him sat a painting like the judges I witnessed before. I began to wonder if they trapped me.

"Senor Barnum. I know you sold out to Judge Bourgeois, I know you want your mother and sister freed. You already broke the arrangement before we made an agreement. You, my son, are in great danger."

"What if I kill the judge myself, or hire someone?"

"The deal is off. Your mother will remain free. However, she must remain in Mexico. You and your sister are on your own, there will be no protection. Tomas, you are no longer a Barnum anymore. You cannot have any contact with her. I understand you wanted protection for your family, and that is honorable, but you do not understand the Bourgeois law. They're wanted by the Mexican Mafia and moved into our territory and attempted to control the entire region. You my friend are what we call a un agente doble. Son peores que Bourgeois. Comprende. Senor Barnum, or Bourgeois, you're a lucky man. I will not kill you; I'm letting you go, but you're on your own. If you think you had a hard time getting down here, wait until you try to return."

I looked the man straight in his eyes. "I want to contact Early Greene. I will pay to have the Judge and Warden killed. I will always be a Barnum. At the time I agreed to switch to Bourgeois, I wanted to protect the remaining members of my family. I acted in haste to preserve their life and the Barnum name. I did not want to see the name eradicated. I beg you, Senor Fuentes, spare my family. Spare me, and with the help of an old family friend, I will have the man killed, along with his henchman. The innocent Bourgeois will remain, since I'm sure there are many. Let me go free, and help me find Early Greene."

"Very well, Tomas." He turned to one of his lieutenants and motioned him away, as if a fly buzzed around. The aide returned in thirty seconds with a man who looked familiar. He looked like a man who lurked around Papi's place a time or two.

"Look at that boy," the scar-faced man said, smirking. "He's a real chip off the old block. Too bad the block's head got chopped off." He hollered at his own joke. "I hope this boy doesn't want the same thing."

He opened a fiddle case and took out an instrument not resembling a down-home violin. He grabbed it by the steel handle, flicked the double-edged sword back and forth, and caused a breeze in the warm office. The utensil looked like it was used for cutting down vegetation, or for decapitation and I doubt he used it for clearing fields. He walked towards me with it in his right wrist, and moved the sword back and forth like a pendulum. My eyes followed his every move. Every time he swung the machete, he grimaced, ready to cut something.

"What can I do for you little Barnum?" he asked when he paused. "I doubt if you can afford my services since all your money was stolen in La Grange." He reached in his pocket and grabbed a wallet.

"Hey, that's mine." I reached an arm out towards the wallet, not caring about the slicing sword.

"How much of this do you want me to take?" He pulled green out my billfold. "I'll take it all with the rest I stole." He turned his face to smile at my second cousin. He stuck the money in his money belt and threw me my wallet. He left me a dollar. "I don't think this will cover it all. I will need a lot more. You federal agents don't make that much."

"How much more? I can get the money."

"Where at? I'll follow you."

"When the deal is complete, I will get you the rest."

He reached out his machete, the blade laid still in front of me. I grabbed it and shook the machete which was an extension of his hand.

"Okay, Mr. Tomas Barnum, I'm sure I know where the money is, and I will meet you with my partner. I think you met him at your Daddy's funeral. You know, your former Uncle Zeke, who's known as your current Uncle, Zeb Bourgeois. We must get on the train to Laredo, you, me, my princesa, Lydia, and that little nigger babe of yours. I will lead the way since I don't trust any of you to do the job right."

We left in the evening, and soon snuck across the border. Early paid some immigrants to try to cross, setting up a diversion for us. The four of us snuck in behind the arrested pair. We caught another freight that took us to San Antonio, hopped the Eastbound, and soon we traveled back to Huntsville. Mi Madre snuck back into prison, while Uncle Zeke, a rather obese man, who struggled to keep his jeans above his butt and wore overalls with a flannel shirt, met us outside the prison yard. The prison sat nestled along the railroad tracks where making a rapid getaway was feasible, once the mass killings came to their conclusion.

"You two go to sleep in the woods, start digging some tunnels to hide for a few days. This will get messy, and folks all over will search for us. So, you need a hide-out for a few days."

"How will I know if the deed gets done?" I hesitated.

"Early Greene does not fail when he's on a job, and this is the second biggest job I've ever done. I'm not going to tell you the biggest since you know it already." He took the machete out of his case, slashed a small tree in half.

Ruby and I took off for the forest where we found some tunnels that were already dug out. I think my father, sister and Miriam created the burrows, as well as countless others.

Ruby and I relaxed underground. We sat in close quarters, unable to move around, with just the sounds of our breathing echoing in our pre-dug tunnel. It seemed like an eternity since we screwed but buried a few feet below the surface of the earth and with limited mobility, we passed on the idea. I wanted her and she wanted me, even though it wasn't the best idea. We were required to run when Early gave us the okay.

The train hollered. I didn't want to stay in no tunnel with my girlfriend and we both stank. It was the same line that went by

Papi's place. I grabbed my lover's hand and we crawled out of the tunnels and snuck out of the forest as fast as our legs took us. The train chugged along at a brisk pace. We dashed to catch it and the two of us hopped on and lay in the car while it took us back to Louisiana where I felt safe.

Part VI

Chapter 12

Sara and Miriam
Chicago, IL.

Miriam kept sending me letters, describing how miserable her life was up in Chicago. She lamented on how terrible it became from the last time I headed North, and how she needed rescued. I kept a file of the letters she sent me and decided to head North.

I had time, since the trip to Topeka was still a month away, and I needed to clear my head. School desegregation was important to me, and I danced around my apartment when picked for the assignment. I needed about a month to go through my files to prepare. When I set my mind to something, I get it done like a knife fight in a phone booth.

Miriam needed me, and I needed time to bail her out. Once again, with my vehicle confiscated, I bought me a ticket on the Trailways. This time, being a good girl, I packed Stella and the Regal underneath, and my marine band harmonica sat in my overalls pocket, next to my knife, itching to create music on the back of a bus. I wore Cisco's fedora that I stole from him. I wanted something to remember him by, or to see if I looked good in it. Fashion wasn't daddy's or Grandpa Cecil's strong suits, so it wasn't passed on to me. My stupid younger brother dressed a whole lot better than me. He's such a Mama's boy.

I refrained from tooting on my harp all the way to Chicago. I assumed Miriam knew I'd be arriving, even though I didn't tell her. The place still appeared like a dump when I arrived. Clothes scattered on the floor like rugs, the dirty dishes lucky to find the sink. Pictures hung crooked on the walls, and I saw a couple of rats jump into the bottom cabinets. Miriam's dark skin displayed patches of purple, appearing like a club or a fist smacked her. She wore ripped clothes, and not from wear and tear. It looked like she got caught in something, or a dirty old blues singer finished beating her.

She hugged me tight, clinging to me like a long-lost lover. I often felt she was the sole person ever to love me, besides my father, and he didn't count. Her soft, sweet breath whispered in my ear. "Oh, Sara, why did I run off with that man? I hate that mother fucker. He's as bad as that fat man in Shreveport, or those clients on Fannin. Take me anywhere but here, honey child." She instigated something she hadn't done in years, and with her soft lips kissed me on my ear lobe. Chills went up my spine, as I did not stop her for a minute."

"What are you doing?" I asked her. I wasn't sure how to respond to her advance.

She took a step back, and I noticed her beautiful face all messed up again. The tears streamed out faster, like when the Louisiana rain picks up in the springtime. "I'm sorry, Sara, I missed you so bad. I think there been two people there for me my entire life. One is dead, and you're the other one."

"Just hug me." She wrapped her arms around me again. She wasn't going to let go.

"Sara, we've done it before. You know, before you went off to college."

"You was showing me stuff and teaching me things for the boys I might meet at college. I didn't meet any."

"I wasn't showing you stuff Sara. I want you to feel good."

"You did, and I enjoyed it, but I think I like guys, at least I don't like any other girls. I want this as our little secret."

"It can still be a secret, but get me out of here. I'm going back home for the last time."

"How should we get there? I got me a one-way ticket here. We can take the train, hop a freight, take a bus, or them car salesman back home won't sell me a new car, since I'm one of them commie activists their mother warned them about, so I can buy me a car up here. I'll get me a good one, and we can drive back South. This lawyering money got me itching."

"Buy a car, plus I need me some stuff. That dirty old man don't spend nothing on me anymore. He don't buy me any new dresses, spends all the music money on cocaine, reefer, prostitutes and booze for himself. I'm lucky he's in a rehab place getting clean. He's coming back to an empty house, except all this garbage."

"I'll buy you a couple of pretty dresses, and some good traveling clothes. We got a month. Watcha want to do?"

Her eyes devoured Stella the entire time. Stella, like me, always responded to her touch as she slashed her knife or bottle across the strings. She always sang edgier, matching Miriam's pretty and soulful voice in two-part harmony. Miriam's soul mate became my guitar. I wanted to gift my darling guitar to her for keeps, but Stella, also was my soul mate.

"Maybe we'll find you a baby like this." I pointed to my beautiful beat-up guitar. She loved my Stella guitar. I'm not sure why. Papi picked it up for me when he made a run to Mississippi right before we picked up Miriam.

"Sara, I can't keep a guitar in da house. You know that stinker would take it or crash it on my head. That man can sure play, but he's a bum also."

"Leave him this time. Let's grab everything."

"I got everything I need. You and Stella."

"Do you know where the nearest Chevrolet dealership is?"

A smile came on her face. Her yellow and crooked teeth showed their beauty for the first time. She laughed, at first a little snicker, and her tears of sorrow became tears of laughter, as she came up to me again and wrapped her arms and right leg around me. "Sara, do you think I know where the car dealerships are? I ain't never gone car shopping in my life. I'm sure we can take the train uptown."

"Can we hop it, or do we have to pay?" I chuckled. It resembled a smirk.

My friend didn't know I kidded her. "See up there? It's elevated. We can't hop it."

"Okay, let's go. I'm not sure if I want a truck or a wagon."

I got another Buick wagon with wood panels on the side. I desired that Chevy truck, but wasn't sure how long Miriam and I would stay together. After I made my big purchase, we hit the big department store, where I decided to upgrade Miriam's wardrobe. Two pretty flowery dresses purchased. One yellow with red flowers, the other was blue with yellow flowers. I also got her a tight red dress and a few pairs of overalls, along with the appropriate undergarments. I admit she looked sexy in that skin-tight red dress. I stared at her pretty but innocent face, and followed down to her bare feet.

I glanced back up; old feelings rekindled. "Anything else you need?"

"I need me a new Stella, one of my own. That way I don't play yours."

I licked my lips, chin on my right fist. "Miri, you can always play mine anytime. You play it like a maestro. Plus, I like Daddy's old regal and feel more comfortable with it. Also, honey, they know nothing about Stella up here. We need to get back down South. Up here all they want to do is electrify the music. That little gal of ours does it without them fancy chords and amplifiers."

Miriam struggled in the passenger seat. Her tight dress refused to move along her petite body. I looked over to my right and giggled at her.

"What's so funny, Ms. Sara? You like to see me struggle."

I stayed in the same position. "Oh, Miri, you're so cute. I love you. Bend your cute bottom with the dress, and let's head south. We ain't got any worries about getting kicked-off any damn buses."

She worked that bottom of hers into the passenger seat, and I started my new machine up. I called her Woody II since I purchased another wood panel wagon, and we soon departed Chicago, across Illinois, and home. I wasn't sure where a dark-skinned and a light-skinned Creole mix of people stayed. In the south I couldn't share a hotel with Miriam, since she's as dark as a piece of charcoal, and folks, clueless to my heritage. I'd drive until I couldn't drive no more, and then find a safe place to park, where we'd sleep in the back of the wagon.

Memphis became our goal for the first day. We made great time, but my eyes got heavy and keeping my peepers focused on the road became a struggle. I stole peek at my little friend who wore her skin-tight red dress along the way. All trip long, she kept trying to get comfy. She clutched her body, trying to stretch it out. I smiled. Half-way across Illinois she asked me the question.

"Are we going to do it again or not?"

"Do what again? Play some shows?"

"You know what. I wasn't showing things you needed for college I was showing how I felt."

I took a hard swallow and digested my pride. I gave her a wry smile. The left side of my mouth came up, and my teeth clenched, not in anger but confusion. I took a breath. "You were Papi's lover, so you were like my mother. No one explained sex to me before you did, and you explained it perfectly. I'm not sure if I like girls that way, or even guys.

"I see you staring at me, plus you didn't mind way back then."

The words came out of my mouth like a turtle crossing the walk, and flowed like cold molasses flowing upstream. "I was learning things. I got Cisco whenever I want him."

"From what you say about him, you need some more learning."

She adjusted her dress, trying to make herself comfortable. Her big brown eyes focused on me. She licked her mouth a little, and my eyes gleamed over her face and body and not the road. We swerved to the left a little, and a Northbound car honked, bringing me back to my senses. The next thing I knew Miriam attempted to lay down in the front seat and struggled removing the flimsy material from her petite body. She squirmed and wiggled, and once again my eyes noticed her, and not the road. The car bumped along on the shoulder, and missed a stationary object, which turned out a tall pine tree that protected the main highway from the Ohio River.

I straightened out the car again, reduced my speed, and kept my focus on the road, that until she completed her clothing removal, and sat back naked. Those old feeling came back, where she showed me how to love and received love in a delightful sinful manner. The emotions I desired from her little brother years ago, back when Papi still lived, when this boy kissed me, down in Morgan City, and when I went up to his room to learn the art of sex, only to receive humiliation from a couple of hookers who screwed a fourteen-year-old boy.

I wanted to match those feeling again, and I met Cisco Greene. Cisco couldn't match Miriam or her brother, but he had something that I craved. I needed more teaching, so I'd be able to teach him the art of lovemaking, at least the way I wanted it. Miriam knew what I liked.

Even though we both slept naked in the back of my station wagon, nothing happened between the two of us. She refused to cross moral boundaries this time. I wanted her to, but she refused me. She played with my hair, kissed my forehead, and held me through the night, before she plopped her pretty head on my stomach and drifted off to sleep. I think she wanted to do more, and I know I wanted her too.

At breakfast, at a colored diner across the state line in Mississippi, she told me while she downed a cup of coffee and smoked two cigarettes in succession.

"I'm sorry Sara, I don't smoke that much, but I'm nervous. Sometimes these things calm me down."

With the second smoke extinguished, I noticed she twirled her thumbs, and made little churches out of her pointer fingers. She raised her right hand and twirled her hair into a braid.

"Sara, I'm not a girl who you gonna use for sex, I don't want to be a side lover for you. If you love me, love me, but don't go running off for some guy. If you make a choice to be mine, I'll be yours only, and I ain't gonna have no other lovers. Sara it would be me and you living in the bayou. What I'm saying is that, if we make love to each other ever again, you or me ain't being with anyone else."

I sat across the booth from her, wiped the coffee from my lips, dumped some gravy onto my grits, and took a swallow. I kept my eye trained on her. "Miri, that would not be a good arrangement for you. I don't know how to love. Everybody I ever cared for in this world ends up gone. Mami, Papi, my best friend back home. Hell, I haven't see my squirrelly brother for years either. That's why I came up to see you. I need a friend. Maybe I needed you all the time."

"I want to move back with you, but what am I moving back as? I'm not moving back as your lover, if I ain't going to be your lover forever. We can't touch each other one night and be sisters the next. I love you more than a little sister. It's all or nothing."

I shot a hash brown potato with my pointer finger across the diner, upset at her response, and poured the coffee down my throat too fast. Choking a bit, I retorted, "I'm unlovable."

"You're loveable, Sara. No guy is good enough for you."

I stabbed my toast with my knife. I took a bite with the toast still attached to the knife. I rested my chin on the toast and stared at her. A small purple stain displayed on the bottom of my head.

"Sara, you can't coax me with them big brown eyes of yours." I smiled. "I must be able too, I wasn't trying to coax you into nothing," I lied.

I paid the bill and left the waitress a giant tip and we headed out the door. We entered the vacant parking lot with nobody in sight, so I put my arm around her waist and opened the car door for her, like a gentleman's supposed to. I watched her wiggle into the seat, shaking her little behind at me. She gave me that smile, that lead me into her door, her eyes wider. I heard rustling from the shrubbery around the parking lot. As a multiracial woman, who spent the last eight years in and out of the swamps of Louisiana, I knew the score. The sixth sense of rape or lynching develops like tornado, and I knew how to defend myself. Miriam knew, too. She reached under her seat, grabbed, and put it in my hand. I felt for the lever and the blade came out. I almost always carry two knifes with me. One for Stella and one for protection. I wasn't playing the guitar this time.

The man, tall and fat, smelled like a pig and resembled an ox, the same as all the other white men I whooped on the last few years. This time, I didn't whoop on him, since I smelled his breath, body odor, and felt his sweat drip onto my torso. His tobacco breath stank my overalls. I spun to face the rapist with the knife blade extended, and it went straight into his chest. I pressed it further and the man fell like timber in the forest. I climbed in through the passenger side; crawled across Miriam and soon the engine started. I crossed back into Memphis, West Memphis, and Helena. We went home through Arkansas, since I detested driving through Mississippi after killing a man in Southaven. We crossed the bridge into West Memphis, and Miriam started humming already. I watched her climb into the back and grab Stella. My girl strummed the shuffle and sang the blues. Next that little gal start shredded and hollered the blues. She grabbed the murder weapon with the blood stain handle and blade, and slid along Stella's steel strings. She woke all the lynched Negroes of Mississippi, all the raped black girls rose from their graves, and came out of the woodwork to confront their attackers. I let her sing by herself the first two times through, but soon joined her. She created this song:

I killed a man down in South Haven
I killed a man down in South Haven
I killed a man down in South Haven

He tried to rape me, had no time to run
he tried to rape me, had no time to run
He tried to rape, but I had no gun

He could of killed me, had no time to run
he could of killed me, had no time to run
he could of killed me, but I had no gun.

The knife went in straight through the heart
Switchblade went in, straight through the heart
Had no time for a running start

I killed a man in South Haven
I killed a man down in South Haven
I killed a man down in South haven

On the run, got a place to hide
On the run, but I got a place to hide
Cant confess, police think I lied

On the run, got a place to hide
On the run, for the rest of my life
Can't confess, jury will think I lied.

Home in the Swamp, I'm forever free
Home in the swamp, I'm forever free
Down in the swamp, I'll always be free

I killed a man down in South Haven
I killed a man down in South Haven
I killed a man down in South Haven.

"We need to record this as soon as possible, while the energy and emotion is fresh. Is that recording stuff still at Cecil's?" Miriam asked.

"Yeah, we'll stop at pawpaw's on the way down. It's right on the way, and let us get this thing recorded, leave it somewhere, and split. We'll clean off the murder weapon and drop it in the lake. That slide of yours will play the blues and haunt the bayou forever. You don't need to collect no beer bottles anymore."

"That was your knife Sara." She smiled at me, and gave me a quick pucker, and a wink. I winked back and smiled as we high tailed it across Arkansas, but I obeyed the speed limit. Folks of color in the South don't like cops pulling them over for nothing, especially after killing a white man.

Across Arkansas we sped on, one eye focused on the road and one gleamed at her. When she put the guitar in the back, she turned her butt to me and her cute bottom rested inches from my face, and when she stretched her arms and body, her top rose to expose her bare back and bits of that bottom of hers. She knew how to entice me, she looked down, wet her lips with her tongue and smiled. She plopped back in the seat with her back against the car door, and her legs spread. "After we record it Sara, after we get this song down, we can get down."

"What about?"

"We killed a man. I'm as responsible as you are, Ms. Sara, since I watched you stab dat motherfucker."

"Miri darling, I'm starting to wonder. That guy might not been no mother fucker and wasn't trying to rape me."

"Sara, honey. He had him a knife, too. I seen it with my eyes. God knows this was self-defense, and God's on the side of us colored folk. Let's get down to Cecil's and quit staring at these legs." She puckered her lips, and wrapped her tongue around them as her legs went a little further apart. I ain't saying what her hand and fingers did.

We scooted across Arkansas and took our sweet time in Texarkana. I knew we were close. I missed daddy a lot, but I'm sure he'd roll over in his grave about me killing a man in Southaven, Mississippi.

I crossed the state line on the back road, let out a deep breath as I knew we returned home to Louisiana. Like Papi, I always felt safe here. Invincible as a hurricane that hit New Orleans, or the peninsula with a thunderous roar, and winds that will take a house from Houma to Monroe. The next time I exhaled, I gave Miri a long pucker as the breath came out. She still sat with her back against the car door, watching me drive. Her smile shone as large as the state we didn't cross into, while her hand, rested above her thigh, a nice big grin on her face.

The new car meandered through the forest, and along the shores of The Black Bayou. I took a left towards the dirt road, and hung a right down the muddy path, and we drove along Pawpaw's lengthy driveway, covered in gravel. The car bounced like Miri and I traveled across the country as pioneers, hopping across the great plains in our covered wagon.

I stopped the car at Grandpa Cecil's in my usual spot. Pawpaw's old jalopy sat parked, and the lights of his place shut off. Walking around, I noticed the light in my old room turned on, and I thought that odd since I hadn't returned for a while.

Miriam rose and moved over to me. She put her finger under my nose and slid it down in my mouth, so I received a whiff and taste of her, and gave her digit a little kiss. She reached over the back to get her stuff. Her butt exposed, and I gave her ass a couple of swats.

"Sara, after I record this, we got us a classic. You're playing guitar and singing harmonies, aren't you?"

I tried to think of some double entendre, but the best I came up with was, "I'll pluck your strings and you sing, and we'll harmonize." I winked and puckered up for her, while she looked at me as if I ruined my chance.

There weren't no dogs there to meet us, but we thought we heard a dog bark somewhere. In a flash, a couple of lights came on in the house. I saw a head bounce through the luminated windows of the parlor room and kept my eyes peeled on the shadow as it crept through the house.

The lights turned on, throughout the house and I got a good look at my grandfather, who met us at the wooden front door. The man did not look well. I knew he suffered with cancer, and that explained why I didn't come to see him. Watching another family member die, after witnessing my father tumble from a freight train into the Sabine River while it crossed into hell, would be heartbreaking.

Chapter 13

Grandpa's nose worked well, since he sniffed around Miriam after he gave her a hug first. Miriam put down her bag and my guitar and hugged him back. His eyes always reminded me of the raccoons that scavenged scraps of food from the family down by the docks. He hunched over as he looked at me.

"How's my big-shot lawyer, baby girl, doing?" His voice sounded blocked a little, as he repeated himself, after pushing a big spot on his neck. His voice came through clearer, but I became terrified to hug him. He looked so fragile as he was not well. Once I put my arms around him, I did not want to let go.

"I'm doing good papaw; I might be in big trouble though. We need to record something quick. Do you still have Papi's magnetic tape machine?"

"Yeah, it's in your old room. I set it up as a recording studio in case you ever wanted to record some stuff." The old man repeated himself after he pushed the lump on his neck again, and the sound came through much clearer again. He continued to fiddle with that lump, as he spoke. He hobbled towards his chair. "We soundproofed your room. Go make your record. Do you want anything to eat?"

"Any crawfish pie?" Miriam asked.

"We got a bunch. I can't eat much no more, but Angeline still cooks for me like you kids still live here, and I ain't got the stomach and I got me throat cancer. I can barely swallow."

"I'm sorry Cecil, anything we can do for you, name it."

"Make that record, that's what you can do for me." He swung his walking stick at us, as we ran down the hallway. I heard a thud as the man fell, but I also saw the geezer pull himself up.

Miriam sat on the bed and unpacked Stella. I got my Regal out of the case and turned the knobs as I tuned it. Who's doing the slide? If I'm doing lead, I'm changing the tuning."

"Ms. Sara, you is right about one thing. You can't show love, can you?"

"I thought we were recording?" My eyes dampened, and I tried brushing the tears away when Miriam wasn't looking at me.

"Sara did you see Grandpa? He don't look no good."

"Of course, I saw him. He doesn't smell good either. He smells like that fat guy in Mississippi after I killed him. He ain't going to make it long is he?"

Miriam bowed her head, shaking it. "Nope. He ain't going to last long. Say let's share a secret with him. It's good to spill your guts to someone. It's even better to share your guts with someone who ain't going to live long."

"Tomorrow. Let's get this thing down and do whatever else we gonna do." I stared deep in her eyes.

Possessed with large brown eyes, that penetrated my soul when she focused them at me. Her lips curled up, and as I looked down her body, she spread her legs a little wider. There wasn't any touching like in the car. Pushing her body up, she rose like poetry in motion, and she shook her head. Her long-braided hair swished back and forth.

"C'mon Ms. Sara. We need to get this song down while the blood is still on the knife, and dat fat man's spirit's still haunting dat diner." She stayed in Spanish tuning, while I tuned mine up to standard.

I started the shuffle, while she snapped the blade open on the evidence. I noticed a couple of red stains on it.

I started singing. "No, no, Ms. Sara, I'm singing this. You can do harmonies with me, on *I Killed a Man.*"

Three takes later we completed the song. It sounded like nothing I ever heard before on the radio down here, or in little juke joints across the South. "We need to toss this thing in the lake, unless you feel there is still magic to it."

"Oh, Ms. Sara, there is magic in this slide. It's going to haunt us forever too. It's going to haunt the bayou here, or wherever we ditch it. I want to record a few more while I still got it."

"Do you got any more songs?"

"I got me bunches of material, but I'm going to do one more. It's one I shared with your daddy the night I came back, a few nights before your daddy died. Bobo's the only one I played it for. It's got a similar theme. Start the shuffle again, baby."

We did the next song, too, and I know for a fact that Miriam killed that man in Texas before she crossed the river and found Daddy. Miriam became better off without that pig, but I we became fugitives. Low profiles were required. Once we finished recording both songs, we pressed the records, and put them in the paper sleeve. I stared at her, and she returned the look. An awkward silence settled. She still held Stella by the neck of the guitar, the body rested on the ground. I took a few steps before and Stella fell, as Miriam no longer wanted my favorite guitar. She wanted something else and so did I. I walked towards her, to where she sat on my childhood bed. Her eyes remained on me, as I took my time strolling forward. I leaned down and gave her a soft kiss, nothing more than a peck. We repeated that several times. Our hand worked across each other's body, and soon, clothes scattered on the floor, and Miriam cuddled on my breast, while I thumped her braided hair.

"So, we ain't gonna part? We're always gonna stay together?"

"I hope so, but you don't want to love me that way. Nobody wants to love me that way and you know why. We're both wanted by the police, and we have two sets of evidence. One a 78-rpm record, the other a bloody slide."

"Ms. Sara, my hands are all over this too. I'll take the fall for you, besides," she paused as if to reveal some secret, and turned her head from me. She caught her breath and continued, "it's my song, my voice, and your slide. That's how much I love you."

I took her face in my hand, leaned up and kissed her. "What we gonna do?"

She kissed me back and whispered. "Go to Baton Rouge and try to live a normal life, Ms. Sara."

"You don't call me Ms. Sara. Makes me feel like I'm your master. Besides, you're older than me. I'll call you Ms. Miriam." I gave her a nice long kiss that lasted until sunrise."

Angeline, Grandpa's lady friend stood in the kitchen making breakfast. Bacon frying and coffee brewing are the best way to wake up in the morning. The woman walked in on the two of us laying naked together with no blankets on, and Miriam using my right boob as a pillow. I wasn't sleeping, with all the drama from the day before. I looked up at the woman, who I always thought beautiful, and smiled. She smiled back at us.

"Your secret's safe with me, Sara. I knew about you guys for a long time, but didn't tell a soul. I made you girls a big breakfast of biscuits and gravy, grits and, bacon and eggs. I hope you girls are hungry." She paused and looked around, looking for Grandpa, I'm assuming. "It looks like you worked up a pretty big appetite."

"Oh, we're getting up. Once I get this girl off my boob." I lifted her head up, wrapped my left arm around her and pulled her across my body, so she faced Grandpa's lady. She covered her face up, embarrassed of what Angeline saw. Miri waited for her to leave, leaned over and kissed me. She stood up on my bed, her small frame stood above me, so I noticed everything. She crawled across me, gathered her clothes, and departed to take a bath. I followed her. The incredible sensations we gave each other while bathing, since we washed each other's bodies, and kissed and fooled around in the tub. We came out and ate breakfast.

"Your grandpa's still sleeping. Sara he's real sick and at the most has a month to live. Your best bet is to say goodbye to him when you leave."

"We're going to stay for a few days, and I need to get back to work. Miriam's moving down with me, but we're staying here for a few days. I want to take her out fishing. I also want you and Grandpa to hear what we recorded last night, and we need to distribute the record, anonymously. When you hear the record, you will know why we need to hide out."

"Baby girl, what happened?"

"How's Grandpa's hearing? I want him to hear this. Miri wrote it and it's da best damn blues song you've ever heard. Should we play it live or play it on the record?"

"We can play it live for her. Last time we gonna use this switch." Miriam snapped the blade open. She closed it and went back to get Stella and my Regal.

"I'll go get your grandpa," the beautiful dark chocolate skinned lady told us.

It took a few minutes but back came grandpa. He smelled kind of moldy, like books that sat in the basement a few years too long, and he hobbled with a cane, when it looked like he needed a wheelchair to move around. Somehow, on his face sat a smile. He always loved to hear my parents sing together, but I knew he liked my songs the best, and especially when Miri and I got together. The music we made, more passionate than my parents, and Grandpa Cecil always smiled. His lady friend whispered to him, and her pouty lips went near his ear. He looked at Miriam and smiled. His attention turned to me, and a little scowl came on his face, soon replaced with his grin. He arranged his tumor again, so his voice became clear. "Play this song for me girls."

"Miri introduced it. We can play this one more time. Something happened on the way down here. We need to hide out for a while." She looked at me. I started the twelve-bar blues shuffle, and Miriam popped open the blood-stained switch blade. Grandpa sat back in his rocker and attempted holding his head up. The man no longer had teeth, but an amazing smile appeared on his face, with me playing the shuffle, and Miriam lighting up Stella's steel string with my blade. Grandpa tilted his head back, nodded in rhythm to our playing. Angeline also grinned as Miriam started singing, and once she sung killed a man, both their mouths opened, astonished, but Barnums were no strangers to this life. Angeline left the room for a moment, while grandpa continued to enjoy the show.

When we finished the extended version, with Miriam went crazy on the slide inventing new arrangements. She knew full well my knife would soon rest at the bottom of the Black Bayou later today, and if she tossed it out blade first, it may imbed in an alligator gar.

Angeline came back into the parlor room, which sat by the lake, with some of Grandpa's best fishing poles. "Get out on the lake and do some fishing, you better get out now since the law's been snooping around too much. It's those damn Bourgeois deputies. They're letting Grandpa go in peace I think, but you two better watch out."

"Great song you two." Grandpa said after arranging the tumor in his throat. "Miriam is that the weapon in your left hand?"

"We're going fishing. I'm gonna need a new one when we get back."

"I got a few in the old store. Angeline will get you some." He cleared his throat, arranged his neck again, and respoke so we heard and comprehended the man.

We went down the rickety steps of the dock and out to the water. Grandpa's boat sat there, tied up, and the Evinrude outboard hung off the back. I pushed the primer button to allow the gas through, pulled the chord and it started. Miriam climbed into the boat and fell into my lap. I hoped she stumbled on purpose, and we soon hopped along the waves of the big lake. We passed Cypress trees, that looked like death won them over, and a couple of alligators cruised on top of the water. We got out amongst a couple other fisherman, and I cut the engine. Miriam climbed up front and hoisted the anchor. I saw her bow her head to give a little prayer. She popped the blade open, tied the slide to the anchor rope. She tossed the anchor overboard and the murder weapon, and the musical accessory descended to the bottom of the lake. In this spot, the lake dropped to about nearly thirty feet deep, I remember Papi told me one time. My gal came back and sat on the seat next to me and kissed my lips.

"Sara, I'm hoping we will stay safe. Ain't nobody gonna find the weapon."

I leaned over and kissed her back. The kiss, amazing, as it ended with my tongue probing the inside of her mouth. She returned that kiss by licking my neck.

"My luck, it will get stuck in a fish, and some fat redneck will catch it and find it and get with the deputies."

She put her hand under my top and moved it up, squeezing my boob ever so gentle. "That ain't happening, besides I'm taking the fall for you."

I put my hand between her legs, slid my finger up and down her privates. I blew in her ear, "I want you, baby." I backed off and told her, "you ain't taking no fall. I love you, Miri and we're going to stay together. Let's catch some fish and head back to the shack."

She looked around while we drifted to an area where no boats floated near. The witnesses, only waterfowl, alligators, and fish don't tell tales.

"Let's cast these lines out and get cozy." I put my arm around her as we set the fishing poles down and drifted across the lake, oblivious to anything around us, we gazed into each other's eyes.

We didn't catch any fish, but remained hooked on each other. I took the boat back to the dock and needed to return to Baton Rouge, and get Miriam settled in her new home. I also needed to check my agenda. I knew that Brown vs Board of Education, approached. An important case for me, especially after getting booted from LSU for having Negro blood in me. Some folks down here went by the one percent rule. That eliminated all the Creole people, but if you possessed light skin, some folks passed and allowed to enroll in the state schools.

After we returned, I noticed the essence of fresh crawfish boiling. Angeline made us a good dinner of my favorite pie. "Did you gals catch any fish?"

"Ma'am," Miriam answered. "We didn't even try fishing. We relaxed together."

Grandpa sat nowhere near, but we found him asleep in his rocking chair. He paced in a steady rhythm, the rhythm of our song. I'm positive he didn't approve of a relationship between his granddaughter, and his youngest son's former girlfriend. He didn't join us for dinner. Later Miriam and I retired to the tub, and bed.

Chapter 14

Tomas and Ruby
Near Zwolle, Louisiana, that same evening.

"Baby, we need to get to my grandpa's. I know where he keeps the money, plus he says he's got something for me. It's the recipe for the whiskey and I'm going to make it legal, and distribute it all over the south, and America. Hell, it's going worldwide." I stood ahead of her and flexed arms wide, looking like Charles Atlas carrying the world. "Hang with me, baby. Once we get past Shreveport, we'll be fine."

Ruby smiled. "I know, baby, I'm going to make a good wife."

"Yeah we got to get this started. It's going to take a while, but I think we're going to be rich."

"We don't need them Bourgeois folks either, do we?"

"Nope, we' going to do it."

We sat alone on the freight train as it slowed down to a bridge. I knew the bridge well, but not as well as Sara, or the rest of my family.

"C'mon, baby, we need to jump."

We both tumbled down the hill, and pa's old jon boat still rested there, hidden on shore. I hoped the engine still worked, since we needed to float upstream. If the engine didn't start, I knew where to get one downstream. We had an old redneck neighbor back when I was a kid, who got his kicks by taking his boat up the river, and he'd shoot up our place a little. I don't think he liked the house parties.

Well, the damn Evinrude never started for me, so we drifted down the Sabine. It was a few miles to the neighbor's dock. Ruby and I relaxed, and she did that thing I already loved about her and craved from Miriam, but that bitch only has eyes for Sara. Ruby made me forget about Miriam's lack of desire for me for the time being, as she crawled up on her knees, and rested between my legs. She yanked my pants down, while the sun and soon other things stood straight up.

The neighbor's boat lay tied up on the dock, so I confiscated it like any FBI agent would. The Mercury engine started, and we soon headed back up the Sabine River to Logansport. In Logansport, we borrowed a car from some stranger and sped past Shreveport to the Black Bayou. I knew Grandpa Cecil's health was failing, and I needed to see the man off to heaven. We headed up to my Grandpa's as the sun began its descent.

It took us an hour to get up there, and another half hour to wander around the back roads. Ruby rubbed my thigh and licked my neck and ears the entire drive. Both of us were oblivious to anything around us until I could not take it anymore. I pulled over in a forest, a few twists and turns from Grandpa's place. Ruby and I got into the back seat and she took care of herself rubbing herself as she knelt between my legs. Her soft lips and tongue did wonders on me. Once finished she sat up and smiled.

"I can't wait to meet your Grandpa. He sounds like a good man and you won't be as distracted." She twirled her tongue in my ear.

Arriving at Grandpa's, I noticed a strange car parked there. I had never seen the vehicle before, and the hair on my arms stood. It could have been Sara, but she was much too busy attempting to change the world. I noticed there were no lights on, except in the back room where a faint glow illuminated the lake. Sara's room overlooked the lake, since it always had the better view. I relaxed a bit, assuring myself she returned. I've enjoyed my time on my own, and real lucky, I've been unable to visit her for an eternity. Damn bitch got everything I ever wanted, except the whiskey recipe, and long talks with our mother.

Ruby and I walked into the house and everyone slept. We went to the bathroom, and got undressed. I turned the water on, found some soap to make a nice bubble bath. Ruby grabbed the toothpaste out of the medicine cabinet, squeezed the tube, and the paste came out on her finger. She brushed her teeth with her middle finger, took a cup of water, rinsed and spat. She did the same to me. With the tub halfway full, she tested the water, by sticking her big toe in.

"Get in with me, Tommy." I held her hand as she climbed into the tub. Her long leg went over the edge of the white porcelain tub, and the bubbles cascaded over her body. I joined her and sat down on the far end, watched her move that sexy bottom plop on my lap. We washed each other and kissed some more, got out of the tub and dried each other off with towels and mouths. The towels wrapped around our privates as we snuck towards the dimmed-lighted room.

We stopped at the sound of giggles. Ruby raised her browsed at me and smiled. Her hand brushed my face and she whispered. "I heard two ladies giggle. Let's listen for a bit." The giggles turned to soft moans, and not one set. "I think someone likes girls. Shall we peek?"

The moaning got louder, and small shrieks of pleasure erupted. Again, it wasn't Sara. The other girl sounded like Miriam. Ruby opened the door. The creak was quiet enough not to interrupt the love birds, as she pushed it ajar. I stood behind her with my body pressed up against her behind. My hands caressed her breasts. She continued to nudge the door open, until we noticed the bed. There, I recognized Miriam, who straddled the other woman's face, her face between the woman's legs. I couldn't make out Sara's face, but I recognized her voice. My breathing got heavier, as my hands caressed Ruby's breasts faster. I stiffened up as we watched a little longer, and then led her by the hand as we went to my old room and made love all night."

Chapter 15

Sara and Miriam

We woke up early the next morning.

"Miri, did we forget to shut the door last night?"

"I don't think so. I thought I locked it."

"Let's get going, honey. I want to start our new life together." We went in and brushed out teeth, kissed like an old married couple, a sweet little peck on the lips. We gathered our belongings and soon arrived in Shreveport where I traded the car in for a similar model, and returned to Baton Rouge. Miriam approached her happiest home to date, where one person loved and cherished her. I'm still not sure about her and Daddy's relationship. I know he liked her. I know he wasn't using her, and treated her good. I don't think he loved her like I did. I wanted to give her my world. She sat in the car as we drove through the swamplands of Central Louisiana, passing the old Barnum plantation near Natchitoches, near the area we first met her. She sat there staring at me. Her large brown eyes appeared bigger as a small tear descended her face, and a small smile appeared. Never more beautiful, I took a breath. My heart skipped beats.

"I love you, Miriam. I ain't ever said that to anyone, except Papi, Mami, and my little bratty brother."

"I love you, too. I can't wait to get to my new home. I'm gonna cook for you, keep the house clean, and take care of you. I'm gonna be a good wife."

I rubbed her leg as she adjusted in the front seat. She sat with her back against the door panel and legs spread. I massaged her calf and lower thigh as we smiled at each other. The new car rolled south.

Chapter 16

Tommy and Ruby

I went up to Angeline and hugged her. "Was Sara and Miriam here last night? I thought I saw a car parked here when we got in, and we heard giggles and moans from her room."

"Yeah they stayed here for a few days. They must have taken off early after I made them a nice breakfast."

"Are they lovers?"

"I don't know, but it ain't any of your business Tomas Barnum. Now who dis purdy lady?" Angeline looked her over good and smiled at my young little friend.

"Oh sorry. This is Ruby Wilson, damn purdy little thing, plus she plays a mean guitar once we get her a new one. Everything we owned got stolen down in Texas." I looked over the house. I knew who and what was coming how we're gonna do it and I required confirmation. "So, how's Grandpa?"

"Not good, but that son of a bitch is too stubborn to die."

"Well Gramps and I got a plan. Some important folks are searching for me, and one is Mr. Greene. Hopefully, Grandpa has the recipe ready."

"Tommy, he's ready to give it to you. He doesn't want to carry it to the grave and wants to make sure it gets in the hands of the right part of the family. He wants to make sure it remains in Barnum hands. It ain't going over to no Bourgeois."

"We are going to hang out here while I'm still with the Feds. I do need to hide out. So, did Sara and Miriam say anything?"

"Tomas, whatever they're doing together is none of your business. I knew about them years ago."

"So did I." I wanted a plug of tobacco, I never spat in Grandpa's old brass spittoon that sat on the wooden floor. I found his bag, and stuffed a wad in. Getting dizzy and grabbing the wall, I chewed the tobacco, and got my mouth full of the juice. I spat the entire wad out. "So, you agree to this immoral stuff?"

"Tomas? You ain't the one to talk. I heard you last night, and this house has seen a lot worse, and so did that house your daddy ran. Lawd, have mercy, Bo ran them whores through there as folks go prostitutin around. Your sister and Miriam always loved each other ever since she went to college, and I'd rather see two folks loving each other good, than seeing all these whores running through."

"Ruby and I are gonna get married. I ain't being with no one else. Hoping we can find a place down here."

Angeline wrapped her arms around me, squished her big ones into my chest, and kissed my cheek. "Well, congrats. It shouldn't be a problem. You got enough Negro blood in you to make it legal, but you gotta marry as a Negro."

"I don't know if I can do that. I want to be a white man, since I got so many more privileges. I can't tell you since I've been out on my own, how I get by. Folks don't even look twice at me, and they don't know that I'm half Mexican, and part slave. Guess I'm blessed to be light skin."

The right hand struck my face like a high and tight fastball. "Tomas Barnum, I know your daddy didn't raise you like that. It ain't the color of skin that makes you who you are, but what's in here." Her right finger poked my chest. "Let me check on Grandpa. I know he ain't doing good but he's waiting for you. Grandpa's got everything you need."

I was assigned a case regarding Pa's murder. They wanted me to talk to Mami and the Feds think she was involved. I think skanky Miriam had something to do with it, but I can't talk no more about it. Ruby agrees with me on it."

I felt the right hand again. This time it was followed by a left. Next thing I knew, she pushed me against a wall. The few books that Grandpa and Angeline displayed in their house fell on to me from the bookcase. "Watch your mouth about that girl. She was your daddy's girlfriend."

"Yeah and my sister's. I don't think I can trust her. She comes back, Papi goes and gets Mami, and gets himself killed. Fed's ain't got anything on her, except that murder in Texas, but I got a suspicion."

I struggled to get up, and Angeline stared right above me, daring me to try to stand. I noticed her hand reach out, ready to give me another combo. In the nick of time, we heard load groans, and some bones creaking. The woman pulverizing my face turned and walked away. She turned her head back towards me as I attempted to rise. I stayed on the ground. Another book fell on my head. It read, "The Adventures of Huckleberry Finn."

She returned, as my dear old Grandpa limped up to Ruby and I. Ruby assisted me to my feet. I saw Angeline whisper to my grandfather. The man hobbled towards me and pushed at the lump on the side of his throat. It looked habit forming, like combing your hair, or picking your nose.

"You came for the recipe, cause I ain't taking it with me to the grave. Let me go get it, Tomas." The old man turned and went back to my old room.

Angeline motioned for Ruby and I to follow. We went back there. The floor creaked an evil sound like something cutting loose in the bayou. The type of noise that Grandpa, Papi and even my stupid sister enjoyed. To them, they might as well have sat on the dock, smoking a corncob pipe and fishing when they heard it. To me it sounded like a critter got stuck in a trap, mauled by a fox. I didn't like screeching. I looked at Grandpa, and he motioned Angeline into my old closet. Once again, I followed her.

"Help me move this old dresser," she told me.

I pushed it out on the main floor and looked at Grandpa. His eyes never focused, and the tears were real. He knew the end was near. He adjusted the lump again.

"Tomas, it sat in your room all this time. I always wanted you to carry this on. I want you to, "he coughed bad. …. "carry this tradition on. Make it legal for everyone."

His face showed lines, that resembled bad sketching when he smiled. The old man lost his teeth, but there was still something in his grin that showed sincerity. He proceeded giving me the family treasure, the family legacy. Papi had it, but Papi died before he passed it down. Angeline bent to the floor. The man watched his friend bend down and his eyes followed her bottom as she knelt. The toothless grin got even bigger as she removed the floorboard and spun a combination lock. She pulled out a manila envelope that papers peeped out of the edges. The woman smiled at Grandpa who returned a toothless grin. I looked at him, our eyes met, and I noticed that tears exited his eyes.

Angeline passed Grandpa the folder. The entire Barnum legacy of Grandpa's shine, nothing better in the three states, and I knew in seconds I'd inherit the fortune. I planned on legally making it and distributing the hooch around the world. Grandpa refused my uncles to continue the legacy. One remained a recluse, and the other aligned with the other family and became Klan. Of course, Gramps did not know my recent affiliations either; I felt like a fool. I couldn't betray the man. I needed to betray my new affiliation, and I believed my trap was prepared. Hell, I was in so deep, I might need Sara's help. I already had her set up, she didn't know it.

Angeline exited my old closet. She carried more goodies for me. Brown paper sacks full of something. She handed them to Grandpa. Grandpa squinted as he peered into each of the three paper sacks. He stretched them out to me. He tried to talk, but couldn't. The tumor in his throat, unable to be shoved aside, when he tried to clear it. He hugged me, and believed he said "Skedaddle Tomas. I love you. Make your grandpa proud."

I wrapped my arms around the coot, never wanting to let go. I thought that if I kept on hugging him, he wouldn't die.

Startled, we heard a crash like raccoons knocking over trash cans, but the footsteps resonated much heavier. In a burst of energy, Grandpa flicked his hand, shooing me away like a bug. Angeline bailed as if the place got raided by the real feds, and she returned to whoring. Ruby and I escaped to the dock, where we watch the action as Early Greene and my Uncle Zeke arrived. Part two was now in effect.

"Where's the recipe, Dad? It's all mine, since Bo died."

Grandpa wasn't talking. He pointed to his neck, looked at Early, and nodded. Early carried his fiddle case with him, but he wasn't packing a musical instrument. It took one swing, since expensive government assassins never miss. The head stayed attached.

Angeline already snuck down to the dock and hugged me. "This is what he wanted, Tommy. He's hurting so bad and no longer wanted to suffer. You two run off and make a home and don't worry about me. I'm getting myself out after we bury your grandfather."

Ruby and I took off and arrived back in Monroe by midnight.

Chapter 17

Sara and Miriam

I didn't know how to live with someone and the thought of Miriam staying around me all day was a good thing, as if God prepared me for her. She's an angel, but again, the thought of that woman prancing around me all day nauseated me. I mean, anyone hanging around me for the rest of my life made, me want to clear my guts out like I swallowed a chaw of Beechnut. I mean, I had no idea what we would do all the time. Eat, play music and enjoy each other's treasures. I still worked as an attorney and wondered if she'd prepare dinner for me every night. Would she smother me with kisses, have a nice warm bath drawn for me? What the hell would this be like? I called the suits from the NAACP.

"I want to go to Topeka. How soon do you want me there?"

"As soon as you can get there, Sara."

"I'm leaving tomorrow morning."

"Ms. Sara, we just got back here. Why you leaving so soon? We can't spend no time together, like girlfriends should. You say you going to take me shopping. I need me some new clothes."

"Miri baby." I leaned over and kissed her. "This case is something that's always been important to me. They want to integrate the schools. No more black schools, no more white schools, damn baby, I could attend anywhere I want and so could you."

"Ms. Sara, you know I didn't go to no school. I told you what I was doing when I was fifteen."

I hugged the little woman. She rested her head on my breasts; looked at me and smiled. "That's why I love you too baby, but I got a big world I need to change. This case is so important to me; I can't believe I'm going."

"Can't you wait another day? I want to see what it's like to be in love again. I want to be with someone who cares about me and treats me good. I haven't had that since your daddy."

"I'll wait another day, baby. I'm still tired from all the driving, and all the stuff that happened." I caressed her face, still nuzzled in my boob and leaned over and kissed her. She returned the kiss. "Maybe we should relax."

"Again? That's the fourth time since we got home."

"Baby, I'm tired, and I got a long drive the next day. You need to help me relax." I leaned over, and my lips reached for hers again. This time they missed their target, hit her pretty cheek as she turned her head.

"Ms. Sara, I want everything you do but baby we need more. I will do things to you when you want it. I might not got no education, and whored around in Shreveport and to that fat man up there, and I let those dirty ol blues singers have their way with me, and let them beat me, but I want everything different with you. You said you love me, so baby, I want to feel the love, and that's not by sleeping together. It's not buying me stuff. That fat man bought me some clothes and he raped me. Ms. Sara, I hope I'm not here to please you."

"Miri baby, I want to lay down with you. We can relax together. We don't have to do nothing but cuddle and take a nap. I think that I'm trying to show you how to love someone. I'm new to this, too, so I need to figure it out. So, baby, let's go relax. We don't have to do nothing."

"I didn't say I didn't want to do nothing. I need this no to base on always doing stuff."

I tried to look in her eyes, but my eyes rolled as I let out a louder sigh than I wanted to.

"What's wrong, Ms. Sara?"

"Stop calling me Ms. Sara, for one thing. If we're going to do this, we're partners. When you call me that, I feel like I'm your mistress. I ain't your mistress, I don't own you."

"If we're going to do this?" You told me we are going to do this, and you were rolling them big eyes of yours. You think I'm some poor country girl." She turned and walked away.

The door to my bedroom slammed louder than normal. I started sweating like a whore in church, since our first fight happened, in our second night together. I didn't know what she wanted. I know why daddy spent a lot of time writing music, or at the still when he cooked some shine. I grabbed the regal and played a tune.

We spent the next few hours with Miri locked in my room, which I guess became ours, while I practiced some scales. I didn't feel like writing anything new, or at least anything I wanted to share with loved ones, or the public. I got up and knocked on my bedroom door.

Silence.

I knocked again, and nothing. I turned the handle, and I didn't see her at first. I noticed the little lump under my blanket adjacent to the pillows. Miriam, a small girl, resembled a lump of pillows, next to the other stack. I pulled up the covers, and I saw the wet splotched under her eyes.

I stroked her face. "Miri baby, I'm sorry if I made you cry. I'm nervous about this. I don't know how to love a guy, and now I'm trying to love a woman. I want more than friendship with you. You're not a little play toy that caters to my wishes. I'm sorry that you feel that way. Seems like the two people who want to treat you like a woman, is me, and before that my daddy. I don't know how yet, but I'm not stupid. I'm gonna figure it out."

"I'm sorry, too, Sara baby." She let me brush her tears away and rested her head in my chest again. I held her soft head, ran my fingers through her hair, and refused to let her go. We cuddled up like that all night, deciding to make a fresh start in the morning.

I woke long before Miriam and couldn't find anything for breakfast. I strolled down to the market a few blocks away. I passed the bars, pharmacies, and paid attention to the parked cars, as I hurried past them. The market, a couple of blocks away had everything I desired. I bought some flour for the biscuits and gravy, some eggs, sausage and a package of grits. Mami, Papi, Angeline and my sweetums taught me how to cook, and I prepared to spoil my love with a big breakfast.

I got back from the A and P and started making a mess. The flour scattered everywhere in the kitchen, resembled a Nebraska blizzard.

The pots and pans disappeared. I don't think my little vixen deserved the abuse, since she wasn't around long enough to rearrange the whole damn place. I did anyway as my sometimes-potty mouth and quick temper decided to roar its ugly head.

"Miri, where the fuck is the biscuit pan? God damn, I'm trying to make you some grub girl. What the hell did you do with everything?"

"Sara," came the voice from our bedroom. "What the fuck ya talking about? I ain't touched nothing. I didn't even cook nothing yet."

"Where the fuck my pots and pans at?"

"I don't know. I wondered that, so when I cook you something, I know where the hell they're at. Let's take deep breaths and look for them."

"You find them, since you put them somewhere. I need me a bath, and you can start it for me, too."

"I ain't starting shit for you bitch. You ain't no better than that fat man, or them dirty ol singers. You say you ain't gonna act like that, but first sign of any trouble, you blame me, and act like them dirty ol men I screwed with. I wish your daddy was still here. He didn't raise you like this. Start your own damn bath. I might head back home and see my cousins."

The bedroom door slammed as my little apartment shook like a hurricane came through.

I sweated like a whore in church as I figured I screwed up one of the few good things that happened to me. I burnt tracks like the throw rug was on fire as I raced towards my bedroom, our bedroom. I heard the poor woman crying, and knew I fucked up. I needed Miriam, and tons of pride craved swallowing, something I didn't do well. I needed to apologize. I gulped a few times as I stood outside my bedroom door, counted to ten and repeated my swallow. I needed to say it and mean it with conviction. I had never felt this way in my adult life.

The humid air in my apartment soon located my lungs as I held it there for ten seconds or so. I took another breath, this time a little bit longer, and knocked on our door. I tapped on the door at first, barely hearing the rapping. I doubt if she heard anything through her tears that sounded like a riverboat chugging down to the Crescent City. The knocking continued, this time louder. She did not open the door. I turned the handle and it wasn't locked, so I went in. Miriam laid face down on the bed and she did not acknowledge me. I walked to the bed, sat down beside her and rubbed her back near her missing bra-strap. My hand caressed her back until she acknowledged my presence. The petite little woman rolled over on her side, away from me.

"Sara, don't touch me. I don't want touched now."

"Miri, I'm so sorry. All I wanted to do for you is make you breakfast, and I made a mess with the flour and forgot where I put the pans. I blamed you for it." I put my head in both hands and covered my face. Gasping for air, I took deep breaths, continued raising my head. "Miri, I'm sorry I blamed you. I'm frustrated with myself. This damn flour bag ripped and spilled flour all over."

"That ain't no excuse." She glanced up and returned face down.

"I know!" My words came out louder than I wanted. I stared as she turned her head and stared right at me. "Before I came to get you, I rearranged the kitchen, and the pots and pans placed in a different cupboard. I remembered that. I'm so sorry. I mean it, Miri. I really mean it." She rolled over and faced me without bending her pretty little neck. She sat on the bed with her legs crossed. The tear stains still around her eyes, but a small smile appeared on her lips. I stared at her pretty face and she remained silent, waiting for me to finish apologizing. "Baby, I'm also sorry for asking you to draw me a bath. I'm not sure why people want that done for themselves anyway." I motioned with my left hand to follow me. I Turned my head over my left shoulder and saw her rise from the bed and followed me towards the bathroom. We walked in and went straight for the white tub.

"Why would I even ask you to do this?" I peered in her eyes, while reaching for the stopper, and placed it in the drain. I turned the water on, and dumped some of the bubbles in. I smiled as the tub filled up.

"Why should you do this for me? I'm capable." I spread my arms and waited for a hug. I loved when she stuck her head in my boobs, and I held her tight. She moved, and her face first made contact, while my arms enveloped her. Her face squished between my breasts as she tilted her head to gleam into my eyes. She smiled.

"You're forgiven." She glanced down at the tub, which filled up with water, slower than a turtle sliding on molasses uphill, and against the wind.

"We can make up soon and make breakfast together." Our lips met, and we went to the kitchen to get things for breakfast out, and I cleaned up the white flour off the white stove.

"You look all pretty cleaning stuff up." I smiled realizing I survived a possible breakup situation.

Chapter 18

Tommy Black Bayou. Shreveport.

I already dropped Ruby and Angeline back at my secret spot a on Black Bayou, a place I shared with an old friend, and prayed I wasn't followed. I snuck back to Grandpa's, looking for Early and Uncle Zeke. It required the odd couple observing me. I needed to pay my debt to that fiddle-playing assassin, and I knew I'd be able to outrun the scar-faced bastard, but I needed an edge. I grew up here, knew the roads around grandpa's place better than anyone, except Grandpa, my dike sister, and my father. I worried about my fat uncle, if he knew his way around here like Papi. One look at his beer belly and the suspenders holding his pants up, told me he did not contain the intelligence or speed. I spotted the weakest link between Uncle Zeke and Early, and it wasn't the shifty hit man. The weakest link was born a Barnum.

They snuck around the property, still looming around the house looking for pieces of the still, any drunk coon dogs that ingested Grandpa's shine. They spied for any clues to discover the recipe, so they'd move the still to wherever they chose to set up camp. Little did they know the crap sat down the lake, all but a fake copy of how to make it. That rested in my overall's pocket, along with the money I promised Early to take out the judge. The still remained hidden, so was the dynamite.

The borrowed car, strategically parked heading out to the main road, sat a good football field away from the lake. I snuck down to the dock where we kept the boats to rent, grabbed one and tossed in into the lake to make a large splash. I sprinted to the borrowed vehicle with the speed of a Grambling football player returning the opening kickoff against Southern for a touchdown. I lit the fuse

"Get that double-crossing son of a bitch."

"He's your fucking nephew Zeke, get that little shit yourself."

I heard Zeke say something like, "he ain't my nephew, but your son. You get him." I did not think anything of it, since I sprinted like a deer. I heard a car start up, and I raced towards my vehicle. I lost the speed I possessed, making me a reserve defensive back and special teams' player at Grambling, but I knew outrunning these jokers in the bayou would be a piece of pie. I grabbed the wheel, and the car tumbled down the muddy cart path of a road. I learned the fine art of driving down here, and it was now second nature to me. Soon, I bounced down the muddy path, cruising the back roads to Papi's old place. I already hid evidence that could convict Early Greene of my father's murder. Sara would be summoned, either by spirits or by subpoena, and her revenge finalized. I required additional time, since the feeding of Mr. Greene and my uncle sat on my schedule for tomorrow. It was fortunate coincidence that I knew the best hiding places on this old land. Cletus Tree, overlooking the Sabine, became my favorite little spot in the world. I desired that Miriam take me there and climb in the hollowed-out cypress tree to teach me about sex. Instead she took Sara, and I gawked at them in dumbfounded.

It took me a few hours to get down there, and I went to the river. I climbed up Cletus Tree and got comfy. There, I carved a Klan cross inside the tree, dropped some horsehair, and there sat the old machetes. I kicked back on the bench listening to bullfrog's chirp, owls hoot, and the sharp trill of the raccoons with all kinds of other critters howling away.

I even heard two human voices. "Let's get back in the morning. We know he's here." I sat back and smiled. So far, everything worked as planned.

The next morning, I drove into town. I went into Sara's and my favorite little cafe that served us. I don't think she's dined here since we moved out, and I knew she would love to see it. Sometimes nostalgia got the best of her, and that's when I liked my sister.

"Little Tommy Barnum. Is that you? Boy you're all grown up." The waitress gave me a nice big hug.

She's the same one that wanted Pa, but Papi wanted nothing to do with the fatty. I did not either, but I used her help to make sure Sara, like a like a largemouth bass jumping on a fake frog, was lured into my trap, and about where Early and Zeke hung out. I required timing, and so far, everything fell in place.

"Let Sara know that I'm here if she stops by okay?"

"Sara is around? Heard she's a bigshot down in Baton Rouge. I knew that little girl would amount to something."

"Yeah, tell her I'm working the land here, and that I need to talk to her."

"Will do, Tommy. Come here and give me another hug." She engulfed me with her boobs and stomach.

My face twisted a little, when I broke the hug from her. "I got me some important things to do with Pa's land. I need to head back."

The car remained parked behind the diner as I chowed down my biscuits and gravy. I washed myself off in the washroom and hitched down to the river, by the old homestead where climbed the tree and waited.

A woman came wandering down the path towards the tree ,and I hopped down. A woman of average height and little top heavy, wore her usual overalls. She also wore a straw hat that blocked off the miserable Louisiana sun. She had her sunglasses on, and gallivanted when she walked like a prized filly. If she weren't my sister, I'd assume she's a looker, that is, if she bothered fixing herself up. Daddy's spirit talked to her for, she came straight for the tree. I climbed out and took a tumble to the ground. I felt like rebuilding a new house on the old land.

I hugged my sister and kissed her cheek. "I heard you're a big shot lawyer. What else have you been up to."

Her eyes soft, stared at me. I peered deep hers. I trusted her.

"I've been traveling. I ran up to Chicago a few times to see Miriam. I did some civil rights training out in Tennessee. Hey, say we go down to the riverbank and toss some sticks in like we used to."

"Yeah ,we always did that. My favorite memories as a kid were you and me talking here, skipping stones and tossing wood."

"I always skipped more than you." She took off her hat and flipped her long auburn hair. She always bragged about herself.

"Yeah, but I beat your record once."

She glared at me. "How many?" She stalked the riverbank for the flattest stone, picked up rocks, examined them like a federal agent investigating a murder scene, and grabbed one. She turned at me and smiled. It wasn't a cordial smile as she raised her sunglasses. I saw the wickedness in her eyes. Her nostrils flared with the competitive nature she possessed. "How many?"

"Thirteen," I lied.

"Here goes fourteen." She lowered her arm like a sidearm pitcher in baseball and tossed the perfect skipping stone out into the Sabine.

We counted the times the stone skipped. When it hit fourteen, I lowered my head in shame, and missed the last two bounces of the rock.

"Sixteen." She grinned. "I beat you again." She lectured on the potential damning of the river, and mentioned it needed stopped. "We'd protest by standing in front of the bulldozers."

I wished she rest her body on the land, so I'd receive the pleasure of watching her sink to the bottom of the lake, as well as the rest of this place that was my childhood. I wanted my youth to vanish.

I did noticed a mark on her neck that looked like the one on mine that Ruby gave me. "What's that there on your neck?" I pointed at mine. "It looks like this here. You met someone?"

She appeared startled, like she forgot it was there. "Oh, I have, I got me an older lover who makes me happy. I see you got someone."

"Oh yeah I met me a singer while investigating a case. She's a blues singer from Texas. You might remember her. Her daddy sang at Papa's place when she was little. She remembered you and Miriam." Her poker face flinched when I mentioned that bitches name. "Actually, sis, Ruby reminds me a lot of Miriam. She's short and skinny and plays a mean guitar. Damn pretty also."

"You always liked her, didn't you?" Once again, she smirked liked she assumed victory over me. Her sassy smile and hair flip, a little too much for my ego.

Moses developed a plan and so did I. It required patience, since framing time approached. I prepared for Uncle Zeke and Early Greene. They both would go down, while Sara Barnum assumed the guilt. We wandered up the river after more conversation and searched for the skiffs and boats Papi used to own. We talked about them.

The sun crossed further into the eastern sky in a place Daddy dreaded so much; that gigantic state of Texas which we all loved taunting so much. Grumbles in my stomach called me, so I headed back to the café. I got Sara a Po Boy, and grabbed a chicken sandwich while Early and Zeke waited for me.

"I did the deed. The judge, the warden and the deputy, they're all gone. Zeke got a picture of it. So, Tomas, where is the money and recipe?

"I left it with Sara. She's back at the old place."

Papi always told me to look someone straight in the eye, that way they knew you told the truth. My short time with the police and feds, taught me that the best way to lie to someone needed the exact eye contact. A damn good liar I was when it became required of me, as Early Greene's eyes and mine made solid contact.

"I trust my sister with the money, and I trust her with the still. I only trust family, and to me she's my family. My Mami is gone, and I don't know my uncle." I pointed to the fat man standing beside the assassin. "Drive me down there, I'm sure you know the way. Give me an hour to eat and to get the money from Sara. That girl don't like giving stuff away."

"Okay. We'll grab some grub, too, and eat up here." I shook Mr. Greene with a firm handshake. The legendary hitman would never complete his final assignment.

I got back, and Sara and I went up to a rusted old picnic table that sat along the riverbank. We stretched out on the bench and ate our sandwiches. She ate the Po Boy in her usual sloppy style. The sauce covered her face, leaving patches all over. She went through all the napkins I packed for her, and she used the back of her hand when the napkins became too greasy.

"I was always jealous of you." I told her as I strolled towards Cletus Tree. "Papi seemed to give you everything, including his old girlfriend."

She looked up at me with her eyes big and brown, but she didn't budge. "What do you know about that?"

"I saw you two diking out before you left for college. I heard you in her room moaning and stuff. I opened the door and saw you getting it on."

"Tomas, you punk. She showed me stuff, so I knew what to do with a guy coming along. We were playing. Did anyone else know?"

"I think they did. We arrived at Grandpa's a week ago and watched you. Angeline knows, and that might be Grandpa's last memory, that his precious granddaughter is a dyke."

"I ain't no dyke. I like Miriam. Too bad she didn't do crap for you. Maybe you would have respected girls, if you would have met yourself one instead of chasing whores." She squished her face, and I knew the time was perfect to put my plan into action.

My sweet smile that turned the ladies crazy, turned into the evil smile of the bad guy. Feeling sinister, my plan still worked to perfection. We strolled up to where the house sat. An old green trash can still sat half-full by the old frame of the home. Sara tossed her wrapper in the rusty green canister and prepared to burn the trash. She lit a match and tossed the flame in, then looked down and saw another sandwich wrapper. Mine rested in my hand.

"We're not alone," she whispered while blowing a kiss to the burning match. The small flame went out and soon the men chased after her.

My sister, brilliant as always, trapped Early in one of Papi's old gator traps. The traps only Sara knew about. I guess our Father took her out trapping on several occasions. He never took me. I already cuffed my uncle without a problem. Papi was right about this brother.

I prepared myself to watch Sara in action., marveling, as she flung her machete, while I hid. She sliced Early Greene, carved crosses, added scars to his face and body. Watching her in action, mesmerized me. She evolved into a warrior. Early went down as my sister held a machete in hand. She pointed it at him, made crosses, and slashed down on the man. It appeared she went for his privates with the extended knife. When the girl turned brutal, everything fell into place.

Sara continued the torture with the wielded machete. I heard the brutal hitman whimper in the background. He sounded like a puppy that got stuck in a Louisiana thunderstorm, and attempted to get back in the house. He sounded like any other wounded animal that knew his final breath approached. He sounded like he saw his future, and there was nothing left.

I went up to Sara. "We got Papi's killer."

She took off her straw hat and shook her hair. "These clowns didn't do it." She looked at me, confused but satisfied. She shook her head and her auburn hair tossed all over. She placed the hat back on. Do you know who did?"

"It was them. They got the killers. What are we going to do with the fat uncle?"

"Guess we'll frame him for this. Let's prepare for Grandpa's funeral. We'll call the sheriff from up North somewhere."

"You ain't gonna kill him."

"Nah. Gators do get hungry; they'll take care of him." She stomped away and I followed her up to her station wagon.

Chapter 19

Sara. Black Bayou Caddo Parish

We took Grandpa into Shreveport for cremation. Tommy and his girlfriend excused themselves that morning.

"I got a surprise for ya, Sara. I need to run back to my house in Monroe. I mean it sis; you're going to like this."

Even as a crooked fed, who lied through his beautiful smile; I witnessed sincerity in his eyes. They softened a bit, and not as penetrating as normal. His lips refused curling up; they sat stationary, as he tried to give that devilish grin. And I knew he was honest

"What's the surprise, little brother?" I put my arm around him and hugged tight and long, like I should have been doing the last several years since Papi's murder.

He grinned again without showing his perfect teeth. "You will see. Ruby and I are heading off to Monroe. We will back in a few hours. Someone's waiting at my house."

"Who?" I pushed him back a little harder than I intended, and he fell into the davenport. "Tell me. Is it Mami? Tell me, Tomas Roberto."

"I ain't gonna tell ya if you keep shoving me. C'mon, Ruby, let's go." He started out to the car and kept walking."

Miriam came out of the kitchen, where she helped Angeline prepare meals for the expected guests. We weren't sure how many folks planned on attending, and I was unaware of The Bourgeois. I leaned over to my sweetums.

"I think Mami is coming. Tommy left with that little girlfriend of his. He said he's got a surprise for me."

Miriam's eyes got big as if she saw a ghost moving down the hallway towards the linen closet, or she saw pawpaw sneak around the corner and into the parlor.

"Your Mama hates me. She knows I was screwing your daddy when she was still living and breathing. What would she think if she knew you and I are doing each other? Sara, I need to run off if she's here. Plus, that little skanky bitch girlfriend of your brother hates me. I remember her from years back. She hated me then and hates me now. I can tell these things."

"Miri, you need to stay." I ran my fingers though her hair. "I need you here. This is grandpa's service, the lone grandpa I ever had. I ain't got no family, except my brother whom I don't trust, and my mother, who has been in prison for years. Believe it or not, that woman escaped back to the prison farm." I hugged kissed on the lips. "Baby, you are all I got. I need you." I exhaled.

Her eyes got wider. "Ms. Sara, I really gotta run. Nobody needs me. I'm the one who needs you and I can't stay here." She bolted out the door, like someone shot her from a cannon.

I stood, wondering why I had spilled my guts to her. Too stunned by her response, I stood with my hands on my hips, mouth wide open, while she darted past my shattered self. I always figured every creature sought someone to love and need. I found that person, and she bolted when I needed her most. I've burnt bridges in the past, and all who was left was Miriam, and I hadn't the foggiest idea where she departed to. Her clothes remained on our bed. Was she going back to Chicago to live with that disgusting Blues singer, who I never met, but read about in her rescue me letters? I witnessed the marks he left on her. Or did she head back to the peninsula to visit her mother or father? The longer I waited the further the distance between us grew. I turned to run out the door to chase her, when Angeline stopped me.

"Let her run, Sara, let her run." Angeline was known in New Orleans before she moved up here as a voodoo queen. Papi sometimes called her a witch, since he didn't believe in no voodoo crap. "She'll be back. She doesn't want to start any trouble."

"She's my family, and all I got is you and Tommy, and he says he's bringing a surprise. The last I saw my mother she escaped back into prison because she didn't want no part of us."

"Stop, child." Her voice raised a few octaves. "You and your father don't believe in this, but I do believe in the spirits. She wants to go, and she's not your lover. She's your friend, at least for the night. There is a reason she needs to go, and what that is I don't know at this time. The girl does not want to interfere with the family. Maybe you will stay together again, and maybe not, but she does love you. And it looks like she may sacrifice something for you. What it is, I don't know."

I went into my old room, and Miriam's stuff remained in a pile on our floor. I hoped she departed for the service. The poor girl didn't realize her inner strength and perseverance. She needed the pampering, but I required the love, and where the hell did she go? I demanded a nice hug, and she fled to the unknown. The old guitar sat in my hands as I played some twelve-bar blues. The blues engulfed me more than ever. The Regal sat in the stand, Stella rested on the bed, and Papi's favorite guitar hung on a stand on the wall. I captured the old beat up Montgomery Ward's special. My old six string. The repetitive shuffle flowed like the tears in my eyes. The blues refused to release me, I played louder, deeper, but the lyrics refused to come out. I couldn't sing, it became a girl and her guitar.

Once again, salty tears sprang from the orifices of my face as I refused to sing what I thought. Grandpa got me this guitar, and I wondered if the kindling worked for his cremation, or mine. I eyed the wall from my bed, and hurried across the room, with the neck of the guitar in hand. My hands clenched the neck tighter and tighter as my left hand strangled it, and I held it like Joe DiMaggio. I took it back when I heard commotion in the other rooms. I heard Tommy's voice, I heard Ruby's, and I wanted to see my Mami. The last time I saw her out of prison, she hopped a freight train by the old place. The last time Papi hopped the identical freight train, I killed the alleged murderer, even though I knew he didn't do it. I decided facing my mother was out of the question, and I grabbed the Regal and Stella; leapt out the window and headed towards the dock. There I got in one of Grandpa's rental boats. The same watercraft Miriam and I taunted each other a few weeks ago. Damn, she's missing also. I started the Evinrude, after priming it four times and floated past Cypress trees and water moccasins. I found a nice quiet place on the bayou, where I considered jumping out and drowning, or where some sort of critter feasted on me for its dinner long before I'd swim ashore. My spot, Miriam's and my spot, also the ideal spot to play the blues. If the music didn't flow, my blood carried flowing capabilities, since my slide, also my knife served many wonderful and useful purposes. The song needed to come as soon as possible since I noticed a large gator swimming towards the boat.

I wish I didn't get Early Greene, and wondered if someone with a machete drifted by, slashed my head, tossed me into the murk. The long green critter looked like it desired some flesh for dinner and searched for blood. Stella's neck rested in my left hand. I squeezed the life out of my guitar. The knife rested in my pocket. I never leave home without it. I reached in my pocket and felt the handle. I wanted to pop the spring, while it rested in my pocket, hoping it poked me. I didn't. With more caution than I intended, I removed the blade. I looked around again, realizing the last knife I owned sank about thirty feet down, tied up to an anchor, as it carried the blood of a fat white potential rapist on it. The blood of another man I murdered. Stella, on the floor of the boat, and my left hand laid flat on the seat of the boat. The knife rested in my right hand, and I released my grip from my beloved Stella guitar.

My eyes dashed between the knife in my right hand, and the bare palm of my left. Back and forth, I saw the blade shine, and I looked at the lifelines on my palms. They appeared to reduce in size to a point of my life disappearing before my eyes. They grew shorter and shorter by the second. I took my focus off my hands and my slide, and saw another nice juicy gator cruising the river. I considered stabbing my hand and tipping the boat, becoming lunch within minutes. I looked at Stella sitting in the seat of the boat, and realized what beautiful music comes from her, from me or my lover, or former lover, or however you described our relationship.

Spinning my head away from the cypress trees, I wondered if I heard a noise. At first, the noise reminded me of a bug, a hornet, fly, or some insect buzzing around the bayou, but there was nothing. The noise resonated louder. Recognizing the hum of the Evinrude, I peered out into the lake. Spotting a boat near the horizon, I contemplated my next move, my future. The boat chugged my way, and I hoped my dickwad little brother drove the watercraft.

I took five seconds to capture myself and realized his creepiness, with his acknowledgement of spying on me, but still he's family. My brother, the lone family I had besides my mother, and my doubts about her still lingered.

I looked at the knife, my hand, Stella and the boat racing up the lake towards me. The boat drew closer, and I reached for Stella's neck. My blade, also in my left hand, I soon performed what came naturally. G chord to C to D, over and over. Something different and magical happened on my solo. I looked over the lake, and the chubby gator froze. An alligator gar swam towards the boat, and snapping turtle jumped off a log and swam. I played faster, cutting the strings with that blade, and in that moment, I felt I knew life had meaning.

Thank you, Daddy, and thank you Miriam for teaching me the Blues. Magic soon exited the boat as swamp creatures surrounded me. They sang unintelligible lyrics. This song did not need them. I played it over until the boat stopped adjacent to mine.

Tomas arrived, accompanied by Ruby and a Mexican woman in a fancy dress who resembled my mother. I bowed my head in shame. I shut my eyes, as I looked down. Gathering strength, I raised my head, and stared at my mother and smiled.

"Mami, hug me when we get ashore."

She smiled back. "Of course, dear."

Tommy tossed me a rope, the last thing I needed. A tiny part of me wanted to tie it to my ankle and jump, however that part drifted away. I wasn't sure how or why someone went through with suicide, but I'm sure more and more people like me chickened out at the last minute.

Tomas spun the boat around, backed up to the front of my favorite watercraft, and connected the two boats. My little brother, like a knight in medieval days came to the damsel's rescue. I wasn't sure how I felt about it. My head still hung in embarrassment; I did not need my family to see me this way. I wondered if they knew the real reason why I sat on a boat, in the middle of a large lake, I hope they didn't, but my brother, employed as a cop and federal agent, a young man capable of deductive reasoning may figure it out. My mother understood because from what I heard, mother's always do. Ruby don't know me, so I doubt if she gave a damn.

The boat got to the dock, and Tommy tied it up in one of his famous knots that he used to brag about. Ruby eyed Stella and smiled.

"Can I carry that for you?"

I knew she played. With caution, I handed her my baby, or Miriam's and my love child. Miri, the one person I'd let touch Stella, and again I betrayed her. I felt like I committed adultery once Ruby held Stella in her arms, and fingered the strings with her left hand as the girl stood on the dock. She handled it with poise and grace, looked the thing over and. strummed my baby.

"Is this open G? Can I play a little number for ya, Ms. Sara?"

"Go ahead." I looked at the girl, and she resembled Papi's lover or my lover in a younger version. Short, scrawny, but thicker than Miriam, but looked like a guitar goddess as the shadow cast over the dock and stretched over the black bayou. Once she started playing, I knew I became second or third best guitar player here this weekend. I'd be third if my sweet Miriam returned to me.

Grandpa's service was small, as it was family and a few neighbors. No preachers, reverends, or any other man of the cloth attended to give him his last rights and wish him off to heaven. No old customers, and none of his children showed up. Two of them gone, as one preceded him in death, one incarcerated, and the other child, my Papi's oldest brother's whereabouts and identity still unknown. I wondered if he evolved into the mastermind behind the Bourgeois Barnum affair, the last man I killed told me about.

Three Blues men, who played at Grandpa's place, two that I recognized. One guy, who migrated to Chicago, where he made a name for himself. Another man, whom I didn't recognize, performed with him. He said nothing, but played the harmonica throughout the service. He played beautiful, and I wished I brought my guitar or harmonica. The third sat in the shadows, and covered his face with a large straw hat. I smelled the tobacco from his corncob pipe. Performing with them would make me smile.

Angeline addressed me. "Sara you got such a pretty voice. Your grandfather cherished the song, *Michael Row the Boat Ashore.* Walter and Sonny, can you accompany this angel?"

The song became one of my favorite hymns, and I went up and stood next to the musicians as I sung the words to an old gospel song. I never knew Grandpa adored the hymn, and the three of us, who never played together before, performed it as if da devil taught us. The sparse attendees gave us polite applause, because at a funeral setting, hootings and hollerings are not encouraged.

"Lydia, we'd like you to sing. Walter, can you let Sara play something? I know she played this amazing." Walter stood up. When he stretched, he towered over everyone, and handed me his Regal.

I smiled at him acknowledging the beauty he played. He smiled back, trusting me to handle his baby and I started playing an old Mexican standard *Las Golandrinas*.

"Cecil started listening to Mexican music, the day Bo brought Lydia down. He wanted to know more about their culture and music. This became his favorite and he called it The Swallow."

I played it as Mami started singing. Tears descended my eyes. I played wondering if Mami had stayed put, Papi would be alive and kicking, and making Grandpa's funeral a family affair.

Again, polite applause from the folks, and the ashes were presented to us. Angeline read the instructions.

'*Sara, Tommy please go out at midnight. Take my boat out to the spot. Sara you know which spot I'm talking about. Please, play some devil's music on your guitar, nothing in particular. Make something up, and finish with a gospel song. 'Michael Row the Boat Ashore' has always been my favorite. Dump the ashes in the lake and say goodbye. Make sure Angeline kisses the box before you leave.*' The woman wiped her eyes since she cried too hard.

The musicians came to the house after the service. When we got back, a feast and an all-night jam session commenced. I noticed the door open, and a pretty young lady sat with my Stella guitar there. We looked at each other, smiled and rushed towards each other in a passionate hug.

"I got a bunch of cooking to do for the party," Miriam said to me as she tilted her head and batted her eyes.

The feast and the music went all night. Miriam and I snuggled up, but we did break out my Regal and she fingered Stella like a true artist. Mami and I did most of the singing behind Ruby, Walter, Miriam's and my guitar playing. We sat on the dock and looked up at the full moon. Clouds covered the moon, but not as it appeared and soon vanished behind the gray clouds. Bullfrogs chirped, owls hooted, and the other critters hollered away as we played.

A rivalry brewed which I knew nothing about. It commenced between the two dark-skinned ladies, one a few years older than me, the one who I claimed as my lover, and then the young woman, who may become my sister-in-law. Ruby, from what I heard from Miri hated my girl. "You ain't shit on dat guitar, Ms. Miriam Landry."

"I can play you under the table." My baby said as she snarled her lip at Ruby.

"We gonna fight about it."

"Hell no. We gonna cut heads. Scales, followed by solos at midnight. Sara's gonna be the judge."

"Hell, you two are lovers, make Walter, Sonny and that other man da judges."

"There can only be one judge bitch. The judges might not agree. You're a stupid kid."

"Well, you're a dyke and a whore. I know you hooked when you just fifteen."

"I ain't sold myself since I turned eighteen, so we would use Walter, since he's a guitar player."

They looked at each other longer than I preferred as my heart beat faster, and my face turned a beet red.

Tommy, who ventured inside and out of the house all evening, left the place carrying a box. "Sara, we need to go. It's near midnight. Angeline kissed the box goodbye; I gave her a big hug. We need to head out."

"Tommy, our girls are fighting. They're cutting heads at midnight. Walter's friend is judging, so we need to wait a little."

"It's Grandpa's wish to be dumped at midnight."

"It can be at 12:15. He ain't gonna know any difference."

I heard a sigh, and he shouted. "Sara you can't fuck with the spirits. That's why you are so fucked up. Our ladies can battle, while we dump the ashes." He paused. "You know they can also wait until we get back. Scattering Grandpa's ashes is more important, especially dumping them in this lake. You know it's haunted. If we don't abide by Grandpa's wishes, he might return to haunt us."

"I don't believe that shit Tomas." I shook my head and my hair swished.

"Do you want to take any chances? Our lives are haunted already. We don't need anything extra."

I looked at my brother under the full moon. We carried a few lanterns, allowing us to see where we walked. "Okay let's go. I'll steer the boat, since you don't know the spot."

"I know the spot. It's the same place I found you at earlier today. Same spot I heard you and Miriam went fishing at, and the same spot where a certain knife dropped."

I looked at him and through the lantern lit sky, I noticed his eyes hardened. "How do you know? You weren't there?"

"I was a fucking FBI agent. I know a lot more about everything than you know. I'm quitting the goddamn feds though. I intend to run a whiskey business soon."

"Let's get going."

He looked at his pocket watch that Papi gave him. It one of the few things I didn't get. Next, he looked at the full moon. "We got about seven minutes. This damn Evinrude better start." He pulled the chord, and the engine did not start the first time. He pressed the primer button a time or two.

"You're gonna flood it!" We'll never make it. C'mon Tommy, we don't want midnight to arrive until we're there, so hurry up."

"You start it then. You're better with these things."

I walked to the back of the boat. It shook as if we floated in the deep blue sea. I pulled that chord with everything I possessed, let go, and fell on my butt. The engine started and Tommy took over the driving. We bounced our way to the spot. The exact location I tried to off myself, the same spot I dropped a knife, and the same spot where Miriam seduced me. I still wondered how Tommy knew about the last two.

"Grandpa also told us we need to have a good talking, too. No better place than this. We haven't talked for ages, since we've been busy with our lives. I heard you hit the big time and didn't want it. I'm as crooked as they come. I double crossed everyone, you, Mami, but more important, the Bourgeois group. I did get Early Greene to get the Judge, and the Warden."

I interrupted my brother. "Do you know the deputy killed Papi?" My eyes widened, a smile burst on my face. I knew something my baby brother didn't know involving the murder.

"That's ol news sis. I knew Early didn't do it, but that dang deputy didn't either."

"So, you made me torture him like that for nothing?"

"It wasn't for nothing. I got rid of witnesses. I think they are all gone."

"Why us, why Papi?"

"You know Bourgeois used to be Barnum's don't you. They are the Barnum's who turned Klan way back and been terrorizing us, since the 1880's. You know that motherfucker Cletus Barnum started it, so he'd live in peace. He changed his name to Clarence Bourgeois. All his kids but one kept the Bourgeois name."

"The Cletus Tree guy. He turned bad. Well, good thing they gonna dam up the Sabine, and flood that place. I want to protest it, but if Cletus Tree is an evil thing, I say flood Papi's land."

"Bourgeois folks are all rich. They wanted Pawpaw's brew but gramps wanted daddy to keep it. That's why they killed Papi. They killed him so Early and Zeke would get the recipe and da still. Only Pa, Grandpa, and me, knew the recipe."

I looked at my brother through the light of the lantern. We approached my secret spot, and I looked up and saw that moon, high in the sky, as once again the clouds surrounded it like an eclipse.

"Move the boat over there Tomas. You're missing the spot, and there's a bunch of trees."

He guided the boat in the right direction, and we crept up just as my brother cut the engine. I sighed, since this became the place I always went to when I needed my reality checked.

Tommy whipped out the pocket watch and held it under the light of the lantern. The lantern casted a shadow over it, that looked like an owl swooping down on him. "Before we dump the ashes, we need to come clean with each other also. I already told you I set you up to kill Early. You might be in trouble. The Feds wanted him dead, but he was also paid by them. It's no skin off nobody's back."

"But I killed a man."

"From what I heard it wasn't the first time."

My eyes fixed on my brothers as he held the lantern and peeked at Papi's pocket watch. "What do you know about that, and how did you get Papi's watch?"

"You tell me what you know. It's midnight though. Hold the box with me."

He held the urn out to me with his right hand, and I grabbed it.

Our pleasant but depressing conversation took a sharp detour. "Tell me about the man in South Haven. I know that Miriam wrote the South Haven song I've heard on the radio. Tell me." He snatched my wrist, holding a firm grip on my lower arm. I thought I was about to go swimming with Pawpaw.

"It was self-defense. That mother fucker was going to rape me. I didn't give him a chance. Miriam wrote the song and she says she's taking the fall. How do you know about it?"

"Because you killed a fed. The guy was FBI all the way. He attempted to infiltrate the Klan, and was a good man." Soon the ashes went overboard, and I did not. Tommy loosened his grip on my wrist, while we sat bouncing on the lake in the moonlight shadows. We were in no hurry to go back. "I'll protect you on that sis. You don't know who's gonna come after ya? More important, when did you and Miriam start to dyke it out? Tell me!"

"No, it's your turn. Why do you care? Tell me. Truth or swim little brother."

He took a deep breath, and a short pause followed. I heard his heart beat over the hooting owls. He swallowed. "I wanted her. I wanted her to teach me things, too. I went to college a virgin, and my Papi ran a whorehouse. Imagine that."

I laughed. At first, a quiet snicker, and a short time later I busted one out, falling over on the floor of the boat. My brother joined me on the floor laughing also. "I don't know if we lezzed out back before I went to college. I thought we were experimenting. We did not get together for real until this last time I picked her up and we agreed that we can't be lovers since we fought already. It ain't going to work Tommy. I'm unlovable."

"You ain't unlovable. You have to know how to give and how to receive love."

"Tell me how?"

"Sis, I don't know, I'm going to figure it out once Ruby and I get all settled in."

"Hey, you didn't answer about my pocket watch?"

"I swiped it. I didn't get nothing from Papi."

"That was mine."

"You rode a freight train with him. He taught you harmonica and guitar. He let you smoke and chew. He taught you how to drive, you were his everything, and I swiped a fucking pocket watch. I guess love would be about letting the other person keep it." He shut the watch and handed it to me.

I collected it and took the lantern to get a better look at it. I checked the back and saw the engravement. *"To Bo, from your father, Cecil."* I handed it back to my brother. "I guess I learned something about love. Can we go back? I might share my knowledge with someone."

"Me, too. Start this thing will ya? I can never start an Evinrude."

Chapter 20

We returned to the house, and Ruby sat alone. Miriam departed with one of the men, maybe all three. Whom she left with became anybody's guess.

"So much for practicing for my love. I guess I'll stay here with the critters."

"Who won?" My brother asked his woman.

"She did, but I'm calling for a rematch. I think she's a more technical than me, but I'm a lot flashier. She' s mighty fine on the scales, but she can't do this." She lifted the guitar over her head and spun it around. She ripped blues licks that made the swamp come alive, as owls hooted, fish leaped, and bullfrogs croaked. I forced a smile on my face, knowing my brother found a keeper.

Tommy looked at me aware my smile was forced. My lover ran off with another blues musician. I lowered my head into my hands, and the forced smile all but disappeared. My head came out like a turtle, and my brother snickered.

"Sis, do you remember when we got back to Omaha, and our house burnt down?"

"Yeah."

"Papi started laughing. You reminded me of that day. You even look like him."

"Thanks, little bro. I'm thinking I'm thinking of moving up here. The place is mine if I want it. I'm going to share it with Angeline."

"Yeah, Gramps gave me what I wanted. I ain't going to be no fed no more. I think they fired me anyway. Legal whiskey making. We can become partners if you want too."

"I don't want to. The whiskey killed our family."

"Don't forget, sis, that the whiskey made our family, too. If it wasn't for Grandpa's and Daddy's whiskey, we wouldn't be here."

"Yeah, I know, maybe you can cut me in on a small percent. I will need some money, since I'm quitting lawyering. I'm sure I got warrants out for me, too. I'll be disbarred, so I need to hide out for a while."

"Ruby and me are heading inside, you gonna come with us?

"Nah. I'm going to down to Baton Rouge and pack some stuff up and head back. I like night driving."

Working with the movement, doing some sort of work, freeing people of color, trying to halter racist minds. It would become, tireless, and the fighting will never end, but if one or two people a day changed their way of thinking, life can commence changing. I regretted not going to Topeka. I knew that Brown vs Board of Education would become a landmark case. The idea was to get folks while they learned in school. You ain't born prejudice, you learn it from those around you.

I got in at six in the morning and started packing everything that fit in my car. I slept on the floor and planned the rest of my life. As history dictated my life, planning for a future becomes useless. The future changes without notice. The possibility of spending my life in Angola prison, or at Goree across the river haunted me. God forbid they send me to Huntsville and toss me in a cell with Mami. What an incredible way to spend my eternity.

I left and dropped a couple of c-notes behind, and at midnight, took the trip back north. I'd share the swamp house, former bait and tackle juke joint whore house, with Angeline. Still an attractive older woman, I wondered if she'd make a move on me, since the witch knew my tendencies. The thought kind of bothered me. My lover was also my daddy's ex-lover, and Pawpaw's survivor. Ew, nope. I won't go there.

When I got back, Angeline did a great job of taking care of me. Not in that way, but the woman taught me how to cook and sew. She showed me how to make delicious crawfish pie, since it was always the meal we craved. I loved her dinner, but her pie, was not as tasty as Miriam's. Miriam added something special to her pie.

I did what most recluses did. I sat on the dock, practiced my scales, did some twelve-bar blues and wrote. I wrote for about a year with little or no social contact. Tommy and Mami stopped by to see us on occasion but their visits dried up. I played my guitar. I fished and trapped. Angeline and I worked our garden, and we grew and caught everything we needed. Going to the market became optional, which kept us together most of the time.

One day, about a year after Grandpa's passing, her eyes gawked all over me. "Sara, I know you're a woman, a grown woman and a pretty woman. I know which way you lean as far as your preference. I'm a woman and I need touched. I also need to touch someone. She smiled at me as her head tilted to the right, and she licked her lips."

"No! You're my grandma. I can't."

"Ha ha-ha," came her reply. "I'm not talking about us. I'm talking about moving to the city. I can meet a nice person down in Shreveport and you'll be fine by yourself. Besides, your friends are the ones who care for you, and the ones you care for. There's a whole bayou full of your friends."

I drove her into town, dropped her off near Fannin Street, where the hookers hung out. She hugged me tight and said, "Take care of yourself." I never saw her again.

Unfortunately for me, this old whorehouse, bait shop, and juke joint and home of Grandpa Cecil's moonshine became well known by law enforcement. Parrish elections elected a new sheriff in Caddo Parish, Justin Benoit, his name, and the new man in town. Rumors in town said he came from the Crescent City, The Big Easy, or New Orleans. The man looked familiar, dark skin of a Creole, but also appeared like the whiteness of a Klansman. Folks living around the bayou said his platform involved cleaning up the Parish, and another rumor stated he knew this area like the back of his hand.

I trusted a few people on this lake, most of them old timers. The closest neighbor remembered Papi and his brothers running shine down here, before Grandpa moved in. I took a spin in the boat trying to escape any sheriff's raid that might happen, and I ran into an old man. He tipped me off about the new sheriff.

"Sara, you be Cecil's granddaughter and Bo's baby girl?"

Once again, Papi told me about eye contact. He stared at me with soft eyes, but not penetrating my soul. Yet he portrayed a trusting look.

"Yes sir." I looked at him and smiled. A little older than Grandpa, I imagined they once were fishing buddies, and ragged on each other about bagging snapping turtles.

"This new sheriff's here for a reason, don't ya think?"

"It's Louisiana. Of course, I'm sure he's a plant trying to make Caddo a pure white place."

"I saw that man about thirty years ago. Ex bootlegger and he delivered great shine. He came to my place a few times after delivering to the whores."

"Papi delivered here but he's dead. Zeke's in Algona. Wasn't there another brother?"

The old man's head bobbed. He looked right and left, as if people listened to our conversation. His lips mouthed. "It's Jeb. Girl, you gotta watch out. I think you're the reason he's here. It might be best that you get out. Lots of folks round here heard the rumors, and lots of folks believe them."

"I could hang out on the lake, and not go back to Pawpaw's for a while. I got all I need right here in this boat." Stella and my Regal nestled on the floor of the boats, adjacent to my Zebco rod and reel. What else does a swamp girl need anyway?

"No, girl, get enough coppers and they be all over this lake. If these rumors are true, you be looking at the Mississippi with your other uncle from a cell window in Algona. I say, take a vacation and get da hell out of here."

I spent the night on the bayou in my special spot. I'm sure Uncle Jeb knew the exact location of my secret place, hell, everyone else did. Stella rested in my hands as I cranked out another blues song. Like my suicidal march, but slower and more gripping. I produced a little slower rhythm and less pressure on the strings. The years of solitude paid off. I needed to hit the road.

I snuck back into the house before sunrise. I went in and made myself a decent breakfast of biscuits and gravy, and grits and eggs. I wanted to do some writing, so I took Stella into the parlor, and started the shuffle. The identical shuffle I played for twenty years. Papi taught the same goddamn repetitive shuffle to me. The horrendous twelve-bar-blues made most blues songs sound the same. I grabbed Stella by the neck and noticed the artwork in the parlor room. I always hated that picture of the farmer and his wife. It wasn't an original Grant Wood, only some cheap copy of it. I took a deep breath and counted to ten. The door slammed open as I pushed my way through it. I placed the Stella in her proper place, and replaced her with the Montgomery Ward's special. The guitar Papi bought me on my twelfth birthday. The guitar I learned to play this stupid shuffle on.

I played again, and figured the timing was perfect. The imitation Grant Wood painting soon knocked to the floor and a hole went in the wall behind it. The glass vases with which Angeline decorated the room scattered across the room, and shattered on impact with the guitar. I do give that guitar credit as it withstood a Sara induced mutilation. The marble-topped table came into view. The Ward's guitar missed a string and a small dent appeared. More dents would come. Like Paul Bunyan or John Henry, I lifted that Wards six-string far over my head and smashed it on the table. The guitar came in pieces. I swung the neck of the guitar like Willie Mays, and the other half of the neck went flying through the open window. Pawpaw's prized spittoon soon smashed into the remaining body piece, and I threw them both out the window. Back and forth went my head, like I became one of them snobs in Rhode Island watching a tennis match, and I went into my room, packed a bag, and grabbed Stella and my Regal. I left the Black Bayou.

I did not get far, since a tall man in a Caddo Parish Sheriff's car stopped me. The lights flashed red before I got to the main road. I sat in silence as the man approached. I noticed the guy, and struggled to identify his features. The man did not look like any of the deputies, I ever witnessed while avoiding this place. This man was much taller, and through the reflection of the headlights, I started to make out his features. He looked familiar, but he wore a cop costume. His face reminded me of Papi's. He paced up to the car shining his flashlight in my eyes. My eyes snapped shut, as the back of my right hand covered my face. My lips tightened.

"Ms. Barnum. I need to speak with you."

The light still beamed in my eyes. My hand rested beside my face shielding the glare. "How do you know my name?"

"Barnums are well known in this neck of the woods. I saw you leave Ol Cecil Barnum's place. You're living there, I take it?"

"Yes. Are you my uncle? You look like my daddy. His name was Bo."

"Yes I am. I used to be Jeb Barnum, but now I'm Sheriff Benoit."

"Can I call you Uncle Jeb?"

The glaring stare he displayed, dissipated. His head went back a little and he put his hand on his cheek. His gun went back in his holster. "Sara, do you want to get out of your car? We will go sit on the hood of my squad car."

My slide still rested in my pocket since I needed protection, in case he tried to do something. I followed him to his car and I jumped on the hood, sat down and crossed my legs. He stood facing me, but to my left. "So why did you pull me over?"

"Sara, I'm sure you know why. Two murders, one could be self-defense, the other might have been an accident, but it was of an indestructible professional hit man, hired by factions of the Barnum family. Factions I wanted nothing to do with. You're free of those charges. What can we do about the federal agent in Mississippi?"

"He was gonna rape me. That fat dude was all over where I didn't extend my arms or anything to stab him."

He studied my face in the moonlight. "I believe you. You're my brother's kin, and that dumb son of a bitch always told the truth. The feds know where you live, the best thing for you to do is get da fuck out of here, like a bat out of hell, and don't you ever come back. Local cops and feds are searching for a Ms. Sara Barnum. You ain't her no more. I got you some papers and your new name is Sophie Benoit. Get the hell out of here Sophie."

"Uncle Jeb, what if I don't want to be no one else but me? I ain't no Sophie Benoit, but I've been Sara Barnum for 28 years. I ain't gonna be no one else."

"Sara, I mean Sophie, think of yourself as a singer, an actress or a writer. You invented a pen name or a stage name. You're somebody protecting their private identity when they go to the market. Again, remember, Sophie Benoit is your stage name, so take these papers and run. You're a free girl; leave before this place gets raided for the last time. My nephew will gather up the rest of your stuff, and the last Barnum home will go in flames like the Texarkana home. It will go down like your pa's place on the Sabine. I know all about it. I have the power to throw you in Algona or Parchman right now, but I also have the power to give you your freedom."

"Were you involved in daddy's death?"

"No. Leave, and if I ever see you again, I will tell you everything. You may have heard rumors about your mother, your other uncle, Early Greene, or the Bourgeois group. Some of them are true, while others were spread to confuse the family. I know everything. I used to work with the man who set everything up, from your mother's parents' death to your mother's kidnapping, and to your father's death. Leave, do your thing and meet me in New Orleans in a few years, and leave here now. Here is a number to call.

"Why?"

"Sara Barnum will exist only to you, Miriam Landry and Senor Tomas Barnum. She's going to die in an explosion. Get da fuck out of here."

My first thought about my uncle was he was twisted, as I cocked my head to. I jumped off the hood of the sheriff's car and walked to my Chevy truck, started it up and in no time camped out on the bayou. I desired a legacy of my own and was determined to recapture my life. I had places to go and desired a child.

Part VI

Chapter 21

Lafayette Louisiana. 1958

Uncle Jeb wanted me in exile and disappear from life for a while. I do not think he wanted me performing in a popular Swamp Pop band from Lafayette that toured the country. I received my new identity, but I still felt like Sara, so Sara Barnum I remained. Sophie still did not exist to me. I plopped down on the street corner and grabbed Stella. Once again, I popped open my slide and the blade sprung out in a flash. I grabbed the harmonica, put it in the holder and played the blues the way my father taught me years ago. I played the Blues like all of them Dirty Blues singers that Miriam ran away with played. In secret, I wished she dropped by, so there was a possibility of running away together, but unable to make a child. At the present, creating a legacy became a priority, so I searched for a provider, a donor, a man who can fuck me silly. Stella's case lay wide open, and I flipped a few bills in the case to inspire folks walking by. I started a college fund for my unmade child.

I did not want a low down, woman beating, and abusing, alcoholic blues singer. I knew the perfect girl for that, even though I did not want her in another one of those relationships. The guy I rescued her from the last time I went to Chicago became famous. He migrated from the Delta and I remember him stopping at Papi's place long ago.

I sat on the grass with my Regal, which I always kept in standard tuning, unless I performed with Miri. She loved Stella a little more than me, and more than the dirty old Blues singer, with whom she lived with. I played me some local music, the tunes the Cajuns and Creoles all claimed was their music. The straw hat, which I always wore, sat tilted on my head, covering my face. Eye contact with folks passing by became impossible, since no one noticed my eyes. I also wore my horn-rimmed sunglasses. I did not notice the man, who stood in a black and red zoot suit and a matching felt-hat. After I finished a Zydeco song that Miriam wrote, I heard two thunderous hands meet each other. A slow clap reminded me of a Louisiana thunderstorm, and not in time with the song. I looked up at him and met my future child's father. He did not know that at the time, but I assumed the man had no objection to the practice, or opportunity.

"Dem Beans are not salted are they, Ma'am?" The man spoke with a deep voice, deep as a sinkhole, and with a charming French accent."

"Les haricots ne sont pas sales," I replied in a French accent that I did not know I possessed. I felt like a spy giving this beauty of a man the right code word.

"You got some talent, miss...."

Dumbfounded, I stuttered my name. "S-S-. Sophie Benoit." I never introduced myself that way never exited my lips. "Barnum. Sara Barnum's my name."

He reached down, shook my hand, and pulled me to my feet. I trembled like a California quake, and my heart beat way too fast. It did not feel this way with Cisco Greene, and the other time I felt this way, a young naïve fifteen-year-old girl tried to get with the man-child little brother of my other lover to this date. More than ready to change that, I sweat like a whore in church, and felt I became one.

"I'm Sam Fontenot; you know Sammy and the Mudbugs."

"I like you better as Sam Fontenot. I ain't crazy about that Swamp Pop crap. Give me some good old Bluesy Lala de Creole, and you'll put a smile on this girl's face."

"Oh, I'll give you that and more." He smiled; his deep husky voice made me sweat even more like that tramp-praising Jesus. Not worshipping anyone, but that man in front of me. "Play me another song, Ms. Sara Barnum; The Mudbugs need another guitar player and a lady singer. Play me a gut wrenching, heartbreaking song that people can dance to. Play me something that would want to make me hold you close and feel your breath on my neck, while we dance close."

Playing a stringed instrument was hard enough, but my trembling fingers, due to nervous energy, I figured afraid I'd hit all the wrong strings. I took a deep breath before I started playing and that did not work. I caught Mr. Fontenot raise his sunglasses and glance from my face to my chest as I breathed. I took another deep breath in, this time a little longer, wondering if the man sketched, because I felt this breath enabled him to draw my portrait. Unable to sketch my face, his vision peeked elsewhere.

I worked on the song called Sara's Blues that I wrote in my solitude after Angeline left, and when I sat alone with the critters on the bayou. The ditty made the snappers come out of their shells and wander up to the dock to sit and listen, as well as sun themselves. I looked at Mr. Fontenot and he swayed his hips sideways and again thrust his pelvis towards me.

"Congratulations Ms. Barnum. You've became a Mudbug."

I played him another song, one I wrote back in college, *Cornbread, Crawfish and Me.*

"I'll take all three." The man smiled and once again tipped that hat. "I'm ready for Ms. Barnum and I filled me up a nice brunch of cornbread and crawfish. We are playing over in Breaux Bridge this evening. I think we gotta rehearse a bit before the show."

I looked at that beautiful man. The man stood tall, stretching well above the trimmed shrubbery that lined the streets. The man's complexion, a light-skinned Creole, like chocolate milk that missed a scoop of Nestles, and he glowed like the Louisiana sun setting over the Sabine. I continued sweating like a whore in church. I wanted him to take me to a place of worship, so that idiom could come true. I desired becoming his whore in church or wherever he took me, since I was destined to become his whore anywhere and everywhere, and I ain't no whore. Two people in my life went down there, Cisco Greene and of course, Miriam.

We moved the truck into a safe parking. He gathered the rest of my belongings and off we went down the road to Breaux Bridge to rehearse.

He led me into the club, took me in and into the band room where we rehearsed alone for a few hours. The man, an incredible lover, and I did everything Miriam taught me on how to please this man. Later that day I met the rest of the Mudbugs and played music with them for the duration of the band.

The band lasted that spring and through early part of July. We scheduled ourselves to play in Rhode Island at the Newport Festival. The festival became the biggest gig of my life.

That evening, Sammy struggled to get anything done, but the man still managed to please me, as well as himself. I did all the work, but I wasn't complaining. This man became my horse, and I rode that man fine, and he was all mine.

My monthly never showed for a few months. And that morning, while resting in bed with Sammy, I staggered to my feet and struggled towards the restroom. Hanging on to the walls, I rushed into the facilities, lightheaded, and ready to puke. Morning sickness hit me, and I knew I carried another life. In my reflection from the mirror in the hotel bathroom, I witnessed the glow that I dreamt about. I did not see the depression of a multi-racial confused girl, but of a strong confident woman expecting motherhood.

A loud thud came from the bedroom of our hotel. It sounded like someone flipped the bed over or a large body fell on the floor. Still admiring my glow in the mirror and I wondered what kind of father this man would be. I shuddered, as I witnessed him kicking the bathroom door open. He pulled himself up with the aid of the door handle, took three steps, and fell on the floor. He crawled over to the toilet and spat up blood all over.

"I got something to tell you, Sara. This cancer caught up with me. I can't go on anymore. Give me my pills, love." I got him a glass of water, opened the pill bottles, and handed him his medications. I did not know which ones he needed, but he took everything in all three bottles and two of the bottles sat half full. He mustered up the strength to tell me, "Sam Fontenot never missed a show in his life as long as I'm breathed alive, and I'm still not going to. You gonna perform the show, darling."

My head went into my left hand, and tears cascaded as if the levee broke. I got my strength and looked at the soul of a man facing mortality.

"Sammy, I got something to tell you too, I'm pregnant."

His eyes brightened for a few seconds; a small smile came on his face. I smiled, too, witnessing his final breath.

I called the Mudbugs into our room, and we spoke about Sammy, his life and if anyone knew he lived with the cancer. They all looked at me, and I did not know. I noticed the times of struggle, the coughing late at night, the insomnia, but that does not mean you're expecting to die soon. Personally, I witnessed my father dying, my lover dying, and a potential rapist and a professional hit man who I left for dead. I did not feel like calling the authorities, but I commenced using the name Sophie Benoit. Sara Barnum owned a record a mile long and she'd once again be charged for murder. Sara gave the man the pills he needed for the overdose.

The Mudbugs fought through the show. Music craved emotion to mean anything, and nothing exhumed an emotion more than the death of the leader of the band. We performed better than normal. Even the crappy swamp pop displayed an edge to it, by my haunting vocals and screeching guitar. I received an invitation to perform the following year.

After we piled off the Mudbug bus in Lafayette, we cremated Sammy. I went north to Monroe to visit my brother. He resided in a luxurious home, adjacent to Monroe's version of Black Bayou. His eyes noticing my expanding belly. He smiled his irresistible smile. "Where's the father?"

"Don't you mean who's the father?"

"Oh, you know who the father is. You ain't no whore or never will be. You might dike out on occasion, but you ain't no whore."

My hands clenched, and I realized my brother spoke. I took a deep breath. "Have you heard of Sammy Fountain, of Sammy and the Mudbugs, or Sam Fontenot?"

He shoved me on the shoulders. The nudge, a playful push. "Get out. No way sis."

"Yep, I went out on the road with them. I witnessed Sammy's last gasp in life. That goddamn cancer got him, too. Tommy, I saw him take his last breath." My eyes watered a bit as I told my brother this, but with a swish of my left hand I wiped them dry.

He snickered a. "It follows you around, doesn't it?"

A small smile came to my face. "Remember Papi, when our Omaha house burnt down?"

"Hey, I reminded you of that. Come here. sis," He opened his arms for his older sister and gave me a nice comforting hug. I did not think the weasel knew about compassion. "Hey, Sophie, I got something for you. Park your truck here and I'll drive you down."

I gathered up my junk and threw it in the back of his truck, and we meandered through the bayous of Louisiana.

About two hours south of Monroe, we came to a sign for the Dugdemona River. Tommy pulled over and found a place to park.

"Get out and grab Stella. Grab your Regal and clothes, you're going to your new home and you can't drive there. I bought you a home and two boats. You can hide out here, there ain't no one going to find you."

The boat was already equipped with fishing gear. I started up the engine, since my former football playing and FBI agent brother never could start an Evinrude engine, and we threw our fishing lines out the back, and trolled down the river. Cypress trees emerged from the water like grass in a suburban lawn, and we cruised by them. I already caught three crappie, while my brother caught nothing. We went under a railroad trestle, and my brother yelled at me to steer the boat ashore. There, on the shore, sat a little shack, perfect for one person and a baby.

Adjacent to the house sat a rickety boat dock where we drifted up. Tommy got up and tied the boat down. He reached out a hand and grabbed Stella, and set her down, grabbed my regal and set him down, and my bag of clothes, and toiletries, dropping them on the dock. The dock still looked stable as he grabbed my hand and yanked me up. As we stepped on the dock, it sounded like owls hooting or raccoons bickering, but we still carried the gear inside. He gave me a tour that lasted a few minutes. There wasn't much to this place, but a kitchen, rest room, and sitting area. The hut's plumbing worked fine, in addition, it was already electrified, and I was grateful. I wished there was another room or two, but I kind of liked the place.

"Sis this is the same train that goes by the Zwolle place. Mami's back in Huntsville, but Jeb's got plans. You need to visit her."

The place was mine, all mine. There wasn't a soul around to bother me, so I practiced all night long. After a few weeks of hearing that freight train whizz by my little rickety place and I felt it was ready to tumble, I knew I needed a return trek to Huntsville. Last time I attempted a visit, Mami was missing, and I started a riot playing some spirituals outside the gate. I needed to go back.

Chapter 22

This man came looking for me with Miriam and Tomas. He asked me about Papi and me and the music. I attempted to keep my low profile, but I couldn't. I spilled my guts to him. He recorded me, then recorded me and Miriam, and in his car drove the five of us including Berto to Rhode Island.

Tommy grinned at me while the three of us sat in the back seat; he may have been responsible. Miriam sat in the front seat, peeking back at me, also grinning, maybe it was her. The man, a perfect gentleman all the way blared the radio, while we sung along to the tunes we enjoyed.

Miriam and I played some tunes on the big stage, while Tommy held my baby. Afterwards, we returned home. The man dropped me off at Tomas's place while I craved for Miriam to reenter my life.

We gawked at each other; our big brown eyes lost in one another. We stood staring at each other, while Tomas took Berto inside his two-story home. The folklorist sat in the car.

"Sara," Miriam told me, breaking off a hug, "I loved playing with ya on da big stage, but I don't wanna play no more, nothing serious anyway. I want to teach dem girls in Shreveport and play on my porch."

"We can do it, I got rights to Sammy's songs, we got our own, and you're the best musician I ever heard, I grew up in juke joints." I came close to grabbing her chest. I wanted her to grab mine. I did reach around and swat her ass, in a loving way. "I miss you, baby." I whispered. "I still want you that way."

"We can't. I trying to be with The Lord now and ain't doing nothing with no one ever again."

She stepped back. I tried again pulling her to me. I so much needed her petite body pressed against mine.

She shoved me back. "Stop it, Sara, I'm going back. You acting like are you trying to rape me, and believe me, I know what that's like." She never looked back at me. She made a mad dash to the car where Lomax and she sped off towards Shreveport.

I stayed with my brother overnight, before he took Berto and me home.

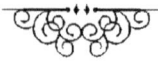

After two years, and fighting my brother about raising my son, Roberto Barnum, I knew the train schedule like the back of my hand. I knew when it slowed to a crawl, and when it accelerated again. I climbed up and hiked across the rickety trestle.

On a windy day and I clung on to the bridge, like I clung to Miriam when she gave me her special hug. I crossed the bridge and sat down with Stella and my harmonica, and reflected since my baby boy stayed with his uncle. Sara's Blues part two was composed in a bayou overlooking my river shack, where I sat on the dock naked and played guitar, interacting with the critters. I gawked at this old Cypress tree on the flood plain, and noticed some unusual carvings on it. I walked up to the tree, and the markings looked familiar to the ones near Zwolle. A KKK cross carved in the side of the tree, and an opening, not as big as Cletus Tree, but it did appear a person climbed in through the bottom. I crawled in and lit a match to look around. A note hung inside, stabbed into the tree, written in my brother's handwriting.

"You're so close to finding Papi's killer and we're right the first time. Look on the other side of the tree. Initials are carved in like two young lovers. It will reveal something no one knew."

Damn, a mother fuckin heart carved deeply into the ripped bark off the tree. The cuts, wide and deep like a machete carved them, and the initials displayed EG, and LF.

"Early Fucking Greene and Mami? Early Greene and Mami," I repeated to myself as I kicked the dirt with my bare feet. Soon, I heard a boat coming down the river, the train appeared through the tunnel and it kicked up rocks and gravel along the steel rails. I knew another ride passed along in another four hours.

I prayed the person in the boat was Tomas. Alone in this little forest, I'm still under suspicion for two murders, and even though no other killings were linked to me, I knew I had the potential for at least two more. The sound of the boat disappeared, and I heard something walking through the forest. Twigs snapped as if a campfire stirred, and the rustling leaves made me think the velocity of the wind blowing through the bayou increased. Of course, the sound could be anyone or anything, but I sure as hell hoped my brother strolled up, the lack of trust I had for him accelerated every minute I sat alone in my hut.

The young man emerged from the forest and entered the clearing. "Can you believe it? Mami and Early shacked up. Those Early Greene sightings we saw, was him and our Mother. You know they spied on Papi. Our mother told me she knew that Daddy bonked Miriam. Pa screwed the pooch when he went after our mother. Mami knew the way to ever stop daddy from chasing after her was to get rid of him. There ain't any Bourgeois conspiracy. That shit is all made up."

"Did Mami tell you this, or did you make it up on your own?"

"Mami did. She said she needed to go back to jail. This time it's for good. Go see her, she will tell you everything."

I bowed my head like I prayed. "I want her to be innocent, and damn, I will make her innocent. Mami could not kill Papi."

"Oh yeah, she could, that damn Ruby is killing me already, but I do not think Mom killed our dad. Honestly, sis, I think Miriam was responsible."

"No way. She had no motive. Why would she run back to Papi and let him know Mami was still alive?"

"To set him up. Jeez." Tommy shook his head.

I rolled my eyes a few times on that. "Miri ain't no liar. She might run off with a dirty ol bluesman from time to time, but she got no MO. What would she gain for having Papi dead? I mean the lone motive you have for Miri's involvement was she wouldn't fuck you." I shook my head and my long hair swished in the wind.

I continued. "The theory of Early and Mami having an affair does sound right. I'm not sure when it started." A sly smile came to my face. I tried to wipe it off with the back of my left hand. It did not work. "You know, Tommy, you might be Early's kid. You're much lighter than Daddy. Papi was a dark-skinned white guy, while you're a light-skinned dark man. You gotcha lot of Mami's Mexican features, but little Creole or Native features. You're half gringo, kiddo. I bet Early is your father." I busted a gut laughing, unable to contain myself and saliva dribbled out of my mouth, as I rolled over into the mud. I turned and stretched on my back staring at the sun as it peeked through the trees. "Do you want me to ask Mami who your true father is?"

I noticed Tommy getting mad. His cheeks flushed as if he chewed big wads of tobacco, and his face turned scarlet as he swallowed them all. He turned away, stomping towards the river without a word. I got up and followed him.

"Tomas, I'm sorry. You've done a lot for me; you're keeping me from a life behind bars, or a life of working on a prison farm. I hate humans, but I still need some human interaction. I'm having fun at your expense. You also made a record of Papi's songs, giving me a recording. I will love you forever for that. I'm teasing you, it's my birthright to pick on you, and if we live to turn eighty, which I doubt we will, I'll still tease you."

"I guarantee I will survive longer on this planet. I'm getting out of the South first chance I can. This whiskey is going international."

"I don't care how long we live. As long as I'm alive, I'll tease you, and when I'm gone, my ghost will haunt you forever. It doesn't matter what the hell you do for me either. Tell me everything you know."

Tommy turned and faced me. "Sara, I love you too. You and Mami never nurtured the relationship we had. I need you to talk to her to see if my plan will work out. You guys need to speak, so go see her while I head back to Monroe." My brother got back in the boat and tried to start the engine. He failed, so I climbed in, shoved him into the river, gave the Evinrude a solid tug and the thing started right up. He got up and squeezed his clothes dry, and I the green water dripped from his shirt. He sped up the river, and I went back and to grab Stella and my traveling bag and headed for the railroad track. The next train sped by and I did not bother catching it.

My family heritage came from betrayal. My Paternal grandmother set up Papi and Grandpa Cecil, my Mami cheated on my father and conspired his murder, as least that's the way the current story goes. The same person who I regarded as the current killer of my Papi killed my maternal grandparents. Was my mother responsible also? What would happen to me if I got on the train to Huntsville? Tommy seemed a little over eager having me hop the freight. I waited for two trains to pass before I hopped on. Nothing happened to.

Chapter 23

Huntsville TX. Women's State Prison.

I jumped off the train and waited at the usual place. The tunnels we used years ago must have been refilled with the Texas mud. The fence we plowed under for the escapes was also repaired, so I walked back to the forest and hiked around the place a good two or three miles, until I found the main entrance.

I walked up to the clerk. "I want to see Lydia Barnum, or Lydia Fuentes."

He looked through a stack of papers a foot high. "No one here by that name."

"Lydia Greene?"

"No one by that name either."

"Some fucking L first name with Bourgeois as a last?"

"I'm sorry, miss. There's nothing."

"Lupe Benoit?"

"Don't you know who you're here to see ma'am." The clerk rolled his eyes at me, looked down at the paper. He looked at it again. "Who should I say is visiting?"

"Her daughter, Sophie. By the way I'm an attorney, too." I knew I lost my rights when I lost my license and when my identity changed, but deep inside I remained Sara Barnum. I was as bad as my great grandma. Ain't anyone taking that away from me. They led me to her cell and the door clicked as it locked, the clicking sound loud, like I'd be there through eternity. Looking around the cell, I wondered.

"Sara Maria, come give me a hug."

I hugged her and whispered, "you know I'm not Sara anymore."

She whispered back. "You will always be my Sara Maria." She spoke aloud, "Sophie, thank you for visiting. What brings you out here?"

I whispered, "Do they know who I am?" I followed up in my loudest conversational voice, making sure everyone heard me, "It was requested by my uncle through my brother." I leaned back on the bed that was made of stone and put my hands behind my head.

"Some do and some don't, but please tell me, why are you here. Baby, you could and should've written me off years ago, but you didn't."

"Okay, I don't want small talk. You and Early had an affair?" When did it start? Papi is my actual father and Tomas's too?"

My mother took a hard swallow. Her gulp tremendous. It resembled Grandpa Cecil's when he battled his throat cancer. "Baby, yes, it's true. It did not start until the Cinco De Mayo festival in Omaha. He introduced me to his friends Paulino and Torreon and we kept contact. The affair did not start until I ran off with Early at the San Antonio show, and we kept it going until his mysterious death in Louisiana. I was informed that alligators devoured him, but I think someone set him up. There's more to the story isn't there? Do you want to tell me, honey? I told you something?"

"I knew he killed Papi, I always knew, but you confessed to me that he did it? I don't understand. Were you feeling guilty, or attempting to hide your involvement?"

"That was your father. The man I loved, and I watched him fall to his death. I watched his head cut open, and Zeke push him out."

"There wasn't a third person, was there?"

"A third person?"

"Yeah. When I came to visit you that first time, you said Papi killed someone."

Mami teared up, as she wiped her eyes with her thumbs. The confession I sought from my mother was coming. "Sara Maria, I was the third person. Tu Padre nunca mato a nadie. It means your father never killed anyone."

"I know what it means, Lupe." I tossed my hair back and walked the fourteen feet across the cell, plopping my ass on the cement floor. "You lied to me then, and you will lie to me again. I don't know what to believe Lupe." I walked up to her grinding my teeth. I bit my lip. I grabbed the striped uniform that she wore, above her breasts and tried to lift her up. "Why? Por Que Mamacita, Por Que. Tell me, mama Dime, Mama, Dime."

"Sara Maria." She smacked my face after I grabbed her.

I wanted to attack her, but the last thing I desired was to be stuck in here for life with this liar and murderer.

"Papi became everything I ever wanted out of life, y esta princessa destruyo mi familia." I turned and faced her. My eyes scrunched together as my lips puckered up, but not to kiss her. The eyes soon slanted, and I felt like a cat with a fur ball as I hyperventilated. "I will never forgive you mother. You cheated on my father. We helped you escape prison so his throat would be slashed. That was no escape Lupe. Was it? The escape was nothing but a set-up. Early and Zeke waited by the track, and you knew the exact time to run. I hope you rot in hell on this farm and you never sing another note." I pounded on the door for the guard to take me away.

The guard took his sweet time arriving. I'm sure he banged one of the prisoners, to give her favors. I felt arms around me. The arms this time possessed a gentle hug, but I shoved my hands back and pushed the bitch away.

"Sara Maria, Sophie Benoit, what if we have a chance to start over? Will you ever forgive me?"

My head tilted right. I glared at her, rested my head on my right fist. My tone lowered "I don't know, Lupe. I guess we follow Mr. Benoit's plan. Otherwise, I'll remain in jail for killing your lover, and you will remain imprisoned for killing my father and your husband. They got me for killing an FBI guy too."

"You need to forgive me for this to work. I need to hear you say it, and I need you to mean it, I need to hear it with the feelings of passion you were born with. I can tell you, Sophie, that I forgive you for killing Early. The words are easy to say. However, they're not easy to mean, my love." Silence happened inside the cell, for a few seconds, and out of nowhere she screamed like a maniac, doing her version of the rebel yell. "Tell me you forgive me and mean it! Tell me, my selfish daughter." Her loving hands that enveloped my back soon clenched my throat, while her grip on my neck became tightened. She threw me to the ground, as I looked up at my mother. I saw her arm cocked as her fist approached my face. My hands went up to deflect her punch, I came close, but did not quite. Her fist repeated, and my right cheek received a fist and my jaw joined in the party as mi madre continued the attack.

"You killed my lover, you little media caste bitch."

"Well, you killed your husband and my father, and the man I allegedly killed also killed him. I came here to make peace with you. I guess you don't want it."

The woman I used to worship still stood above me, arms on her hips, she opened her mouth. Droplets of saliva formed on her lips, and soon my forehead felt the precipitation, as if rain fell in the jail cell. I wiped her spit off my forehead; rubbed my hand on the concrete cell room floor.

"Guard, Guard!" I screamed.

"What's the matter hija? You can't get out, can you? The guards can't hear you, so they're not coming. It's only you and me. You ruined my life, Sara, and I will destroy yours. You stole my dreams when you entered this world, I could have been a singer, that's the dream I always wanted, but I was to stay home and raise you. I'm a famous singer in this prison band, and you want to take that away from me."

"Let me go, and you won't hear from me again."

"Papi's little princessa is all you'll ever be. You'll try to bust me out of here. Get this through your head Sara. I do not want you anymore. You're a grown woman, so let me be, hija."

"I'm trying, Lupe. Let me go."

"Oh, my little Sara, there's one way I know you won't come back for me."

Her lips curled and her eyes narrowed as she came for me. Prepared this time and with both hands, I grabbed her left wrist, pulled it behind her back, and marched her towards the door. "Mami, you know I always carry a blade with me, and I'm sure there's a reason the guards didn't search me for weapons. Let me go."

"You're going to kill me, so you'll do life, plus you murdered my lover and fed him to the alligators. Your life should be spent behind bars also."

I pulled on her arm. It came close to breaking. "I ain't going to kill you Mami, and I ain't doing no time either. Get me the fuck out of here." I pulled the arm a little higher with my left, while my right arm clenched around her neck. I moved close and whispered. "Mami, I came here to make peace. We need to remain together, so we can find freedom. People made a plan and we need to follow it, so are you in?"

She made noises as if she lingered in pain, soft whimpers turned into quiet screams. I kept my grip, as I knew I was winning.

"Mi hija, I can't right now. If you see Tommy, let me know and I will get the guard." Her speech, rough and stuttering but she called the guard, while I still grasped her arm like a vice.

The guard released me, oblivious to any of the trouble that happened but again, I'm sure he knew everything, and with this prison in Huntsville, no one could tell. I gathered my stuff from the front desk, hiked back to the woods and waited for the train that always took me back to Louisiana. Amends needed to be made with one more person before I took off for the unknown.

Chapter 24

The freight train crossed the trestle, as I played some old folk songs. Something made me wait and jump on the next train; damn deputies crept all over the area, but if they wanted to know where I lived, my uncle and brother knew where to find me. I'm sure they knew what I did every second. Sara Barnum or Sophie Benoit ain't no fool. I decided to hop the next train.

I might seem a bit crazy and getting a little paranoid, or simply overreacted, but while waiting for the 1600 train, which arrived at 2100 due to a derailment and explosion on the normal freight, I hopped. Deciding against hopping the freight to Zwolle, I felt best I walked, hoping to confuse my relatives. Through the clearings in the trees, I peeked out and witnessed a perfect view of my little rustic river shack, and watched two men come down in a boat. I made out the shadow of a man in a sheriff's hat, and recognized the shadow of the other man, since I seen this man for over thirty years. As grown folks, I saw him off and on, and as a child I saw his birth.

They doused something on the house, which I figured was gasoline and the sheriff threw a burning log on it. And like I heard stories about Papi's life going up in flames and all what remained as ashes, that's all I had. In my possession, Stella and my regal, one change of clothes, my harmonicas, some food, and of course, both slides.

The ground shook, steam ascended the sky, while the mode of transportation echoed throughout the air. It crossed the trestle and the speed accelerated. I knew my brother and Uncle thought I'd hop this freight. When they stopped the freight at the next town, Sara Barnum, Sophie Benoit, or whatever my new name was going to be, would not board the train. I climbed on and jumped out the other side. I made other plans; however, I had no clue what they were. I made them up as I went, but I knew I needed to get back to the Sabine, where I once was a warrior and could become again. Living next to the railroad tracks, I knew there would be a westbound coming, but due to derailments, that train would delay. The freight I planned on hopping exploded, causing the delay.

The two men remained by my old home, as I still made out their shadows. Certain that they saw me board the eastbound, I waited in the mud. My butt felt like I peed my pants, wetter than a whore in church while I sat on the ground. Critters scattered around, but they were my friends as I made eye contact with my brother and uncle. My choices were to wait for the westbound, and I had no clue how long it would delay, or to hike along the railroad tracks. Waiting for the train seemed like the best option.

I waited for hours, glaring at my brother and Uncle, who remained by the house. *"What were they doing?"* I thought. *"They need to go find me. I'm not there. I mean, Louisiana law enforcement is no match for the late Sara Barnum, alias Sophie Benoit, and maybe Sadie Broussard."*

In the shadows, I made out the sheriff with a rifle or shotgun in his hand. My slide, no match for a gun, unless I stood within arm's length. I already found out what a switchblade can do at minimal distance. I was nowhere near Jeb. I crept behind the trees which lined the railroad tracks, and kept a careful eye on my two relatives. Each clearing I snuck by with my eyes on the two. I'm sure they're setting a trap. My house, nothing but ashes in the wind. I approached the trestle, and the train still nowhere near. They still fumbled around the remains of my shack. The logical decision was to wait for the train to pass, but they'd expect me to wait, and patience wasn't a virtue of mine. The bridge was humongous and one of the highest in the state. The crossing required me to keep low as I carried both guitars and a bag. My mobility reduced. After Rhode Island, I crossed it a time or two for shits and giggles, which wasn't easy. My feet stuck in the railroad ties a time or two, yet I hauled a canteen and a camera.

Today, I carried my life's belongings. My knapsack strapped across my back. My guitars rested in their individual cases, one in my left, the other in my right as I snuck along the rails. My arms hung low from hauling them, while I crept as low as possible. I looked like one of them Neanderthal's they taught us about during the study of evolution, as I snuck across the trestle. Relieved about the silence of the tracks, I knew the freight might pass anytime. I moved on, crept along but at the present, jumping remained a possibility.

Relieved that clouds covered the moon, I don't think my brother and my uncle saw me, as I moved one step closer to the other side of the river. I inched on. I knew I'd hear the freight before seeing it, so my eyes fixed on the other side. On occasion, I peeked down at my sibling, and my father's eldest brother, and they still refused to notice me. Soon over the river, it must be a hundred feet down to the water, and the water a mere six or seven feet deep. A plunge meant a death sentence. No signs of the locomotive, and the damn songwriter in me started thinking.

"Hoping that train, don't come too early, hoping that train, don't come too early, hoping that train don't come too early, it will be the last of me."

I wanted to sing and play it, before I forgot it, but I ain't stupid. I mean, I row a boat with both oars in the water. The steady pace of my walking increased as I approached the riverbank. The trestle still stood 100 feet above the ground, and the rocks and surrounding objects were capable of piercing holes in a woman.

Further I went, step by step I crawled. The two men were soon in my rearview mirror as I quickened my pace. The rumbles in my stomach told me I needed food. The rapid heartbeat informed me that I'm either scared, tired or even needed a drink of water. It was probably a combination of all three and I did not dare stop. I took another step and the track gave a little. The tie did not break, but I weighed a hundred and fifteen pounds. Clueless on what it might do to a steamer, I moved on. The next step, a bigger break, but I did not fall through. I looked down, the ground inched closer, and the trestle came to an end. I still needed fifty yards to cross, and thirty feet to the ground if I leaped. I debated jumping but moved on. Again, the tracks broke, and I made a run for it. I only needed about twenty yards, before I felt reassured the jump was safe. I got there in about eight seconds.

I tossed the guitars, and followed them, twisting so I landed on my side. I hit the ground with a solid thud. My side and my ass hurt, but nothing broke. I lay motionless in the grass wondering if to continue was an option. My left leg stretched out first, my right followed. I grabbed a tree branch; use it as a crutch to aide me to my feet.

Walking was no problem. I grabbed my guitars and hid behind some bushes. Tommy and Uncle Jeb still made no acknowledgment of their niece and sister.

I strolled through the bayou along the railroad tracks, with my relatives in my rear-view mirror. I skipped hopping the freight and walked to Zwolle, where I was once a warrior. Free at last, I sung to myself, but again, who the hell knows, anyway.

The train never went by as the aging trestle crumbled to the ground like a house of cards. Everyone on board must have died, and the destitute, vagrants, homeless and migrants never would be accounted for. Those folks liked to hop freight trains for their transportation. They were also my friends.

I figured the next wanted poster with either one of my names, and my beautiful portrait would be for the destruction of the railroad. I loved the railroad. I hitched rides on it all the time. No way I'd want it destroyed. My goal became moving on down the line, and I still wondered how making peace with Miriam would come. I knelt in the muddy bayou, and even though I'd never attended church since I left the movement, I still prayed. I prayed to our Lord and Savior, or whoever listened that Miriam searched for me.

I also knew that Tomas waited for me somewhere with his former FBI brothers, and I'd be sent to Angola, Parchman, or any federal prison. That can't happen, because Sara Barnum, Sophie Benoit, or whatever my name, was created for this purpose. I'm a fugitive and destined for exile. I walked at night since I'm a fugitive, and this is what fugitives do.

Morning came and I took shelter in the forest, cane breaks, or wherever hiding was the best. West Central Louisiana, best known for its bayous, forests and alligators. The Barnum family history near Coushatta was also known for Slave escapes and beheadings, and secret caves. I found a place to stay easy, but the ones chasing me were also descendants from the Barnum family legacy. I knew more about the family secrets than my brother, but I believed Uncle Jeb taught him everything he knew. If Uncle Zeke ran the show, I wouldn't be worried, but Uncle Jeb ran this, and I recognized his intelligence, his shiftiness since he was the oldest sibling and I knew the oldest child was the smartest.

I slept under a small bridge that crosses a little creek. No trains went through to the destruction of Devil's Crossing Trestle. Legend has it, and I know these tales got twisted through time, but an old bluesman crossed the trestle to meet the devil. I adored these tales, on how they get spun around and told to the younger, dumber generations, and become wonderful tales. I hoped to tell Roberto some stories.

I got to the brand-new highway about sunrise the next morning. I found a place to hide out for the afternoon, a place where I hoped I might grab some rest and relaxation. I desired some deep reflection. East of the highway, I noticed a perfect location, a cypress tree, I'd crawl into. I shut my eyes and slept longer than planned. There was no concept of time.

A Greyhound bus screeched to a stop on the west side of the highway, as I stood in the gulley of the East Side.

"Get off this fucking bus," screamed someone inside the vehicle.

I lowered myself further down in the gulley. Caution must be followed; the person getting booted off the bus might be a serial killer, a rapist or a fellow fugitive from the law. I know first-hand not all fugitives needed feared. Some started out as normal people living on the lam. I also heard living on the run makes one feel desperate, hungry and tired. The grumbling of my stomach might expose me.

The person's screams became too much for me as I approached the highway. Her voice, hauntingly familiar, as the screams reminiscent of days past when an old bluesman tried to rape the woman, when she attempted to return as my father's lover. I waited for the bus to pull away and streak down the highway. She came back to me.

Destined to make amends with someone, especially Miriam, even if it killed me, I walked towards the woman. We hugged in the gulley as I had no idea how to act. Should I kiss her? Well I stunk, I smelled like a varmint. My clothes, my face, my teeth all caked in mud. She looked nice in a fancy dress, and fancy hat where the lace came down over her eyes.

"My daddy passed away. Damn diabetes took him. They're having a big ceremony for him in Morgan City. We were riding down near here and I heard someone, maybe your daddy scream, so I screamed, and that stinky fat driver tossed me off da bus." It was Miriam.

"I thought I heard something too. Tommy and my Uncle Jeb are out there somewhere chasing me." I figure they are gaining on me with every second that ticked.

I turned my head but didn't see anything We continued walking southwest to the old place where I was once a warrior.

Chapter 25

Sara and Miriam. Sabine River

"Come to Haiti with me."

"How are we going to get there? Don't we need papers or something?"

"Not the way I'm going. I knew this guy from Narleans who I defended. It was a set up, so I won the case and the wise guy still owes me a favor from nine years ago. I imagine the interest is changing our identities."

We walked by the old homestead. The houses were still there, but in ruins, and uninhabited. It looked like a scene in one of those Dracula movies as the clouds passed the full moon, and the abandoned buildings looked like no willing human spent the night in there. Miriam and I strolled towards the river, and she carried Stella.

She dropped to her knees and prayed. She struggled as she rose to her feet in a beautiful dress, wrinkled from the walk and wear and tear. Small drops of salt-water cascaded from her eyes when they stared at me.

"Ain't this where we buried Bobo?"

"Yeah."

"Where are the flowers and stuff?"

"We ain't never got him any. Besides this place is getting flooded soon."

"You should still put flowers on his grave Sara. You are right. You don't know how to love."

"You could have put some on, too. We spent time down here together." I looked at her, befuddled. "You coming with me?" I smiled as I answered her.

"I need to go to Morgan City. My Daddy passed away. That's why I'm down here," Miriam repeated herself.

"We can get over there somehow. I figure we can borrow a boat, head to the gulf and hop on another one and get over to the city. Guess we can stop at Morgan City on the way. I'll do my business in the Easy, and you can go to your Ol man's funeral. I'll meet you back on the peninsula somewhere. We'll work that out."

She gave me a sweet hug and whispered. "You always got the answers Ms. Sara. That's why I love you. But I do need to get back to Shreveport."

"Miriam, are you wanted by the police or anyone? You might have to gets us some supplies somewhere. The law is after me and they burnt down my little river shack and blew up train tracks. All my plans went up in flames and came tumbling down. I'm a damn fugitive, and I love it." I took a few steps in front of her, turned and spread my arms like the Messiah, holding the regal in my right.

She cuddled her head in my breasts and I hugged her.

"I don't think I'm wanted here. Let's get us a boat."

We walked along the riverside, passed Cat Burrow. For old time's sake, I climbed in Cletus Tree and pulled myself out.

"Miri," I hollered. "There's stuff at the bottom of this tree. It's too dark to see, but can you crawl in the bottom there and grab it?"

I looked down, and she crawled on her hands and knees like a little critter. She went into the tree, which stood on its last limbs anyway. I watched her pull out an old chest. "Look what I found. I remember this from Bobo's."

"Don't open it yet. I'm jumping into the river."

Tomas and I did this many times. We climbed inside Cletus Tree, which hangs over the river, crawled out the opening, and took the plunge. I wanted to do this one more time, since I knew I'd never return, and this whole damned area one day would evolve into a giant reservoir, enabling Sabine Parish, East Texas and the rest of Louisiana to enter the 20th century with hydroelectricity.

My butt squeezed through the opening, and I grabbed the end branches with both arms. I let one arm go, and hung on like the monkeys you see on television or at the zoo. I let go, splashing into the river feet first. I fell far enough down, that my feet hit something solid. I floated to the top, unaware of what my toes touched. After all, this was the Sabine, so I might have landed on a gator's snout. I swam ashore. Folks from here used to call me River Rat or Swamp Girl. I missed this place.

"Let's try to carry this somewhere and open it in the light. We need to find a boat."

Further down the river we strolled. Miriam carried Stella in her left, while I hauled the Regal in my right hand. We both carried the trunk with our other hand. The ground remained dark, but a few houses down the river from our old place, we found a nice new jon boat with an Evinrude engine. I grabbed my trusty slide and cut the rope as Miriam loaded it with our stuff. I pushed the boat into the river and lowered my back. Using the force of my legs, climbed in and stumbled my way to the back. The current took us downstream, and soon I pulled the rope and the Evinrude started up as it always did for me. Even someone else's engine ignited. I laughed to myself, as I knew Tommy struggled to start an outboard. Closer to freedom we floated.

The boat was already stocked with fishing tackle for survival. Since I became a fugitive, eating became essential. I cut the engine, and we baited up some hooks and cast them out the back of the boat. There we trolled along the river. Our goal, the bridge near Lake Charles.

Miriam caught the first fish, a smallmouth bass, and I got a few more smallmouth that were a little tinier than hers, and as the sun rose over the Eastern skies, we rowed the boat ashore, like Michael in the song.

We built a fire off the banks of the river. No one was around, so we ate in peace and hid everything on the East banks of the Sabine. Like my Papi, and Pawpaw before him, the west banks of the Sabine remained enemy territory.

Miriam and I found a place to cuddle up, but I stank. While squinting her pretty brown eyes, she raised her wide nose when we attempted snuggling. On the run for a few days and adoring my new lifestyle, I desired smelling pretty for my girl. I snuck out of the bayou butt ass naked and took a quick splash in the river. I turned to find Miriam gawking at my every move and smiling.

She took my hand and led me back to our campsite. She leaned to kiss me, but I ain't brushed my teeth for days either. She kissed my cheek and forehead and tried to sleep. I slept comfortably next to her.

That evening, as the red ball submerged on the western horizons of Texas, the borrowed jon boat pushed out into the Sabine, right after a large fishing boat came up the river with flashing lights. Miriam and I hid under the water, acknowledging the police or we'd be busted. Once the cruiser floated out of sight, we swam with the boat and climbed in. We drifted down to freedom towards Lake Charles.

Chapter 26

We reached the mouth of the Sabine, and cruised the big lake at the end. The waves rocked the boat all over the place. I felt like lawn chair in a tornado, as we bounced our way near the gulf. At our resting place, we planned on opening the trunk. The resting place sat west of Lake Charles under the bridge.

We opened it up while we sat under the bridge of Interstate 10. There lay a sealed note on top of a smaller box. We read the unsigned note.

'Meet us at the airstrip in Houma on June 14. This is where when you can see what's inside'.

I showed it to Miriam. "This shit is weird, Sara. Do you want me to run off with you?"

"Of course, love." We hugged under the viaduct; giving each other a quick peck on the lips.

"We're gonna hitch?"

"Yeah, who can resist two ladies, one that has been on the run for five days, and hasn't showered or changed clothes?"

"They got showers in truck stops. We can hop on with a truck driver. Let us carry this up to the highway and shower. I'm going to steal a few pair of overalls for you, Ms. Sara and get you a new hat."

We walked in a truck stop that sat on the side of the highway. It was a good place for two fugitive looking girls to walk through since we saw skinny, ugly women walk by talk to different drivers.

"Sara, I don't want to do this, but I'm going to get us a ride east also. Go in and shower, I'll get you some new clothes and a ride to the peninsula."

Miriam never said what happened, or what she did, but I knew what she did. She reverted to her days back on Fannin Street in Shreveport, where young, poor, black or Creole women did what they did to survive. Miriam once told me there were three ways for a young black woman to get out of the swamp. She'd become a whore, work as maid for a rich man and become a whore to him, or she might learn to play guitar and sing the blues. The girl did all three. I admired her.

The Peterbilt bounced down the round as Miriam and I rode in the back. I took in her sweet aroma all over the back of the cab. Our eyes met as she looked down, embarrassed by her heroic deed. "Sara, I had to."

"I know," I told her, as my head bobbed, and my speech silent.

The truck got to Lafayette, and I wondered what the Mudbugs agenda was, but the diesel sped down highway 90. I returned to the New Iberian Peninsula, and I think the last time I visited the area, I kissed a boy for the first time. Twenty-some years ago, but it did seem like yesterday. Miriam Landry's baby brother stole my heart, and lucky for me, he didn't steal anything else. My heart shattered when I met him again.

The fat white man backed the rig into a dock at a Piggly Wiggly. "Okay get. I got you as far as you wanted to go."

"How's she getting to Narleans?"

"I don't know. That bitch is on her own." He paused and smiled at me and exposed four missing teeth. He grabbed a bag of chewing tobacco, stuck a wad in his mouth, and commenced chomping. The brown leaves formed a little trail down from his left lip. He chewed the leaves for a minute and with the loose leaves inside in his mouth, the trail replaced with tobacco juice. He continued. "Unless she wants to fuck me." He smiled; I saw the brown tobacco juice covering his yellow teeth. He spat that crap on me and laughed. "I ain't fucking another nigger for at least a year. I might even call the cops on you." He shot another wad of tobacco in my direction. This time he missed.

We disappeared into the streets of the smaller peninsula city. We crossed a major bridge and soon were in this place reminded me of that city in Italy with streets of canals. We walked around, finding her family. Automobiles sat parked all around her home. I knew someone could drive me to the Big Easy.

Miriam ran up and hugged this big fat man. He looked older as his face was worn with abuse of his body. The man limped with a cane, as if diabetes took an early toll.

"Apologize to her. Go." I heard Miriam scream at the man, as she pointed right at me. Go."

He hobbled up. "Sara, I is sorry I played you many years ago. Look at me, I'm a dying man. Drugs and whiskey can kill a boy quicker than a gun can. I can still play, but my fingers are fat and hit wrong strings." Like a gunslinger, he pulled the guitar over his head and started shuffling.

Miriam grabbed an out of tune Stella, and played the slide with him, while the Regal came out of its case. The three of us played until the local police came. I smiled since this reminded me of my father and my youth. We went inside the house and Miriam whispered to one of her family members, and soon I went to a car with a cousin of hers who drove me to the Crescent City.

Chapter 27

New Orleans, Louisiana

My agenda, I needed to meet a certain man at a Jazz club on Toulouse Street. He owed me a favor, and getting me out of this country with my life defined a favor. I wasn't familiar with the mob scene in New Orleans, only the case I assisted on back in Baton Rouge several years ago. What knowledge I obtained, was this man, an informant for the Pantaglia gang which operated near the old fruit markets by the shipyards. They since moved out and settled in the white suburbs of Metairie, and received Klan involvement. My contact, even though groomed and brainwashed by his gang, was morally opposed to the Klan activities. A lover of Jazz and the Blues he needed to meet me in the Quarter. That's another reason why he requested me to work on his legal team back in 1955.

The club rested on the corner of Bourbon and Toulouse, and I walked in. The man covered his face with dark sunglasses, and wore a Fedora hat that covered up a shady face. He knew I needed him, even though I met him briefly, it looked like he attempted to disguise himself. The man wasn't fat, not like the truck driver and my first crush, but he carried an extra roll or two in his belly. Eating generous portions of New Orleans food and whacking people ain't much exercise so even though he fashioned a loose suit on, I recognized the soft stomach.

He turned up and looked at me. His stone face broke, as his lips cracked a smile. Something in the smile seemed familiar. I mentioned earlier I met the man briefly in the 1950's for the first time. Seven years later, but it seemed like I encountered him in an earlier meeting, and it seemed possible that I recently seen him. The rendezvous meant conversation with a long lost relative.

His hand moved down from his dark sunglasses, to cover the widening smile on his face, and his head tilted down. The man's identity revealed, and I wondered if he knew it. I took of my straw hat, the one Miriam bought me in Lake Charles from the money she got for screwing the truck driver. My long dark hair swished around, and a smile grew on my face. The man still disguised, tilted his head lower, as I gallivanted towards him, like a filly at the racetrack.

I wanted to blurt out "Uncle Jeb," but I didn't. I walked through the smoky haze and muck of the bar, as a poor Miles Davis imitator blew a horn in the background. I sat in the booth across from him. My poker face vanished like outside furniture in the last hurricane.

"Now you know everything Sara. I'm behind a lot of this. Not the death of Bo, I'd never harm my brother, but about everything else. Everything is written in a journal. I want you to meet a smuggler I have connections with, who brings dope into the country. I think you know him". He took of his dark glasses and wiped his brow with his left hand. Back and forth went his hand as if he removed a mask. I saw Papi's face in Uncle Jeb's, and a slow tear ran down my eye, but my grin remained. "Everything will be revealed. There's even more to come, but I am out. I might join you in Haiti; or join your brother in wherever he chooses to distribute the whiskey internationally, or I might not make it through the night."

"Was this all a fucking game?"

"The last part was. Your brother and I destroyed all evidence and checked your survival skills. Have you heard the term ex pat."?

"Of course."

"I'm making sure of your survival skills. You'll be in exile for the rest of your life. Your lover can go with you if she chooses, since she may own a record as long as yours. You passed the test."

"I think I was born to live in exile as a fugitive." I stood and flipped my hair over my shoulder. "I'll see if Miriam wants to join me. I sure hope so."

"Tomas will give you a ride. He's waiting for you."

My face splatted on the table as if I passed out drunk. I'm sure many noses indented the wood here, but booze never crossed my lips. Considering my family upbringing, staying sober was an amazing feat, but the dent was caused by straight out laughter. I soon pounded the table. I sneered at my uncle.

"You son of a bitch." I shook my hair again and strutted out the door like a prize filly who won the derby.

Chapter 28

Tommy waited in his shiny Cadillac on the corner, scheduled to pick me up. The caddy, a dark sedan, and in the passenger seat up front sat his oldest daughter.

"Why are you picking up Aunt Sara? And how come we never see her? Why do you talk bad about her daddy?"

Damn, a mini me. His middle child stared out the window, absorbing the historic architecture of the crescent city, maybe wondering what happened to Storyville, and if the Barnum Legacy went back there to start Jazz music and assist the prostitutes. Beside him sat the youngest and palest of Tomas's kids. I'm not sure how a son of mixed blooded male and a dark-skinned Creole woman would evolve so pale, but I was a lawyer, not a doctor. Next to the albino nephew sat Berto, Roberto Barnum my pride and joy. Tomas took him a few weeks before he forced me to become a fugitive. He told me he'd raise Berto for his protection, and I guess I'm glad he did.

Of course, all their names changed, but I hopped in the back of the large black sedan and picked up my little Berto, or Ricardo Benoit as they called him these days, and held him tight. At three years old, he wrapped his arms around my neck and took off my straw hat, pulled my hair, and hollered choo choo. I knew I wanted to take him with Miriam and me to Haiti. The boy descended from Haitian heritage after all, not the race of wherever Tomas claimed to belong. The problem remained that Tomas wasn't a fugitive. I'd live in exile, so my little pepito needed to stay state side.

We rolled out of the Crescent City and headed towards the airstrip. The town appeared familiar, since I passed through it the day before. Tomas pulled the car over next to a long runway that headed inland from the shores of the gulf.

"Get out!" he ordered me. "Get the fuck out."

"What about Miriam? She's got the trunk, and I hope she's coming with me."

"Get out Sara, Sophie or whatever the fuck your name is. I ain't picking up that whore dyke friend of yours. She's on her own to get here, and I ain't saying this again. Get the fuck out of the car. You're lucky I've done this for you. I should have turned you in a long time ago, or I could have had you killed, or even killed you myself, but you're my sister. I'm through protecting you but I ain't protecting no dyke whore."

I stared down the barrel of a 45 pistol. "You haven't listened. Get the fuck out of the car."

The trigger clicked once as he squeezed it. I wondered if my brother turned crazy, and if he'd blast his sister in cold blood, in front of his nephew and children. I did not test him as I got my ass out of the sedan.

"I want to spend time with Berto, take a walk on the shore, and look at the pelicans. I may not ever see him again. You guys heading are to Africa or Asia, to launch that poison overseas."

"Hey, that poison raised us."

"Yeah, I know. Look at yourself."

The babies in the back screamed as I pulled Berto up and we walked down the sandy shore towards the city. "I'm getting Miriam and taking Berto."

I turned and faced my brother; whose eyes and pistol followed my every move. No little fucking brother would ruin my life. I think I loved three people. Papi, Miriam and little Roberto Barnum, and he carried the Barnum crown. My little legacy. No little dip-shit brother, who changed his name to Bourgeois, Benoit or any other name to avoid the law, and to avoid the Barnum pride, and to control an empire would stand in my way.

"Give me twenty-four hours with my son," I pleaded with Tomas, I turned and walked towards civilization. I twisted my neck around facing the sedan." This is the least you can do." I didn't wait for an answer.

In the background I heard him whimper. "Okay, twenty-four hours. I'll meet you here. Enjoy your time with Ricardo."

"He's Roberto, he will remain a Barnum." I stopped, one more argument remained in me.

"The feud's over, sis," he shouted, but his voice grew fainter as I moved further away from him. "There are no more Barnums."

I strutted my way into Morgan City. Berto rode piggyback over my shoulders as we strolled in town. The weight was bearable, as I became used to carrying two guitars across Louisiana. The clear skies over head switched to gray as a small storm appeared from the Southern skies. Growing up in Louisiana, I knew what that meant. Walking below sea level in a land with a low elevation any amount of rain forced flooding streets.

We noticed the large arch bridge connecting the vast swamp and seashore from a small city. Oil wells filled the swamp as I clung to Berto's legs while he enjoyed the view from above my head. My little boy glanced around like a chicken, back and forth his head went, pointing at everything we went past.

I tickled my baby's knee pit, and he kicked me like a bucking bronco, urging me closer to the bridge. Once we got to bridge, the walk uphill. I dreaded going up, but it must be done. I did greater extremes on this adventure and hiking to the top of a bridge was nothing. Once at the top, it would be smooth sailing, and the Landry's lived close to the shipyard, the industrial area, the black side of town.

Cars sped by us as if we were road signs, or roadkill, whichever came first. I thought somebody might be kind enough to let a mother cross a busy highway, carrying her toddler on her shoulders. But it seemed like these folks had no clue that I hadn't seen the little guy for months. I had twenty-three hours and counting in this country, that's all I had with my Berto, or Ricardo, before the shipment off to a third world country. Hiking up a draw bridge wasn't spending time. Talking, playing with him, teaching him everything I knew needed to happen.

The continued to whiz by us as we crossed the highway in one piece. We followed a long walk, as far from the airstrip to the bridge, the time was right to cross the bay. This lengthy slab of concrete, a drawbridge, wasn't designed for pedestrians. Of course, my fear of it lifting to allow ships into port wasn't going to happen. Not if Sara and Berto Barnum crossed this hunk of concrete and steel. We struggled up the hill, I hummed my old train song, changing train to ship, and sang out loud as we hiked to the top. Berto hummed along with me, clapped his small hands, kicked me in the guts in rhythm. We reached the top, the middle of the bay, and soon the stroll became downhill. My arms and legs wobbled like they had jelly in them and I placed the boy down and together, we sprinted into the city. Ships and boats floating everywhere, and the hyped-up little boy screamed and pointed at every one of them. I squeezed his hand as we jogged down the hill into town.

The sky faded to black as the time approached four o'clock. The rain commenced. At first, a light sprinkle, as if God watered the plants with a water can. By the time we got to the bottom of the bridge, God discarded the water can, and put us under the shower. Miriam's family still lived a mile from the bridge, and by the time we reached her house, God removed the drain and let a levee break as we received a deluge. With nothing to shelter my boy from the rain, I picked him up, tossed him over my shoulder like a small gunny sack of rice, and ran like hell towards my friend's family's house.

I pounded on the door, but seemed not to hear the knock. Thunder soon drowned out any noise I created. I kept beating on the door, hoping and praying someone heard me. I ain't no religious person, and Papi wasn't either even though he got us going to church towards the end of his life. Once I started going again back in Baton Rouge my life changed. I became a target after the bus boycott.

Berto and I took refuge in the carport as the rain kept pouring out of the sky. Lightning flashes and thunder intrigued the boy, but he still clung to my neck. I held him tight, as I wandered through the carport looking for a clean towel but didn't find anything. I walked to the end of the garage and there sat shelves with gas cans, water cans, oil, planters, tomato cages and tools. I spotted a few towels down below just as a door slammed shut while I jolted my head towards the sound.

"There's that ass I could've fucked long ago. Back then I wanted whores, not virgins. Now I want virgins and not whores." The former man child and current fat slob grunted when he spoke. He sounded like Porky Pig from the cartoons. "I see you ain't no virgin no more. I be first in your heart remember?" My former crush unsnapped one of the loops on his overalls and tossed it over his head. He grabbed the other and did the same, and then threw them off. He kicked his pants on the floor of the carport. "It should have been me. I should have popped that cherry way back when. Let's pretend, let's go back to when I just thirteen and you was fifteen." He pulled off his shirt, and his jelly rolls flopped in rhythm to the rain beating down on the tin roof. He inched closer.

Berto clung to me, and I reached for my slide in my overall's pocket.

"Where's Miriam?" I shouted. I didn't want to kill nobody else, but I'd rather kill a man, than become his slave for pleasure or satisfaction.

"You couldn't have me, so you made it with my older sister. Stupid dyke. You want to know what a real man like?"

I reached behind me and grabbed something that felt solid. I didn't want this creep near me, so I didn't want to stab him. With no idea what I grabbed, I felt it, solid, like a wrench or hammer. I tossed it at him. It knocked him off guard enough that my little boy ran like the devil, and we disappeared into the flooding city. The Winn Dixie was a couple blocks away; we sprinted for it.

The rain stopped as rapid as it began, but puddles filled the streets as we splashed down the block. Berto, back in my arms, cried as rooster tails flew behind me like I owned the streets of Morgan City huffing and puffing like a steamer as I entered the grocery store.

"Call the police. This man tried to rape me." I yelled at the clerk. I looked down and saw my love with a cart of groceries. "Never mind." We ran up to her and hugged her.

"Ms. Sara, you're back. I thought you were running away." She hugged me even tighter.

I whispered. "Your brother, you know the one I once crushed on. He tried to rape me. I don't want the cops called, because he'll do life. I didn't kill him neither, just tossed something at him and ran."

"That fat brother of mine got heart issues and diabetes so bad, Sara. You might have given him a heart attack. You know I never did claim him as my brother anyways. Let's get back to the house. I would have been back earlier, but it started pouring when I was shopping."

"So, if God didn't drench us, you would have been home. I wouldn't have been attacked by your asthmatic, diabetic, fat, and former man child crush of mine, who is also a drug addict."

She tossed her pretty brown hair in my direction and smiled at me. "They say there's a reason for everything Ms. Sara. Maybe there is a blessing somewhere."

We got back to her family's house. The boy laid flat out in the car port. Miriam checked his pulse on his arm and neck. "That judge in

Shreveport taught me how to do this. You know in case he had a heart attack while fucking me." She looked up at me and her face displayed no emotion. "My brother is dead. I gotta make some phone calls."

My eyes danced all over the carport. I couldn't focus on nothing. The small can of oil I threw at the dead rapist rolled off his body and into the front lawn like a meatball on top of spaghetti. Was that a murder weapon? I ain't being charged with another murder, even though as far as I knew, Sophie Benoit had a clear record. "Miri, I can't stay here, I'm responsible."

She sat still, next to her obese brother. She turned her head over her shoulder and stared at me with those doe eyes. "Sara, you didn't kill him. The cocaine and heroin killed him. The diabetes killed him. The liquor killed him. The back-child support killed him. He wanted to die. My little brother never got the fame he thought he deserved. He used to play guitar like no other, but he ruined his life. It's a shame, Sara." She stood up and walked at a turtle's pace to me. She put her head to my chest as I held her tight.

Her head tilted back, and she stared again in my eyes. "I need you, Sara." Her head nestled back on my boobs. I held it there while Berto stood beside me and looked at Miriam, too. He put his arm around my friend.

"We need to get to the airstrip."

"What about my brother's funeral? My daddy's funeral is tomorrow. That's why I'm here."

Still breathing heavy, I looked at the shorter girl. "I got twenty-four hours here. The plane will pick me about two in the afternoon. We can leave right after they toss him in the dirt. Your brother, he tried to rape me. Fuck him. Rapists don't deserve funerals. Toss them in a bayou and the hell with them."

"Okay we will hitch to the seashore after Daddy's service. I'm gonna miss the party."

Chapter 29

"Sara, you can't take Berto. He will be better off with me. You're on the lamb. I'm set up good."

"Where are you gonna be, Tomas, and where is Ruby, you know your wife?"

"Ruby went touring with some local yahoo. She won't be back anytime soon. I told you that she's giving me a slow death."

"Well, where you gonna be? I need to know where my baby is."

My baby brother looked at our uncle for guidance. He wanted to tell but he knew he couldn't. After all, Tomas was nothing but a pawn in this game. He turned and hurried back to the car passing Jeb who walked toward me. I noticed a turtle crawling by the inlet that runs next to the air strip and Jeb strolled at the same pace.

"Sara, there is the plane. We must take Berto, but we're going to take him to a place where he can change the world, a place that's further behind the American South, and awaken your opportunist little brother. I worked out a deal in South Africa, and your brother will oversee that division."

"Ain't that where there is apartheid?" My eyes grew wider than usual, but I stared at him, thinking I figured some of this out. I still wasn't sure. The speck that we noticed earlier came into view.

"Yes. It is a test for your brother to see his identity. He does not know this, since he doesn't know jack about apartheid. I do know there is one person in this group who will join the fight, but he's way too young to battle, however he'll have the heart and will to fight. And as he grows up, he will see the injustices through the eyes of the white power. Besides activists like Stephen Biko and Nelson Mandela, change of power needs to come from the inside. This is where Berto Barnum, aka Ricardo Benoit will come to play. He doesn't know this, but he'll always be a Barnum. Your son and Bo's grandson."

"Tommy is a Barnum."

The look Jeb gave me when I said that, woke the dead in the above ground graves in the underwater towns on this peninsula. He continued to stare me down and then laughed. "You don't believe that do you? Tommy is as much kin to that pilot up there as he is to you." He pointed towards the plane, as my eyes followed it towards the landing strip. "Have you opened the trunk?"

"No." I made the word three syllables. "I'm waiting until I get to Haiti." The plane circled again. I didn't want to shout to my uncle, and I knew their departure was upcoming. Tears started their rapid descent on my face. The separation from my baby might be permanent. I didn't know, but he'd be planted into a land even the American South never witnessed. Not even in the days of slavery, where my family proved the institution weak. I'm living proof, and little Berto, destined to set foot in the world worse than 1858 Coushatta, Louisiana.

"We need to take him." My uncle grabbed his hand, but the stubborn little boy refused to go. The plane landed in the gulf with a splash and drifted up to shore.

My baby still clung to me. I stared at him, knelt and prayed. "Little Berto, remember who you really are. They're gonna change your name to Bourgeois, or Benoit, or something crazy like that. You ain't one of them. You are Berto Barnum, don't ever forget your true identity."

"Berto Barnum," he said clear as the blue sky that day. He wrapped his arms around me, not knowing if he'd see me again.

"You have to go. Give Mami a hug and kiss that will last my lifetime." That hug was the hardest thing since pulling Daddy's body out of the river. Jeb soon took his hand and they walked a lot faster to the limo. The limo sped off, just as the pilot walked up.

I'll be goddamned. It's my sweet Latina, sexy, sassy Sara, and her dark-skinned friend. Ain't this gonna be fun?" The pilot fashioned a goatee and wore a wrinkled fedora and flashed his pilot's sunglasses. He looked like a commie.

I rested my head in my right hand for a brief second. My head went bobbed, as Miriam came over dragging the trunk along. It made a nice path in the sand. I burst out laughing as we both looked at Cisco Greene.

"C'mon, Miri, ain't you getting on." I sat up front with the commie.

"Sara, I can't go. I got things to do in Shreveport. I already told ya, I got things to do. Folks need me up there. I'm making lives better. I hope we can visit one another." She stood on the shore holding the Stella guitar. She hadn't packed it.

I looked over at Cisco, he flicked off his sunglasses, got out of the plane and grabbed the Stella away from Miriam.

"I can bring you down whenever you want. Anytime. Here's how to reach me." He passed Miriam a card which she stuffed in her bag.

She wiped her eyes, as I did mine. I bowed my head again, refusing to look at her, my former, stepmom, sister and lover. My son was now gone and off with his and my uncle, and I'm stuck with the man who stole my virginity. I'd make a new life. I'm Haitian after all.

Epilogue

Dame Marie, Haiti, 1963

My life already was prepared for me. This country, one of the poorest in the world, and Sophie Benoit was sent to assist the poor folk down here. It was charitable work, which was fine. I wasn't in the Peace Corps, but did aide the people in agriculture, plus taught Haitians zydeco, while they taught me Reggae. We combined the rhythms and made our own music.

The real reason I was sent to Haiti was the dictator Papa Doc needed to go. My revolutionary past, and my tendency to fight for freedom became a Barnum strength. Heads would soon roll, and not mine.

The sea plane splashed into the water and surfed its way onto the beach. The commie folk singer turned smuggler assisted the woman out the door. I nursed a lemonade, sitting against a palm tree, watching the sunset over the Caribbean.

The two walked up together. Miriam carried a suitcase and a guitar. Gone were the days of hoboing for her. She also dressed much better. She wore a fancy sundress, while my jeans were in tatters. I hoped nice duds for me were packed away. She owed me a few outfits.

The small trunk we hauled down from Zwolle carried all the letters, and some recordings in it. She read the letters and we listened to the music. There were several songs no one listened to before, some she wrote long before we met her. I needed Miriam to verify some facts and hear the certain sections, which her name wasn't mentioned.

I watched the two get closer. I poured her a glass from the pitcher which sat on the small trunk. She set the guitar case down as well as her suitcase. Life finally did her go as she walked with class.

I handed her the glass while Cisco stood beside us. He looked like that fantasy he dreamed of when we first met him in Mississippi was going to happen. It wasn't.

I turned to him. "Cisco, don't you got some dope to smuggle?"

He looked at me, frowned and walked towards town where there sat a little seaside bar he hangs out in, when he visits. It sits adjacent to the azure waters on this pearly white sand beach.

When he was out of earshot, I asked Miriam. "Why didn't you tell me these things? You knew most if all along?" I didn't yell, but it exhumed a shade of bewilderment.

"I didn't know how, Sara. Plus, your Mama don't always tell the truth."

"Did you know Tommy isn't a Barnum? He's as related to the commie unlicensed smuggler over there, as he is to me. Did you know that? Tomas Barnum and Cisco Greene are brothers? Tommy helped me kill his father. Did you know that?"

"I never knew that, but I figured she be fucking da guy from the start."

"Papi was my real father, right?"

"Yeah, she started up with Early after you were born."

"She told you this in prison?"

"She told me a lot more, plus it's in the chest."

"Miri, I read what's in this trunk, but you knew way before me. I'm like the last one to know this shit. Didn't you think it was important to me? We were lovers, best friends, sisters, and mother and daughter. Nothing can separate us but lack of communication. What else haven't you told me? I kept all these letters in here, but I want you to read them to me. Let's go up and talk to Cisco, because."

We strolled up to the cabana where the unlicensed pilot, who ran dope and people from the Caribbean to the USA, and brought young expatriate women to Haiti, sat with a colorful mixed beverage, poked with a small umbrella stirring stick, overlooking a game of chess.

I sat next to the man and shoved him aside with my butt, and with one quick motion of my arm, knocked the pieces onto the hot pavement below. He jerked to his feet and made to leave.

"Sit your ass back down. I need you here for some reason." I picked up some pieces of the chess set and placed them on the board. "Here's the black king, and it's Uncle Jeb or whatever the fuck his name is this week. This here's the white king. That's the fat judge in Huntsville. These two men played a game with our lives." I grabbed both queens. "These two are Mami; she shouldn't have even been playing the game, but she got stuck on both sides of the table." I grabbed the white rook and shoved it in Cisco's face. "This is your father. Mr. Greene was given plenty of green to destroy my family, since they knew Jeb controlled everything." I nabbed a black pawn. This is my fucking little brother. He'd do whatever Jeb said, until he realized who his real father was." I grabbed a white pawn. "He became this fucking little scum, but he realized who his family was. They're the ones who raised you and grew up with, not the ones that sired you." I tossed the pawn into the sandy beach.

"That's one way to look at it, Sassy Sara. But where are we?" Cisco asked.

I looked underneath the table and found a set of dominoes. "Here we are. We weren't even playing this game; we got tossed into it." The dominoes tumbled onto the chess board, as I shook each piece out like I sprinkled cayenne pepper on my crawfish pie. "This is Papi. He's trying to make an honest or dishonest buck." I grabbed another piece. One with less dots on and pointed it at myself. "This is his daughter, me." I grabbed another bone and showed it to Miriam. "This is you, you're too good for this game." It was boxcars, a double six. I tossed it in the sand. "We weren't playing the same game but got caught up in it, so here I am now, living in Haiti."

A short time later while Cisco nursed his second drink and Miri and I swallowed our lemonades, a familiar lady strolled by. The Hispanic was in her late forties and the bitch outlived her parents.

"I knew I would find you here. I want forgiveness from you two. I don't mind that you two became lovers, but this skanky whore stole my husband and my daughter."

"Excuse me, bitch. I didn't steal nothing from you. I picked up what you put down, and you were cheating on Bo anyway. I didn't break up no family. I'm the one who tried to hold your crazy fucking family together." She looked at me and planted a long-wet kiss on my mouth, swirled her marvelous tongue inside. She turned and faced my mother again.

Mami ignored Miriam and glared at me. "Sara please make peace with me. That is why I'm here."

"Mami, I came to visit you at Huntsville looking for resolution. You punched me out, but I can forgive you for that. I will never forgive you for what happened to Papi." I switched to my former lawyer mode. I paced across the pavement looking for a jury. I never found one, but I glared at my mother. I cleared my throat and took a deep breath. "You didn't pull the trigger, or even slash his throat, or shove him into the gator infested Sabine, so my late Papi became gator bait. You may not have known any of this would happen, but I blame you and only you for Papi's murder."

She ignored everything I said, sat down at our table, while Cisco and Miriam went to another table. "Sara, please, we only have each other."

"I said skedaddle bitch, I'd rather live alone." I stood up and walked towards the ocean. A long one-way swim across the Caribbean might suit me. She didn't stop me. I turned while Cisco and Miriam walked towards the straw hut I slept in. The ocean drew closer, while Lydia, Lupe, or whatever da fuck her name stood and watched. I kept walking. I got to the edge of the ocean, where the waves crash onto the sand, spun my head around and witnessed her walking away from everyone, towards the village.

I stood at the water's edge contemplating everything. Part of me wanted to go for that swim. Instead I sat on the beach with my butt getting wet from the ocean saltwater and killed the thought of swimming across the sea. I rose to my feet and strolled back to the cabana, and I noticed both of my former lovers missing. I kicked the cement on the ground and strolled towards my hut. I figured Cisco and Miriam shacked up there. Right as always, I heard some flat-picking guitar with the haunting slide guitar playing which I recognized right away and I heard that whiny passionate voice singing with Miriam in harmony.

You have that long dark hair
and you walk with such a flair
but you have dem
Sara, Sara's Blues

I can't live with them
I can't live without you

Sara, Sara's blues
You got dem
Sara's Blues

Creole Dad, Mexican Mom
Your Daddy got killed
and Mama knew all
Sara, Sara's Blues

I can't live with them
I can't live without you
Sara, Sara's Blues
You got dem
Sara's Blues

Will we stay in solitude
together and forever
or will we part because of
Sara, Sara's Blues

I can't live with them
I can't live without you
Sara, Sara's Blues
You got dem
Sara's Blues

Tears flowed as I crawled into the grass-hut. I smiled, took a seat and joined their song. Miriam returned to Shreveport after telling me her story, but that's for another time. She also gave me a record, I'd hang on to if I lived, alongside some cute clothes she bought me to wear on the beach. Cisco flew her back and he dropped by, sometimes we got together. Most times, I told him to get lost.

Praises for Moonshiner's Legacy
(Barnum Family Legacy Book 1)

5 stars
*****

As a Brit with a passion for rural life in the American South, this book ticked all my boxes. But don't just take my word for it. This book stands upon its own merits, and paints a glorious panorama, rich with three-dimensional characters, authentic dialogue, and a storyline that keeps the pages turning long into the night. Rob Cooke is a masterful author and I look forward to reading the sequel to Moonshiner's Legacy.
Highly recommended
Richard Wall, Author of Fat Man Blues

5 stars
*****

I thoroughly enjoyed cuddling up to this book drinking my hot cups of coffee wrapped in a thick blanket under the AC. I believe Rob Cooke is an amazing and talented author and I have enjoyed this unique piece of fiction with all its southern charm and doses of hard reality that hit America back in those days.
I'd definitely recommend this book to anyone and I can't wait to read Red Christmas and The Long Song of Miriam Landry.
Two thumbs up.👍👍

5 stars
*****

If you're looking for a taste of Southern fiction, this is a must-read. Get ready to curl up and read it cover to cover

4 stars
****

A well executed timepiece of southern fiction starting at prohibition and on ward. A man's redemption comes through his daughter, and life is meant for living in the present and never about falling into the past while wondering what-ifs. Beautifully crafted, I enjoyed this very much.

5 stars
*****

Hang on for the ride as you get a tour of the Deep South in the Prohibition Era with Bo Barnum and his family in this first book of what promises to be an addictive series!

Praises for The Lost Song of Miriam Landry
Barnum Family Legacy Book 3.

4 stars
****

The Lost Song of Miriam Landry' by Robert Cooke is a wild,
unpredictable ride through the Deep South and in particular,
Louisiana, during the early pre-WWII genesis of the
American   Blues.
The main character, Miriam, 'Lost Song' takes us on a
journey filled with potholes and hard-learned lessons. Miriam
is a young, Black teenager caught beneath the avalanche of
Jim Crow, misogyny and her intuitive desire to play the
Blues. Unable to forge her way on her own, both because of
her race and her gender, she's forced to cycle through a
number of predatory relationships with men who simply use
Miriam for their designed purpose until she can find a way to
escape.

As readers, we see her worth and we can hear her talent, and
it's frustrating to watch her transition from one hell to the
next without any real hope of escape; however, Miriam's grit
and backwoods Bayou swagger, are the most provocative
elements of the entire story. We believe as readers that
eventually Miriam will find her spotlight, because she shows
time after time that she can endure her most formidable
challenges by using street sense and an inner toughness that
characterizes Miriam's outlook on life and in the bigger
picture, the Blues. Unfortunately, Miriam's atmosphere is so
suppressive and its odds are so stacked against her, she
cannot help but revert back to dangerous habits to survive,
and it's at these dangerous moments, we fear for her safety
the   most.

'The Lost Song' also reads like a Blues song in prose. Cooke
uses a dirty Southern underbelly as a setting, and each
relationship that traps and exploits Miriam is another verse to
Miriam's lament. I'm not sure, but I think Cooke is a
guitarist. He possesses intimate knowledge of details like
tunings and notes and the differences between Gibsons and
Stellas as well as an intimate knowledge of the Blues scene

from the WWII-era and its most influential artists and songs. Finally, the story is infused in multiple spots by Miriam's lyrics, and her musical struggle to find a platform of her own rather than platforms established by her 'teachers' and I feel like Cooke wrote the entire piece so that Miriam's work would receive the attention it 'should' have received eight years   ago.

That doesn't mean 'The Lost Song of Miriam Landry' is perfect. Cooke's knowledge of Bayou geography sometimes assumes the reader is as knowledgeable about Louisiana towns and locations as him, and Cooke sometimes assumes the reader will be able to decipher his unique Southern vernacular without a Southern dictionary. Also, Cooke's graphic detailing of some of the trials that Miriam undergoes, might be unbelievable for readers unfamiliar with the pre-WWII   Deep   South.

Those small obstacles, however, do not detract from the overall feel and movement of "The Lost Song' from its bawdy beginnings through its narrow escapes to its creative conclusion.

'The Lost Song of Miriam Landry' is definitely a wild ride, but the lessons it teaches and the stories it tells, will have you cheering for Miriam, just like me.

Four stars
****

What a rollercoaster ride! Miriam confronts one problem after another, but she makes it. She is one strong woman--not in your face strong, but a survivor who tries to move forward in the only way she knows how, and I liked that about her. You hold your breath until she's safe. I thought the author did a fantastic job of describing the music of the times, Miriam's music, the music of each location. I could tell he had a musical background, himself. Music passages well-written. Glad I read her story.

Five stars
*****

This book is a swirl back in time when women of color were virtually invisible and powerless. Miriam has all the talent in the world, but she is oppressed by society. To get where she wants to be in life, she is forced to play by the societal norms of the day and placing herself in depreciatory and degrading situations and relationships. How much she endures is overwhelming. However, by doing so, readers are able see just how much inner strength and determination that Miriam has. This book is very much worth a read.

Connect with Rob Cooke
https://www.facebook.com/Rob-Cooke-661803964000938/

www.ingramcontent.com/pod-product-compliance
Lightning Source LLC
Chambersburg PA
CBHW051952220626
47052CB00004B/917